ONE NIGHT STAND

JENNIFER SUCEVIC

One Night Stand

Copyright© 2016 by Jennifer Sucevic

All rights reserved. No part of this book may be reproduced in any form or by any electronic or mechanical means, including information storage and retrieval systems, without written permission from the author, except for the use of brief quotations in a book review.

This is a work of fiction. Names, characters, businesses, palaces, events, locales, and incidents are either the products of the author's imagination or used in a fictitious manner. Any resemblance to actual persons, living or dead, or actual events is purely coincidental.

Cover Design by Mary Ruth Baloy at MR Creations

Edited by Shauna Stevenson of Ink Machine Editing

CHAPTER 1

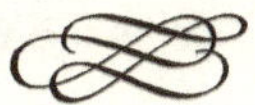

GIA

*I*t's a little after eleven o'clock, and already this place is completely packed. It's standing room only. It might be a crappy, hole-in-the-wall dive bar, but I can't deny its popularity. Although, I suspect that has a lot to do with the cheap beer. Since it's not even half a mile away from Barnett University, and most of these people look young, my guess is that a lot of college kids have taken up residence here. I'm just thankful that Noah was able to reserve a high-top table for the three of us to park ourselves at.

The lights are low, drunken voices pushing in from all sides, and the music… It's even louder than these students cutting loose on a Saturday night. The pulsing beat practically reverberates off the walls. Even though this isn't my usual style of music or venue, my gaze is glued to the four guys performing on stage.

"I had no idea that your brother was so hot!" Harper's gaze never deviates from him. "It must be the whole musician vibe he's got going on."

Um, hello…no sister wants to hear that one of her friends is panting after her baby brother. I scrunch my nose. "*Eww!* You can't go around saying things like that. It's just not right."

In typical Harper fashion, she grins, not taking my words seriously. "Sorry, hon. But it's the truth. He is *definitely* looking good up there." Then she points to the horde of overzealous females crowded around the band, looking as if they might rush the stage before the performance is over. "And I'm obviously not the only one who thinks so." A smirk slides its way across her pretty face. "My guess is that little Noah Monroe is going to get laid tonight. Perhaps by more than one girl."

As soon as those words are released into the atmosphere, I clap my hands over my ears before shaking my head. "That's not a mental image I want or need. So, thanks for that."

Sophie and Harper exchange knowing grins. My brother belts out another lyric, his voice soaring over the guitars and drums. The acoustics may be total crap in here, but he still sounds ridiculously amazing. Another silence falls over the three of us as our attention gets sucked back into the music.

"Hey, ladies, can I buy you a drink?"

Ugh.

Not another one.

Seriously…where do these guys keep coming from? There is absolutely nothing about the three of us that screams *trolling for dudes! Buy us a drink! We're looking to get laid! Come hit on us! Easy targets right this way!*

And yet, they keep ambling over.

One right after another.

They're a persistent bunch, I'll give them that. Why do I keep forgetting this is a crappy bar with drunken college guys who are very obviously looking to get laid?

Even if I hadn't recently extracted myself from a three-year relationship, I still wouldn't be interested in hooking up with a twenty-one- or twenty-two-year-old.

I'm strictly here to watch Noah perform.

Before I'm able to cut the guy off and send him packing, like I've done four times previously, Harper gives him a quick once-over before smiling prettily.

Uh-oh.

I know that look.

"Of course, you can." Still smiling, her eyes turn into chips of green ice. "But understand that there's absolutely no obligation on our parts to do anything more than thank you politely for your generosity." She bats her eyelashes, as if to soften the blow of her words.

The guy is momentarily surprised before an easy grin spreads its way across his handsome face. And yeah, he's definitely a cutie. But come on, he's much too young. He's so boyishly adorable that I'm half tempted to reach over and pinch his cheeks with my fingers.

"You got it, sweetheart." He flags down a harassed looking waitress before whispering something in her ear and then turning back to us. "This round is on me." He sends Harper a sly look and leans a bit closer to her. "Feel free to thank me once you're done enjoying your beverage."

And then he's gone.

Harper's lips quirk as she watches him disappear through the thick crowd back to wherever he came from.

When the three of us remain silent, the waitress slants a dark, uninterested brow our way. "You gonna order something or what?"

Normally, when the three of us head out for a girls' night, it isn't to some low-rent college bar where the clientele barely looks to be the legal drinking age. We head downtown to the more upscale bars and clubs that line the main drag. And we stick to chardonnay and cosmos.

But here, my guess is they don't have a good house chardonnay or make specialty martinis. Everyone seems to be drinking bottles or mugs of pale looking beer.

Well…when in Rome, right?

We order three bottles of imported ale and go back to watching the final set.

When there's about a fourth of her beer remaining, Harper rises to her feet. "As this group's self-appointed ambassador, I shall graciously take it upon myself to thank Mr. Tall, Dark, and Handsome for buying us our drinks."

I give her a look rife with meaning. "Be careful how you thank him, Harp. For all you know, he's not even twenty-one."

I'm not saying that I saw peach fuzz but...

A wicked gleam fills her sparkling green eyes. "Oh, don't worry. I'm planning to do a little recon before I decide how best to express my gratitude."

With that said, she shoves her way through the rowdy crowd. Sophie and I lock gazes from across the table before bursting into laughter. "I wonder if we'll see her again."

I almost wince. "Please, these guys are like babies." They're so damn young.

Sophie makes a point of glancing around before her gaze settles on mine. "Yeah," she drawls, "most of them don't look like babies. *Like, at all.*"

Silently, I have to agree with her assessment. These guys may be young, but some of them are built. Not to mention ripped. I can't say I haven't enjoyed the eye candy tonight.

But it's definitely been from afar.

I can imagine the headlines now: *Nearly Thirty-Year-Old Elementary School Teacher Takes Advantage of Barely-Out-of-High-School Boy.*

No, thank you.

Sophie, Harper, and I all work at North Hill Elementary School. Sometimes it's hard to believe that this is my eighth year teaching second grade. I was fortunate enough to snag a job in this district straight out of college. And since I love where I'm at, I've never considered looking for a different position.

Since the three of us are around the same age, we naturally banded together, forming a tight trio. We eat lunch together and hang out quite a bit outside of school. Especially now that Tyler and I are no longer together.

Even though I hate to leave Sophie alone at the table—because I can practically see the sharks circling as we speak—I yell over the music, "I'm going to run to the bathroom. I'll be back in a few minutes."

With a wide smile, she waves me away before glancing around. "Don't worry, I'm a big girl. I can take care of myself."

"I never said you couldn't." As I'm about to turn away, I spin back around before adding, "Remember—these guys are like the kiosk salespeople at the mall. Avoid eye contact at all costs."

She gives me a cheeky grin. "You worry too much. Just go. I'll be perfectly fine on my own."

With one last nod, I push my way toward the bathroom, which is located at the far end of the bar. The crowd is packed in tight, and it takes a good five minutes to navigate my way to the restrooms. Once there, I'm horrified by what I find.

Has anyone ever cleaned this place before?

I press my fingers against my nose before inhaling another breath. The smell is enough to knock me on my ass.

I do a little self-check and consider not using the facilities. Unfortunately, there's no way I can hold it for another hour or so. The two drinks I've consumed have run right through me.

Attempting to touch as little as possible, I squat over the toilet seat. Once I make it to the sink, I practically scrub the fingerprints off my hands before using a ripped off sheet of paper towel to open the door handle.

Once out of the bathroom, I inhale and fill my lungs with fresh— no, wait. It's definitely not fresh air, but it's a lot better than what was inside that biohazard of a ladies' room.

I'm halfway to the table when someone slides in front of me, blocking my path. Since this place is packed to the gills, I don't think too much about it before attempting to step around him so I can make my way back to Sophie. Hopefully, Harper has returned to the table. She's only twenty-six, which isn't that much older than some of these college students, but I can't see her going home with someone that young. Her last boyfriend was forty.

And a stuffy lawyer, to boot.

The guy quickly sidles in the same direction, which means I find myself blocked yet again. This time, I glance at him. That's when I notice the smirk plastered across his face. It occurs to me that this little dance we're doing is intentional.

As our gazes collide, he offers me a roguish smile.

One that's meant to charm.

It falls short by a mile.

"Hey there, beautiful."

Cue the mental groaning. I am *so* not into this. All I want is to head back to the relative safety of the table. Impatiently, I give him a polite smile, hoping this won't take too long.

Even though it's been two months since Tyler and I broke up, hooking up is the last thing on my mind. When I'm finally ready to jump back into the dating pool again, it won't be with a drunk college kid who has zero idea that women have a little something called a *clit*. Let alone where one might find it.

I dealt with that in college. I'm not interested in reliving that part of the experience again.

At this stage of the game, I'm only interested in men who have, at the very least, a rudimentary understanding as to how the female orgasm is achieved. And who are willing to take the time to prove it. Let's just say that Tyler had a working knowledge of female anatomy but wasn't always willing to put forth the necessary time and effort to achieve those goals.

I met Tyler about three and a half years ago through a co-worker at North Hill. We were introduced at a summer barbecue and hit it off. At the time, he ticked all the standard criteria on my mental list.

Educated—check.

Around the same age—check.

Same core values—check

Not only held down a job but was career focused—double check.

Although here's where I've learned the difference between dedicated to one's profession (me) and obsessed (Tyler). Over the last year, it became a point of contention between us, and was one of the reasons we parted ways.

Not wanting to waste this guy's time—or more importantly, mine, because what he's hoping might happen between us, is so *not* going to happen—I get right to the point. "Sorry, I'm not interested." That being said, I try to maneuver around him. Unfortunately, he shifts his body and blocks my escape.

Again.

Even though he continues to smile, my brows lower. I've just told this guy I'm not interested in whatever he's offering. Shouldn't that be enough?

He holds up his hands in a gesture of surrender, as if to show me he's harmless.

Hey, know a better way to show me you're not dangerous?

Accept when I tell you I'm not interested. That would go a long way toward proving your point.

Is that concept difficult to grasp?

Apparently so.

This guy doesn't appear to be budging anytime soon, which is annoying.

"Hey, I just want the chance to get to know you."

A snort slips out. "Right. I'm sure that's *exactly* what you had in mind." With a sigh, I try one more time to maneuver around him. I don't want to get nasty, but I will if I have to.

Just like before, he blocks my escape route and gives me a knowing grin. My guess is that since the first approach didn't work, he's changing tactics.

"Come on, sweetheart, you can level with me."

His gaze rakes over my body. Even though I'm not wearing anything revealing—we're talking high-neck sweater and jeans—he makes me feel naked.

"You're obviously here looking to get laid. You're a little too..." He pauses.

My brows wing up. I know exactly what word is about to fly out of his mouth.

"Mature," he says with a broad, patronizing smile. "You're a little too *mature* to be hanging out in a bar like this if you're not interested in a hookup." He shrugs, as if he's doing me a favor by laying it all out on the table. "All I'm doing is offering up my services. Plus, I'm into cougars. Or MILFs. Or whatever it is that you are."

Cougar?

MILF?

I'm not even thirty! I'm twenty-nine... and some change. I'm nowhere near cougar age. Isn't that like forty or something?

Instead of going off on him, I draw in a deep, calming breath. "Exactly how old do you think I am?"

He tilts his head and scrutinizes my face. "Twenty-eight?"

Close enough.

Rather matter-of-factly, I ask, "Didn't your parents teach you that it's impolite to point out a lady's age?"

He blinks.

"I'm going to do you a favor—one you don't deserve—and tell you right now that it's incredibly rude to point out a woman's age. And you certainly don't refer to her as a *cougar* or *MILF*." I shake my head. "In the future, I wouldn't open with you trying to do any female a favor by sleeping with her. That's just asinine. If you actually find a woman who is willing to climb into bed with you—especially after you've opened your mouth—she ought to be cherished and revered. Not to mention thanked." There's a pause before I tack on, "Profusely."

He shifts his stance. "So, just to be clear, you're *not* interested in hooking up with me tonight?"

My eyes widen as I shake my head. "Not even for a hot minute. I'm here to watch the band, not get laid. Now that we've cleared that up, you can kindly step aside."

When he doesn't scamper out of my way, annoyance ignites inside me. "Look, I'm not interested. I just want to get back to my friend."

He glances in Sophie's direction before returning his attention to me.

A smarmy smile settles on his lips. If he thinks it ratchets up his cuteness factor, he's sadly mistaken. It doesn't. The only thing ratcheting up are his chances of getting smacked. I have the feeling that whatever words are on the verge of tumbling out of his mouth are going to push me over the edge.

"Hey, if it makes you more comfortable, I'm totally cool with her joining us." His gaze rakes over me again. "The more the merrier, I always say."

Eww.

Guys like this are the absolute worst.

My eyes narrow. "Are you being serious right now?"

He looks hopeful. And oddly confident. The combination is disturbing on so many levels. Especially after everything I've said to him. "Well, that depends. Are you into it?"

Um, no.

I point to all the unhappiness that has settled on my face. "Does it look like I'm remotely into anything you're talking about?"

He contemplates me silently.

Exactly how much has this dude had to drink tonight that he can't pick up on clear social cues? Even my second graders understand that a frowny face aimed in their direction means that someone is unhappy with them.

Note to self—never step foot in another college bar again. No matter how much Noah begs and pleads. He'll have to step up the venues he plays at if he wants my ass in the audience.

Because *this* is not worth it.

As I open my mouth to blast him into next week, a muscular arm snakes its way around my body and I find myself hauled up against a hard male one. Knocked off guard, I blink and stare into the most gorgeous gunmetal-gray eyes I've ever seen. They're crinkled around the edges with humor. He gives me a wink, as if we're co-conspirators rather than perfect strangers.

Even though his comment is directed at me, he turns his attention to the idiot blocking my escape. "Hey, babe. I've been looking all over for you. Where've you been?"

CHAPTER 2

GIA

I blink before it occurs to me that this man—this incredibly gorgeous man, I might add—is attempting to save me from the idiot who won't take no for an answer.

It takes a second to slide into character. "Well, *sweetie*, I was just, ah, talking to this guy who rather thoughtfully asked if I was interested in having a threesome with him." I tilt my head to hold his gaze and bat my lashes.

The hottie next to me drops a quick kiss on my forehead before cocking his head to the side. He takes his time, looking the other guy up and down. A prickle of concern blooms in the pit of my belly. Maybe playing along with this wasn't such a good idea after all. The last thing I need is for a fight to break out.

"Sure, I'm down with that. Why don't the three of us head back to our place for a little bit of fun? We'll need to stop and pick up some extra lube. I'm fresh out." He gives the guy a wink along with a sexy smirk before adding, "I think we're going to need it."

My mouth tumbles open in surprise.

Did...did I hear him correctly?

By the sly expression on his chiseled features, I'm pretty sure I did. A gurgle of unexpected laughter bubbles up in me like a geyser. My teeth sink into my lower lip to stifle the giggles that are desperately trying to escape. The jackass in front of me turns ashen, his mouth opening and closing like a fish out of water, gasping for its last dying breath.

It only gets worse when he stammers.

"I, um, I really wasn't, ah—"

The Adonis next to me eats up the distance between them before running one long finger down the other guy's chest. "I'm more of a top than a bottom, if you know what I mean. Does that work for you?"

Horror flashes across the other guy's face. His eyes bulge before shifting between the pair of us. He opens his mouth before slamming it shut again and shaking his head just once. Without a word, he spins around and darts into the thick crowd. We watch as he knocks into a few people in his haste to escape. My hand flies to my mouth as I die with laughter.

The handsome guy at my side looks disappointed that he's managed to scare off our potential partner, which only makes me laugh harder.

He shrugs his perfectly sculpted shoulders. "Guess I'm just too much man for him to handle."

I gasp for breath. "I can't believe you said that!"

The faux disappointment morphs into a roguish grin that releases a deep dimple in his left cheek. Jeez. This guy couldn't be any sexier if he tried.

"You looked like you could use a little help in fending off that dude's advances."

A few chuckles escape. Especially when I think about the look of horror on that guy's face. It was, in a word—priceless.

Now that it's the two of us, my gaze meanders down the length of him. Believe it or not, he's even better looking than I'd originally suspected. Thick mahogany-colored hair that is shaved close on the sides and spiked up into a fauxhawk. Deep gray eyes that seem to be a color somewhere between flint and silver. High cheekbones that are wasted on a male along with a strong, chiseled jaw. And that smile... no longer does it hold a devilish gleam to it.

It's morphed into something that looks predatory in nature.

I blink at the change in his demeanor. How he went from harmless to dangerous so quickly, I don't know.

His broad shoulders are encased in a dark T-shirt that hugs the bulging muscles of his biceps. Colorful ink peeks out from the top of his collar. My gaze dips to his arms, which are covered in tattoo sleeves, before bouncing up to meet his eyes. What I find is a knowing smirk at my unabashed and thorough perusal of his person.

Heat floods my cheeks. Embarrassed to be caught ogling him so blatantly, I take a hasty step in retreat. The atmosphere changes and, suddenly, it feels too intense. Intuition tells me this guy is way more dangerous than the one he ran off. Even though we'd been joking around a couple of minutes ago, the laughter has dried up in my throat.

"Well, thank you," I murmur, nodding toward Sophie, who is still sitting alone at our table. "I should probably get back to my friend."

He steps forward, swallowing up the distance between us. "Can I buy you a drink?"

We might be separated by at least a foot, but I still feel the heat of his body radiating off him in suffocating waves. Every female instinct inside me sits up and takes notice.

I shake my head. "That's probably not a good idea."

His gaze pins mine in place. It wouldn't take much to drown in those deep depths. They're completely mesmerizing. I have no idea how he's managed to make me feel like a skittish schoolgirl instead of a secure, twenty-nine-year-old woman. The masculinity he exudes leaves me feeling strangely rattled. Certainly more rattled than the jackass who propositioned me for a threesome.

Odder still is the attraction zipping its way through my frazzled body. That hasn't happened in I don't know how long. I hate to admit it, but it's definitely been way more than three years since I've felt this kind of instant, over-the-top desire ignite inside me.

In some distant part of my brain, I can only acknowledge I did the right thing in breaking up with Tyler. We weren't right for each other. What I really want is someone who can turn my insides to mush.

Like this guy.

But older.

So him buying me that drink is definitely not a good idea.

"Oh, come on now," he says.

His silvery-gray gaze stays locked on mine. The sheer intensity swirling in his eyes makes it impossible to suck in a full breath of air. This guy? He may be young, but there's something overpowering about him. Completely male. It leaves everything in me quivering.

"It's not like we're strangers." He holds up his hand and leaves about an inch of space between his thumb and pointer finger. "We were this close to having a threesome. When you think about it, us grabbing a drink isn't really that big of a deal."

I have to smash my lips together so I don't smile. The last thing I want to do is encourage him.

But he's funny.

Why does this guy have to be in college?

He's just so perfect.

Maybe I'm jumping the gun and he's not in college. What if, like me, he's here to check out the music? I mean, anything is possible, right? My brother's band, The Renegades, have their fair share of groupies who follow them from one venue to another. Although, this guy doesn't strike me as a groupie.

I'd bet my salary for the year that he has groupies of his own.

"Are you a student at Barnett?" That's the only college around here, and he's definitely not younger than that.

God forbid.

He cocks his head and holds my gaze, as if silently contemplating the question. My heart kicks up a notch. I can feel the beat of it against my rib cage.

"Why do I feel as if you having that drink is contingent upon me *not* being in college?"

He's intuitive. Yet another redeeming quality.

Can't he just be another jackass with an overinflated ego and horrible pick-up line? That would make it so much easier to walk away.

The breath becomes wedged in my throat as I shrug.

When I remain silent, he sighs. "Yup, I am."

His answer makes hot, tattoo guy with the very sexy hair completely off-limits.

He's too young. At the most, he's twenty-two. Considering I'm coming up on thirty that makes him practically a baby. No matter how much my insides are clamoring for it, I can't go to bed with someone that young.

Holy hell. Who said anything about sex?

We were talking drinks! Disappointment crashes over me like a tidal wave.

I give him a regretful smile. "That's too bad." I take another step in retreat, knowing I need to get out of here and away from him. It's better to nip this in the bud than allow it to linger.

As I edge farther away, he stalks closer. Which is exactly how it feels—like he's stalking me. His predatory prowl leaves me feeling jangled. My mouth turns cottony. My instincts prod me to turn tail and run. Even though we're about a foot apart, he doesn't crowd me. But that doesn't mean I'm not desperately aware of his masculine presence. I rack my brain but can't remember the last time I had such an intense physical reaction to a man.

"Does it really matter if I'm in college?"

Disappointment churns at the bottom of my belly. "I'm afraid it does."

"One drink," he cajoles, "that's all I'm asking for."

It's crazy just how tempted I am to sit down and have that drink with him. But I know better. There's too much attraction buzzing through my veins, prodding me to forget my qualms for just a few careless hours. How strange is it that I'm so attuned to him when we've only met? Even though I know it's wrong to get involved with someone his age, it doesn't necessarily *feel* as wrong as it should.

And that's dangerous.

That's when the lines begin to blur.

Maybe it's his height or the sheer breadth of his shoulders. The way he holds himself, as if he has all the confidence in the world. And yet, it doesn't come across as cocky or arrogant because, clearly, he can back it up. It could be the intelligence radiating from his gray depths. A knowingness. The direct way he has of holding my gaze. As if he knows exactly what he wants and is completely unapologetic about going after it.

There is nothing boyish or cute about him. This guy is completely masculine.

And I want him. More than I've wanted someone in a long time.

That being said, we both know his sweet-talking words are a lie. I can practically feel the combustible heat brewing between us. One drink and a little harmless conversation would never be enough for either of us.

"I think we both know it won't end with one drink, now will it?"

CHAPTER 3

LIAM

She's right.

It won't end with one drink.

I've spent the better part of my evening keeping my sights locked on her. There is no way I'm going to allow this woman to slip through my fingers. If I thought I wanted her from afar, it's nothing compared to the hot shafts of desire spearing through me now.

She's even more beautiful up close. I knew her hair would be a dark, lustrous color, but upon closer inspection, I realize that it's as black and silky as a raven's wing. And long. It tumbles over her shapely shoulders and down her back in thick, full waves.

Waves that I'm already fantasizing about sinking my fingers into. Or wrapping around my fist as I tug her head, forcing her to arch that curvy little body as I thrust deep inside her. That image has my fingers itching to tangle themselves in that heavy mass.

And don't get me started on those eyes. She has the clearest blue eyes I've ever seen in my life. Even in the dim lighting that shrouds us, they shine brightly.

It's almost as if I could glimpse right into her...

Shit.

We'll just leave it at that because me waxing poetically at this stage of the evening will only make me sound like a pussy.

When she was laughing a handful of moments ago, her eyes were twinkling with humor, as if we were old friends sharing a private joke. It had me wanting to say inane things just to see that bright smile overtake her face again.

To be clear, she's no longer smiling.

Nor are her eyes sparkling.

All of her previous lightheartedness has fled. Instead, she's watching me carefully. Intently. As if I'm a dangerous animal she now realizes she should be wary of. Which is exactly how I feel.

Her instincts are razor sharp. Apparently, she can sense my intentions.

Even though there's an interested look in her eyes, she cautiously backs away, as if any sudden movement on her part will cause me to lunge. I have no intention of doing that. Although, I can't say the primal urge to give chase isn't thrumming through me. Maybe I sound cocky, but when I leave O'Brien's tonight, this woman will be in my arms.

"Look," she whispers, sounding desperate, "I appreciate what you did a few minutes ago, but I really need to go."

Without waiting for me to respond, or—more accurately—detain her, she turns, hastily pushing her way through the crowd toward the table she's been camped out at for the last few hours.

As much as everything in me demands I give chase, I hold myself in check. I refuse to be that guy who can't take no for an answer. Instead of taking off after her, I watch and make sure she gets back to her friend safely without any more hassles from the asshats trolling the bar like hungry sharks.

Does that necessarily mean I'm throwing in the towel and moving on to easier pussy?

Hell, no.

I'm nowhere near finished with her. I need to take a moment, regroup, and come at her from a different angle. For the time being, I'll retreat.

The night is still young.

With one last glance in her direction, I head back to my table. It's crammed full of my teammates. The season just ended, and everyone is here to blow off steam. We won the conference championship last week, so spirits are still riding high. The whole university turned out to celebrate for three nights straight. It was complete mayhem. Not to mention, the most fun I've had in a long time.

Boisterous conversations play out around me as I nurse my beer. My attention never strays too far from her. Even with the packed bar, I'm still able to see her from this vantage point. Every time someone approaches her table, or what I consider to be a no-fly zone, my hand tightens around the bottle I'm holding. If I'm being honest, she's been on my radar since she first stepped foot inside O'Brien's. I watched the trio run off every guy who's had the balls to approach them.

FYI, what I'm doing isn't stalkerish or creepy.

Not really.

All right, fine…maybe it is.

Trust me, this isn't one of my finer moments. I'm usually more chill when it comes to the opposite sex. I don't give chase. I don't have to. The ladies flock to me.

At this very moment, a few stray hands are stroking their way up my arm, tracing light patterns over my ink. Two of the girls attempt to strike up a meaningless conversation but my attention is locked elsewhere. I'm barely aware of the chicks who continue to hover, offering themselves up on a silver platter to anyone interested. What I know is that my cock is most definitely stirring, but it isn't for any of the scantily-clad girls buzzing around us like bees.

Once the band takes a break, two of the guys on stage beeline for her table. My body coils, waiting to see how this will play out. This might be another opportunity for me to run interference. At this point, I'm more than willing to do it. I'll happily latch on to any trumped-up excuse to talk to her again.

Within moments of the guys arriving at their table, the four of them are talking and laughing. Almost as if they know each other. Like they're friends or maybe something more. A surge of unwanted jealousy shoots through me when the woman I've had my eye on rises to her feet and wraps her arms around one of the guys.

I grit my teeth. The need to rush over and lay claim pounds through me, which is totally fucked-up. I've never felt this kind of possessiveness rush through my veins. It's disconcerting to feel it so keenly now. Especially over some chick whose name I don't even know.

Music pours from the sound system. Before I realize what I'm doing, I've pushed away from the table and am heading in their direction. I don't know what the deal is between her and this guy, but I'm sure as shit going to find out.

It doesn't take much to bulldoze my way through the thick crowd. Most people know who I am and scurry out of my way. If I'd hoped I would cool down before reaching them, that hasn't happened. If anything, I'm more torqued up than before. Jealousy rushes through my blood, making it impossible to think clearly.

Her gaze catches mine before her eyes flare. Surprise colors every delicate feature. Not bothering to acknowledge anyone else at the table, my attention stays riveted to her.

Oh, sweetheart, did you really think I was going to let you get away so easily?

No fucking way.

A panicked look flashes across her face.

I break eye contact, swiftly turning to the guy parked next to her. He looks a little too comfortable—almost like he belongs at her side. His narrowed gaze collides with mine. There must be one hell of an expression plastered across my face. Before I know it, he rises to his feet.

She slaps a restraining hand on his forearm. That's all it takes for my temper to ignite. I don't like her touching him. I'd enjoy kicking his ass for that alone.

"Noah, please."

"Is this the asshole who was hassling you earlier?" he snaps.

Her fingers curl, biting into his flesh. "No, he's actually the one who stepped in and helped." Her gaze slices pleadingly to mine as she says to the table at large, "I'll be right back."

She releases her grip on the other guy before grabbing hold of my hand. As she does, everything in me settles, and I'm able to draw in a deep breath. I throw a steely look over my shoulder to make sure we're not being followed as she tows me through the crowd. Once we're about twenty feet from the table, she spins around to face me.

Without any further preliminaries, I jerk my head toward the guy. His gaze is pinned on us. Me, specifically. His brows stay lowered. I can almost see the indecision as it flickers across his face.

I don't like that he's this protective of her. And I sure as shit don't like the implication. I don't want to think about her belonging to another guy.

"Who's the dude?" I bite out.

A strange mix of confusion and irritation settle over her expression as she nibbles at her bottom lip. Damn, but that's sexy as hell. I'm tempted to swallow up the distance that separates us and nip the fullness between my teeth before sucking it into my mouth.

Irritation wins out as she plants her fists on the curve of her hips. Her eyes turn icy. "Does it matter?"

I slant an amused brow in her direction. She can't possibly be that clueless.

There is no damn way the attraction careening through me—throwing off my equilibrium—is one-sided. She has to feel it. I can sense her arousal, and it's driving me insane.

"I need to know if we're going to have a problem when we walk out of here tonight."

Her bright blue eyes flare wide as her mouth tumbles open. I'm sure she thinks I'm one hell of a presumptuous asshole. And she'd be right about that. Regardless, that's the way it's going down. Whatever this is between us, it no longer feels like a choice.

"It doesn't matter if I'm with him or not. At the end of the night, I'm going home with my friends. I don't know you. Why would I leave with you?"

The steely challenge threaded through her words has me stepping closer, crowding her personal space, until I can feel the heat of her body. And yet, it's not nearly close enough. It won't be enough until I've peeled off every piece of clothing from her and can press her naked body against mine. Until I can drive myself deep inside her warmth. Only then will it be enough.

My nostrils flare, catching a hint of a light, summery fragrance. As her scent wafts over me, I'm tempted to inhale a big breath of her.

I reach out, trailing my fingers over the curve of her jawline. When she doesn't knock my hand away, I lean in until my lips can ghost over hers. There's a quick hitch in her breathing, and something primal expands in my chest.

All I want is one damn taste of her lips.

That thought makes me snort. Already I know one taste won't be nearly enough to satiate the desire burning inside me. All she needs to do is give me a few hours of her time. Just enough to fuck whatever this is coursing through me out of my system.

And then we'll both be good.

I tell her exactly what she wants to hear. What she *needs* to hear in order to make this happen.

"Come home with me. I'm not asking for anything more than tonight. This is a strictly no-strings attached deal. Whatever fantasies you've kept locked away in the back of your head, I'll make them happen. That much I can promise."

The breathy sound that escapes from her parted lips arrow straight down to my balls.

I take a chance and turn my face until my mouth can feather across hers. Once. Twice. On my third sweep, she opens for me.

Just like I knew she would.

I don't waste a moment before slipping my tongue inside her mouth and causing all sorts of havoc. Teasing, stroking, stoking the fires within. I want her as hot and needy for me as I am for her. My cock is already rock hard as a moan falls from her lips. Before I know it, her slim fingers thread through my hair to drag me closer.

That's when I know she's mine for the night. I pull away enough to rest my forehead against hers.

Not that it matters but…

"I need to know. Is he your boyfriend?"

Her eyes are glazed as she shakes her head. I'll take that as a testament to the affect my kisses have on her. Truth be told, I'm feeling just as bowled over.

My fingers tighten around her hand before I nod toward her friends. "Tell them you're leaving, and let's get the hell out of here."

I'm not in the mood to waste any more time. What I want is to be buried balls deep inside her body.

The haze filling her eyes vanishes as her gaze slides toward the group crowded around the table, staring at us. I hold my breath and wait to see if she'll comply.

Thankfully, I don't have to wait long.

"Okay," she murmurs.

The fist wrapped around my heart loosens.

Good. I'm in the mood to fuck, not fight.

Although, I would have if that was the only way to get her to come home with me tonight.

Hell.

Yeah.

CHAPTER 4

GIA

*H*e pins me against his apartment door. A second later, his mouth crashes onto mine. And then I'm lost to the sensation as his tongue sweeps inside my mouth. The way his hands stroke over my body has shivers scampering down my spine and arousal bursting to life in their wake. A whimper slides from my lips.

He draws away enough to ask, "You like that, baby?" His voice is gravelly. As if he's as turned on by what we're doing as I am.

I can only nod. Any other response feels beyond me.

Playfully, he nips at my lips before growling, "I want to hear you say the words. I want you to tell me exactly what turns you on." He licks and bites at my swollen flesh. "You know what I like?" He doesn't wait for an answer, which is probably for the best. My brain isn't exactly functioning at optimum capacity. "A woman who isn't afraid to tell me what she wants. There's nothing sexier than that."

Gah.

Another moan escapes from me. I'm half-afraid that if I try to give voice to the words, they'll come out sounding like an unintelligible mess.

"Although, I can't say I'm not enjoying all the sexy little noises. They get my cock nice and hard."

My panties flood with heat. I've never been one to be overly verbal in the bedroom. But in all fairness, I should add that I've never had someone do anything worth verbalizing over.

That's not the case in this instance.

I'm already tempted to scream down the apartment building. If this little teaser is in any way indicative as to how the rest of this evening will unfold, then yeah, I'm going to make a lot of noise.

Even though we're both dressed, this is the most turned on I've been in my life, which is...sad. I'm sure this won't come as any surprise, but I've never had a one-night stand. I'm twenty-nine years old, and I spent the last three years with Tyler. I've had four other serious boyfriends since high school and have slept with a grand total of five men.

This guy— Oh my God, I don't even know his name.

How terrible is that?

It's definitely terrible, but it's also oddly exhilarating.

This guy will be number six. And six must be the magic number because everywhere he touches turns me on. This is just a guess, but I'm willing to bet that sexy tattoo guy doesn't need Google Maps to find my clit.

As he kisses and licks his way down the column of my neck, his thumbs stroke across my belly.

"I think," he murmurs, all the while nibbling at me, "you might be wearing too much clothing."

Before I can say a word, the sweater is dragged over my head and I'm standing before him in a lacy pink bra and jeans. My breath comes out in short, sharp pants. He flicks open the button of my jeans and drags down the zipper. The hiss of metal teeth breaks the silence. His gaze holds mine captive as he slides the material over my hips before pushing it down until it pools around my ankles.

He drops to his knees and lifts my foot to slide off both the heel and jeans. Taking hold of my ankle, he pulls off the shoe and then repeats the process with the other side before shimmying the material down my legs.

I swallow down a burst of nerves as I stand in front of this perfect stranger in my see-through bra and panties. When our gazes collide again, my breath gets trapped in the middle of my throat. He's still on his knees in front of me. His hands stroke across my thighs before sliding over the rounded curve of my hips.

"Take off the bra." As the raspy command leaves his lips, he tacks on, "Slowly."

My fingers shake as I reach around my back. It takes three attempts to unhook the clasp that holds the lacy fabric together. As the straps loosen, the cups fall away from my breasts. My heart pounds as I hold the material to my chest.

The air around us crackles with electricity and anticipation.

"That's it, baby," he growls. "Nice and slow."

The way his deep voice slides over the endearment strums something in the pit of my belly, igniting a firestorm of lust inside me. He stares up from his kneeling position as all these strange feelings of power—ones I've never felt before—fuel every move I make.

"Now," he says softly, "you're going to tell me all the naughty things you want me to do to you. All the fantasies you've been too shy to share with any of the men you've gone to bed with."

My heart stutters as his husky words ricochet through my brain. Excitement rushes through my veins and floods my body, stoking my excitement. I've always kept my desires locked carefully inside. No one has ever tried to tease them out.

"You're going to tell me exactly how you want to be touched. How you want to be played with. Your breasts and that sweet little pussy between your thighs. You're going to open them nice and wide for me, aren't you?" He doesn't give me a chance to respond. "Tonight, your body will be my playground."

Why is the sight of him kneeling in front of me the sexiest thing imaginable?

Before I can catch my breath, he closes the distance between us and presses a kiss against my panties before hooking a finger under the lacy material and pulling it to the side. Need spikes through my entire being as his mouth makes contact with my naked flesh. A whimper trembles on my lips as he tongues me.

He pulls away until his breath ghosts over my heated center. "You'll tell me everything. Every wicked little detail. It'll be our secret."

Images of the way Tyler would pump into my body during sex and how I'd lie beneath him, flicker through my brain. I would stare sightlessly up at the ceiling and wait for it to be over. Within a few minutes, I knew there was no way I was going to orgasm given that he was almost there.

What's happening right now couldn't be more different.

Here's this wildly beautiful man, kneeling between my legs, licking expertly at my soft flesh, wanting to know all the sexy things that turn me on. All the fantasies I've never been brave enough to give voice to. The knowledge that I'll never see him again gives me the courage to share them. I tell him everything I've ever fantasized about. All the wicked ways I've wanted to touch a man and have one play with me in return.

I tell him everything.

And then some.

CHAPTER 5

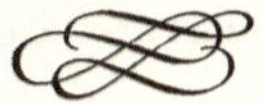

GIA

$\mathcal{A}$rgh.

It's entirely possible that my eyes are cemented shut. At least, that's the way it feels. It takes a few minutes to blink them open. As I do, I realize how gritty they are.

Did I forget to pop out my contacts last night?

That's the only rational explanation I can come up with.

It takes a few seconds for the room to come into sharp focus. As it does, I glance around. My brows draw together because nothing looks familiar.

"What the hell?"

As soon as I mumble the words, last night rushes back at me. The memories are like a torrential rainfall dumped on my head. In shocking Technicolor, I'm inundated with everything.

O'Brien's bar.

The Renegades.

That guy.

No, not the one who wanted the threesome, the other one.

The gorgeous, dark-haired guy with all the sexy tattoos.

My heart picks up its tempo.

Not to mention all the deliciously wicked things he did to my body.

Of course, I remind myself with a small smile that even gritty eyes can't diminish, it's not like I was any slouch in the wicked department.

Nope. I let go of every inhibition. Who knew it could be so freeing to sleep with someone you have no intention of seeing again?

Not me.

Apparently, this knowledge gives you total permission to do whatever you want.

And I did.

Yeah… I *so* did.

For a sliver of a moment, the slight smile widens into more of a triumphant grin.

If memory serves me correctly, he was—hands down—the most gorgeous guy I've ever seen in my life. All right, yes, I'd had a few drinks at the bar. I'm sure there's a small margin of error I need to factor into his hotness quotient for it to be accurate.

Then again, it's not like I can't hold my alcohol. No matter how much liquor I consumed, that guy would still be ridiculously hot. When I left O'Brien's last night, I'd been in complete control.

Furthermore, I can say with the utmost of confidence that I would do it all over again. It had seriously been *that* good. I almost want to lie here for a few blissful moments and bask in all the memories that are dancing around in my head like sugarplums at Christmas-time.

But I can't do that. I'm dying to see if this guy is as sexy and gorgeous as I remember. Carefully, so as not to wake him, I turn my head to where a large male body is sacked out next to me.

Naked.

Air wedges at the back of my throat as my gaze lands on him in all his slumbering glory. Even in repose, he's one hell of a spectacular specimen.

Sprawled out on his back, his face is angled toward me. His chest rises and falls with every deep inhalation.

I'm still unable to wrap my brain around the fact that I had a one night stand with a college guy. A guy who is—hopefully—only seven years younger than I am.

I should feel completely ashamed.

Strangely enough, I don't. If hot sex with a gorgeous younger man were on my bucket list, I could definitely cross it off.

A few times.

I can't help but snicker.

With him still sleeping, it gives me time to look my fill. Something I wouldn't be bold enough to do if he were awake. As my gaze falls to the generous curve of his lips, desire shoots through me, remembering all the lovely things we did together last night.

Or more accurately, this morning.

As tempted as I am to trail my fingers over all the colorful ink that decorates his chest and arms, I keep my hands to myself. I don't want to wake him. Last night was way too amazing to taint with awkward morning-after banter. It's probably best to sneak out before we're forced to endure a conversation.

Before I do that, I want to take a few moments and soak up the sexiness splayed out before me. All those tattoos I couldn't quite see in the darkness, stand out in sharp relief across his muscular body as early morning light pours through the unadorned window. Both his chest and arms are covered in dark, swirling patterns of ink. I would love to take more time and study each piece of intricate art, but I can't.

Time is ticking.

Even as regret fills me, I shove it aside, unwilling to scrutinize it too closely.

I roll to the other side of the bed before flipping off the edge in slow-mo. The mattress squeaks and my heartbeat hitches. As my feet settle on the carpeted floor, I hunker into a naked crouch and pause, making sure the guy is still slumbering peacefully.

I search the surrounding vicinity for my clothes before remembering he practically tore them off at the front door. Another first for me. I almost wince at the thought because it means I need to slink naked into the living room to get dressed.

I mutter a quick prayer that no one is up and about to see my crawl of shame. His deep, rhythmic breaths fill my ears as I move toward the closed door that leads into the hallway. Once I reach the exit, I throw another furtive glance over my shoulder to make sure sexy tattoo guy hasn't woken up.

Nope.

He's still sacked out.

Apparently, I wore him out last night.

Yup. That's right. I did that.

All right…enough gloating.

Time to move. I have to slip out of the room, find my clothing, and get the hell out of here. Once I've safely exited the apartment, I'll request a Lyft to pick me up.

Easy peasy lemon squeezy.

In less than ten minutes this will be nothing more than a delicious memory to savor with my battery-operated boyfriend. Another tiny pang of regret slips through me as I think about never seeing this guy again. He was sexy, funny, and knew exactly what to do with his hands.

And his mouth.

And his tongue.

Not to mention that he was kind enough to prove this knowledge several times over the course of the night. And if that isn't every girl's kryptonite, I don't know what is.

I reach out and grip the gold-toned handle before carefully rotating it. When it clicks, I cringe, and shoot another glance over my shoulder. The door creaks on its hinges as I open it enough to slip through.

As soon as I step into the short hallway, I jump to my feet and spring into action. Air rushes from my lungs as I hunt around for each piece of clothing, which are scattered around the entryway and living room. Twenty seconds later, I've scooped up all evidence from last night's shenanigans. I step into my panties and yank them up my thighs. Once my boobs are encased in my bra, I pull on my sweater before hauling up my jeans.

With my heels dangling in one hand, I tiptoe to the entryway. I'm about to escape from the apartment when I realize that my purse is missing.

Panic shoots through me. That's not something that can be left behind. We have this whole anonymity thing going on. After last night, I would probably die an excruciatingly slow death if I ever ran into him again.

Frantically, I turn the room upside down before spying my bag tucked under the couch. How it got there, I don't know. I snatch it before bolting toward freedom.

As I reach for the knob, it springs open and a guy saunters through the door. Make that two guys. Both are tall and broad in the shoulders. Muscles bulge from beneath their sweat-soaked shirts.

"Dude, I don't know what you're talk—"

Guy number one's words trail off as his gaze locks on mine. In my haste to scurry out of their way, I stumble back a few steps. He snaps to attention before reaching out and grabbing hold of my upper arms.

It's difficult to say who's more surprised by our narrowly averted collision.

Although I suspect it's me by the small yelp I'm barely able to stifle. It feels like I've been caught red-handed. The only thing that could make this moment more embarrassing is if the guy I'm sneaking out on wakes up and joins us.

My face heats as their curious gazes fall on me.

It doesn't take a rocket scientist to figure out what's going on. I'm guessing that's why a smirk tips the corners of the blond guy's lips, which only makes him more handsome. His blue eyes are piercing. He's definitely a cutie.

But he's not nearly as hot as sexy tattoo guy passed out in the other room.

"Hello there. We didn't get a chance to meet last night." The blond nudges his friend in the ribs. "I'm going to take a guess and assume you're the reason lover boy missed his morning workout."

The dark-haired man glances toward the short hallway. "That lazy ass must still be lounging around in bed." He shakes his head. "No discipline whatsoever."

Guy number one's eyes dance with mischief as a grin stretches across his face. Barely is he able to contain his gleefulness. It's almost as if he's settling in for a nice long chat as he leans his powerful body against the doorframe. "I think she's attempting to skedaddle before Liam wakes up." He snorts. "How hilarious is that?"

By the look of the blond, he's really loving that idea. I have a feeling that sexy tattoo guy isn't going to live that down for a long time.

"Can't really blame the girl, now can we? She probably had a bad case of beer goggles last night when they hooked up. I bet she had to gnaw off her arm to get away."

The first guy grins. "Had that happen to you a number of times, huh?"

When the dark-haired one rolls his turquoise-colored eyes, I blink. Staring at him is like gazing into the sun. For the life of me, I can't bring myself to glance away. Sheesh. I think he's even better looking than the muscular blond.

Who the heck are these guys?

"Please. Do you seriously think anyone's running from this face?" He shakes his head, mustering up as much haughty derision as he can. "Unlikely, dude. Very, very unlikely."

The other one gives me an exasperated look, as if we're co-conspirators in this conversation, before rolling his eyes. "You are seriously one conceited motherfucker." There's a pause. "You know that, right? How does Ivy put up with your damn ass?"

The other one shrugs. He's built like his sole mission in life is to pump iron. Just to be clear, the blond is no slouch in the bulging muscle department either. "Explain how it's conceit if it's the truth. And Ivy loves every damn thing about me. Just ask her."

Apparently, these two are going to bicker amongst themselves. With my purse and shoes clutched tightly in my hand, I interrupt their playful banter because, in all honesty, it seems as if they've forgotten I'm still standing here.

Which is just fine by me.

"All right, well...if you'll excuse me, I'm, ah, late for..." My mind goes blank, which I'm going to blame on lack of sleep and three powerful orgasms. "Something important."

Their gazes slice to me. Before either one of them can detain me, I dash past them and sprint down the hall. As I near the stairwell, I stop and jam my feet into my heels before fishing my phone from my purse and requesting a Lyft.

Only then do I inhale a breath, attempting to calm my scattered nerves before hightailing it from the building to relative safety.

CHAPTER 6

GIA

When the car finally rolls up, I practically hurtle myself into the backseat. The man peels away from the curb as if he's the getaway driver for an armed robbery in progress. I peek out the back window, relieved to find there's no signs of life coming from the apartment building. Once we're six blocks away, I collapse against the seat and squeeze my eyes shut.

Since I live on the southern end of the city, and the university is at the northern tip, the drive home should take about fifteen minutes. Although, at this time of the morning, the streets are deserted, and there isn't heavy traffic to maneuver around. As we navigate the streets, my mind tumbles back to last night.

To Liam.

Liam.

I can't say the name doesn't fit him perfectly. There's something sexy about his edgy hairstyle and all the colorful ink that decorates his body.

Did I happen to mention that he drove us to his apartment on a sleek black motorcycle?

You better believe it was cold out last night.

But seriously, who gives a damn?

Hot is hot. Even when it's freeze-your-ass-off cold out.

He's the kind of guy who looks like he belongs front and center in an alternative rock band. Since I know nothing about him—other than the fact that he attends Barnett University—he very well could be. We didn't exactly swap life stories last night.

The only reason I know his name is because one of his roommates (I'm assuming that's who big and bigger were) mentioned it. I kind of wish he hadn't. The last thing I need to do is attach a name to that gorgeous face. The less I know, the better off I'll be. This was strictly a onetime deal. There won't be any encore performances, thank you very much.

Harper has been nagging me for weeks to take the plunge and get back out there again. After three years of a monogamous relationship, I'm a little rusty when it comes to picking up or being picked up by guys.

That being said, I'm fairly certain I rectified the situation last night. A small smile tugs at the corners of my lips. There's a good chance it will be plastered there for the rest of the day.

It lasts for roughly two more minutes before falling off my face as we roll up to my house. There's a man sitting outside on the front porch steps. He's more than likely freezing his butt off even though the sun is already shining brightly.

Tyler.

As in my ex-boyfriend, Tyler.

I shake my head in hopes that I'm having some sort of sleep deprived delusion. When he doesn't disappear from sight, I blink a few times.

Damn.

What's he doing here?

I glance at my phone to check the time. It's not even eight o'clock in the morning. That thought sinks to the bottom of my belly like a massive stone.

By force of habit, my hand drifts to my head, attempting to smooth down the wild tangle of my hair. It's not like I had time to freshen up before taking off like a bat out of hell. I'm lucky I was able to find all my stuff.

"Yeah, that's not going to work, lady."

A deep, gravelly voice knocks me from those thoughts, and my attention slices to the rearview mirror only to lock on humor-filled eyes staring back at me.

Sadly, he's probably right.

I blow out a steady breath as my gaze skitters to the front of my house and Tyler, who now stares at the vehicle. He's the last person I want to deal with. I had my heart set on soaking my sore muscles in a hot bubble bath while sipping a ginormous cup of coffee before slipping between my nel sheets and taking a nap.

I watch in dismay as Tyler trots down the cement walkway toward the curb. My heart sinks with every rushed step.

"Gianna, where have you been? I've been worried sick about you. Didn't you come home last night?" His voice elevates with each question.

It's on the tip of my tongue to pull an excuse out of my ass as to where I spent the night, until I remember that we're no longer together. I don't owe him any explanations. What I do with my time is no longer Tyler's concern.

Instead, I straighten my shoulders before asking a question of my own. "What are you doing here?"

He stares at me silently as his gaze rakes over my disheveled appearance. I have to tighten my hands in an effort not to smooth over everything that is wrinkled, standing on end, or out of place.

His voice remains tempered as he says, "I was hoping we could talk."

I fold my arms across my chest. We've been down this road before. Numerous times. And nothing has changed. And furthermore, nothing *will* change between us.

When I finally worked up the courage to sit down with Tyler and tell him I thought it would be better for us to go our separate ways, he ended up agreeing with the idea. I mean, sure, he kicked up a bit of a fuss in the beginning, but it certainly wasn't enough for me to recon-sider my decision.

Apparently, something has changed during the last month. He's been calling and texting nonstop, wanting to work things out between us. I keep hearing lots of *"it'll be different this time"* and *"I'll scale back at work as much as I can."*

Do I believe it?

Not for a minute.

Tyler loves his job.

And that's great.

For Tyler.

It's not so great if you want to spend time with him and do things as a couple. He goes in early, stays late, and is normally gone on Satur-days. He's even been known to sneak out of the house early Sunday morning before I'm awake.

Don't get me wrong, both his dedication and single-minded focus are admirable traits and qualities. This isn't a job to him. It's not something he's doing to fill time and draw a paycheck.

This is a career. One he loves.

The state of our relationship was slammed home when I tried to picture what our lives would look like a few years down the road. And that was me raising our kids on my own.

That's not the kind of life I want for myself.

Or my hypothetical children.

Better to end things when the stakes weren't so high.

"We've already talked about this," I remind him gently. "Nothing has changed. And nothing is *going* to change. We both know that." I, for one, can accept it. I just wish Tyler hadn't gotten it into his head that we should try and work out our differences. My guess is that he came to the realization that starting up a new relationship requires a time commitment he doesn't have or isn't willing to put forth. There-fore, it's easier to stick it out with me.

That's not exactly a ringing endorsement for us to get back together.

"But I love you, baby."

Even though I'm trying to hold strong, something in my heart softens at the declaration. Tyler isn't a bad guy. Not at all. I just think there are other people out there that we're both better suited to.

I understand that even if he doesn't.

He takes a step in my direction, cautiously closing the distance between us. When I stand my ground, he stops about a foot away. One hand drifts to my cheek before cupping the side of my face in his palm. I cringe at the notion of him touching me when I was in another man's bed less than an hour ago.

"Can we go inside and talk?" When I fail to respond, he adds, "Please?"

Confusion flickers through me as I stare into Tyler's hazel eyes. My decision to break up with him wasn't made lightly. I didn't wake up one morning and arbitrarily decide to end things. I agonized over it for weeks. In fact, I told him a few months before I pulled the plug that I was unhappy with his work schedule. At that point, he claimed there was nothing he could do about it.

Now that he's here, standing outside my house, guilt swirls through me, and I feel myself caving even though I know I won't change my stance on our relationship.

Penance.

I almost groan as the word tumbles through my head.

That's exactly what this is.

This is my penance for last night.

My shoulders slump as I crumble completely. "Okay." Before he can respond, I add, "But only for a few minutes. I have plans with Sophie."

Actually, the only plans I have are with the bathtub, my bed, and a steaming cup of coffee. But Tyler doesn't need to know that.

As we move up the walkway, I take out my key before shoving it in the lock and throwing open the front door. Under normal circumstances, I love coming home. I've spent the last five years renovating and decorating this place. I have everything exactly the way I want it. From the wooden porch that takes up the entire width of the front, and the swing my brother helped hang, to the tiny backyard with its flower beds and neatly manicured lawn.

Tyler closes the door behind us as I set my purse on top of the antique credenza I found at a flea market two years ago and repainted. If memory serves me correctly, I believe Tyler was working that Sunday morning.

Once inside the foyer, his attention slides over me again, and I shift beneath his intense perusal. A dull flush crawls up my cheeks as I head into the living room before beelining to an armchair on the other side of the coffee table. Casually, I do a sniff test, and hope I don't reek of the best sex I've ever experienced in my life, before settling as far from him as I can get and still be in the same room.

I'm tempted to hop into the shower for a quick wash, but I'm half afraid Tyler might ask to join me. I wouldn't put it past him. Not with how much he's been texting and calling. I think he'd like nothing more than to catch me in a moment of weakness and sweet talk his way back into my life.

An awkward silence falls over us as I wait for my ex to get this conversation started. He is the one, after all, who decided to camp out at my house at eight o'clock on a Sunday morning.

With his feet spread, he rests his elbows on his knees before glancing around the living room. "You moved things around."

After Tyler and I parted ways, and he took what little he had brought over, I'd felt the need to change things up. I rearranged the furniture and did a bit of redecorating.

"Yes," I say with a nod.

His brows draw together as he studies all the subtle changes I've made in his two-month absence. "I like it."

"Thanks." Surprised by the admission, some of the tension drains from my shoulders. For a moment, I wonder if he's trying to butter me up. Little does he realize it's not going to work. I'm happy on my own, and sadly, since Tyler worked a lot of hours, his absence isn't as glaringly apparent as it should be.

I shift on the chair, impatient to get this chat over with. He continues to study his surroundings as I silently wait for his gaze to meander to me. When it does, I notice the sadness brimming in his eyes.

"I miss you, Gianna," he admits. "I miss *us*. Nothing has been the same without you." Softly, he adds, "I never should have let you go. As stupid as it sounds, I didn't realize what I had until it was gone."

I can only blink at the admission. Had he said this to me a week—even two—after we'd broken up, I probably would have taken him back. At that point, everything had been so fresh, and I was missing him. Our relationship hadn't been all bad. Tyler and I got along pretty well. What we had was comfortable and solid. My biggest bone of contention was that he was gone all the time.

And...well...the sex. It was mediocre. Routine at best. After that first year, there was absolutely no changing things up. No spice. It was like a well-orchestrated program. One we didn't deviate from. Twenty minutes, two times a week.

Should I have pushed for more?

Tried to be creative and inventive?

Probably. But in my defense, I didn't realize how amazing sex could be before last night.

Know what else I can't shake from my mind?

That I'd never experienced any of those little zings of attraction. In fact, I didn't believe they existed. Before Liam, I assumed all the attraction and ridiculously hot sex you read about in romance novels was a huge, steaming load of crapola.

But that's exactly what it had felt like.

The moment our gazes collided, electricity had shot through my body. I've never felt such an instantaneous attraction to someone before. It's unfortunate that the guy is still in college and so much younger than I am.

When I remain silent, lost in the turmoil of my thoughts, Tyler asks, "Did you hear what I said, Gianna? I love you. I want you back, baby." He sucks in a breath before finishing with a heartfelt, "I want *us* back."

Everything inside me tenses. "Gia," I remind him in a stiff tone. "I want to be called *Gia*."

At first, I hadn't been bothered by Tyler calling me by my given name instead of my nickname. Except, I'd always preferred Gia. For the first year or so, I let it slide. After all, it wasn't a big deal. Certainly not a sticking point worth arguing over. But every time the name rolled off his lips and I corrected him, it morphed into a larger issue.

"I love your name," he responds, clearly not understanding my ire. "You know that, baby."

"I do," I acknowledge, "but I prefer Gia." And he knows it. We've talked about it. Numerous times. Which is ridiculous. It's *my* name. Just call me by it. Is that really so difficult?

"It's such a beautiful name and it fits you so well. Much better than Gia," he attempts again.

His stubbornness on the issue only strengthens my resolve regarding our relationship. It also makes what I'm about to say a lot easier. "Tyler, this isn't going to work. You and I... We're just too different. That's not a criticism," I tack on hastily. "It's just the way things are. I'm not a good fit for you."

Believe me, I've already tried playing the whole *it's not you, it's me* card.

He promptly brushed it aside.

Fine, I'll admit it then—it's you.

It is definitely *you.*

His brows draw together. "How can you say that? We're perfect for each other. We've always gotten along so well. We hardly ever fought."

That's true. We didn't fight very often. The caveat being that he wasn't around that much. When we did happen to disagree on a particular subject, Tyler was an expert at steamrolling over my opinion. And I let him because it was easier that way. Easier to give in and keep the peace. So, in his mind, I'm sure we got along perfectly.

Exasperation bursts inside me like an overinflated balloon. "Tyler, I wasn't happy with how things were between us."

He leans forward before angling his body toward mine. He clenches his hands together until the knuckles turn bone white. A desperateness fills his hazel eyes that I'm not used to seeing. "I can change, Gian—"

My eyes narrow as I give him a sharp look. He promptly corrects himself as a slight flush stings his cheeks.

"Gia." The edges of his lips curl up into a half-hearted smile. "See? Things can be different from now on. I promise."

Unsure what to say, I press my lips together. As I attempt to formulate a response, Tango saunters into the living room before stopping short to eyeball the interloper who now sits in what he has claimed as *his* cushion on the couch.

My ex's eyes widen as he stares at the sleek black animal. "What the hell is *that?*"

"It's a cat," I reply calmly, as if it couldn't be any more obvious.

His horror-filled gaze darts to mine before he whispers in a strangled voice, "When did you get a cat?"

I bite my lip before admitting, "A few weeks ago." Tango may be a new addition, but he's quickly become my fur baby. And guess what else? He's around way more than Tyler ever was, and he doesn't take up nearly as much space on the bed. Or steal the covers in the middle of the night.

So, yeah, Tango is staying.

He continues to eye the cat as if it's a ticking time bomb on the verge of exploding. "I'm allergic to cats."

"I know."

CHAPTER 7

LIAM

I pull my earbuds out as Dylan elbows me in the ribs. I'm breathing hard from our five-mile run. It might be the off-season, but we still workout and train six days a week. Especially those of us who are looking to turn pro. There're only a few more weeks until the NFL Combine at the end of February. It's a four-day event where scouts get a chance to watch prospective players show off their athleticism on the field.

There is so much pent-up energy pinging around in my body with all the family shit going on, not to mention the draft, that I could easily run another five miles.

"Dude, what the hell crawled up your ass? Your aunt Flo come to visit or something?"

I narrow my eyes and shake my head. Dylan can be such a tool sometimes. Honestly, it surprises me that his girlfriend, Lexi, puts up with him. "Yup, you nailed it. I'm riding the cotton pony."

Unable to help himself, he chuckles. "I thought so. You've been in a real shitty mood lately."

I inhale a deep breath and blow it out slowly before turning his words over in my head. He's not telling me anything I don't already know. I *have* been in a crap mood lately, and I'm pretty sure some of it has to do with the chick I brought home a few weeks ago.

The chick who took off before I even pried my eyes open the next morning.

I can't say that's ever happened before. Usually, I have to prod them into leaving sometime after a late breakfast.

Plus, the sex was phenomenal. You can't blame me for wanting to wake up and hit that again before she headed home.

It was a real kick in the ass to be shaken awake only to find Roan and Sam's ugly mugs staring down at me. I'm not even going to mention the shit-eating smiles plastered across their idiotic faces. The two of them had been all too happy to tell me about the woman they'd found hauling ass from our apartment at the crack of dawn as if she were fleeing for her life. Like I was seconds away from making a lampshade out of her carcass or something creepy like that.

Yeah, right…hardy-har-har.

Those two are complete dicks.

Apparently, that's exactly the way it went down. The chick I'd had the best sex of my life with couldn't get away from me fast enough.

After I kicked them out of my room, I shrugged off the whole thing, rolled over, and went back to sleep for a couple hours. I didn't think too much about it. I mean, it was a hookup. We both knew that going in. It's the reason we didn't exchange names.

It wasn't like I was planning to see her again.

Nope. It was more of a one-and-done kind of deal.

Hit-it-and-quit-it.

But that hasn't stopped thoughts of her from creeping into my head at the most inopportune of moments. Like at the gym, during class, or while I'm talking with another chick. Even when I'm lying awake in the middle of the night.

Memories of how damn sexy she'd looked standing in her bra and panties after I stripped off her clothing by the front door will flood through me. The husky sounds that escaped from her softly parted lips when I sucked her nipples into my mouth. How she traced her fingers over the patterns of ink decorating my arms and chest. Or,

God help me, the way her tight-as-a-glove pussy throbbed around my cock every time an orgasm streaked through her.

I'm a little embarrassed to admit that the inside of my shower has seen more than its share of action these past two weeks. I'm like a horny teenager. I haven't jacked off this much since eighth grade.

Which is ridiculous.

So, yeah…that's where I'm at with this.

It's not a good place to be.

To silently answer Dylan's surprisingly astute question—that, my friends, is precisely what has crawled up my ass. Now I just need to find a way to dislodge it and move on with my life.

I've arrived at the disturbing conclusion that one time with her wasn't nearly enough. And the whole *not going to exchange names*, which had seriously upped the whole hotness factor of that particular experience, only means I have nothing to go on.

There's no way to track her down.

Ummm...that is if I *actually* wanted to track her down.

Aw hell, I'd like nothing more than to track down her sexy ass. And I know damn well I haven't seen her around before. I would remember if I had. I knew the moment she walked through the door of O'Brien's that she wasn't a regular. And she's not a Barnett student either. I'm fairly confident she isn't going to turn up on campus. Although, that hasn't stopped me from looking. It's like my head is on a swivel.

The more elusive this woman becomes, the more obsessed I am with finding her.

Wait a minute… Did I just admit to being *obsessed?*

Fuck. It's true. At this point, I'm obsessed.

So where does that leave me?

I'll tell you where it leaves me—up shit creek without a paddle.

Am I necessarily going to confide all this in Dylan?

Hell no.

The last thing I need is to catch any more shit from this guy. And, trust me, I will. That happens to be the beauty of Dylan. You always know what you're going to get with him. The guy is all about cracking jokes, his girlfriend, and football. He doesn't have a serious bone in his body. He's not exactly the guy I'd bare my soul to. If I had to, for whatever reason, bare my soul. So, that leaves one avenue available.

"Nothing. Just some family shit going on."

It's not a lie. There's always crap going on at the old Garrison homestead. It's a never-ending shitstorm, which is precisely why I don't need to get derailed over a hot piece of ass I nailed two weeks ago. No matter how fine that ass was. What I need to do is figure out a way to evict her from my mind so I can concentrate on the important stuff.

Like getting ready for the combine and draft, get my family's financial situation squared away, and look into outpatient programs for my dad. Maybe figure out where Cullum will attend college, and how we'll get Claire through high school.

Not to mention, I need to focus on the rest of my junior year at Barnett. I might be leaving early for the draft, but that doesn't mean I can allow my grades to tank. At some point, I'll finish up my degree. I'm not about to blow off the eighteen credits I'm taking.

See? These are the things that actually matter. Dwelling on a chick who sprinted from my bed like her damn ass was on fire is the last thing I should be preoccupied with.

In an attempt to turn this conversation away from all the bullshit running rampant through my head, I ask, "You ready for the combine?"

For once, the smile fades from his face. "Yup. I've been working my damn ass off."

I nod.

It's true. Dylan has been working hard. Early morning runs, lifting at the gym, agility training, high protein diet, and no alcohol. The guy couldn't do anything more than he already is.

It's just that Dylan injured his shoulder last season, and I know it still bothers him. He never says a word about it, but you can tell when he takes a hard hit. A stoic expression will slide over his features, masking the pain. His mentality is that he'd rather play hurt than not play at all.

Which I get. But that kind of attitude seems a little shortsighted if you ask me. Then again, what do I know? I've never sustained a long-term injury. I've always played quarterback. I don't take hits like some of these guys do. The way they pummel the shit out of each other on the field, it's a wonder their freaking brains aren't permanently scrambled. Once in a great while, a player will sneak past my left tackle before taking me down. It can hurt like a mother fucker.

The question escapes from my mouth before I think better of it. "And your shoulder?"

His lips thin. "There's no problem with my shoulder, dude."

The look he drills me with clearly says *don't ask another question about it.*

So, I don't.

No matter how tight you might be with someone, there are still certain things you don't talk about. And how much an injury continues to affect you is one of them. No professional football team wants to pick up a guy who is injury prone. They want healthy players at the top of their game who are going to go out there and run their bodies into the ground.

Dylan is that kind of guy.

I'm not sure what I would do if I were in his position. I don't want to be one of those players you see fifteen years from now who doesn't remember his name or can't recognize his own kids because he took too many hits to the noggin. Or who has the body of an eighty-year-old from arthritis and joint pain when he's only pushing forty.

For some of these guys, football is the end all be all. They've been playing in a Pop Warner program since they were seven years old. It's all they know. And they won't move on from the sport until they're forced out of it.

"What about you?" he asks, attempting to shift the conversation. "Heard you signed with that big agent out of New York."

Barnett is a cesspool of gossip. And like any other big school with a top-notch football program that pumps out its fair share of NFL players, the rumor mill is always churning.

As soon as I became eligible for the draft, shit was being speculated upon. Who I'll sign with. Where I'll end up playing. Blah, blah, blah. I ignore the chatter. I don't want anything to do with all the bullshit and hype that goes along with being an athlete around here.

So far, I've been lucky. There are other players on the team who get more attention than I do. Like Roan King. He's the real stud on campus. And before Ivy Kaster, the chick who locked him down, I think he was just fine with that. He's like a minor celebrity.

I, on the other hand, am not interested in the harsh glare of the spotlight shining down on me. I don't need people digging up shit about my family and plastering it all over the internet. And I sure as hell don't want anyone's pity.

Ever since I was eight years old, I've been part of a football team. But to a certain extent, I've also been a loner. I keep most people at a distance. No one knows too much about my home life, and that's the way I intend to keep it.

Even though I realize it's a touchy subject, I say lightly, "Nah, I signed with Roan's guy."

His eyes sharpen as we finish up with our jog and start to cool down. "Hmmm."

Rumor has it that Dylan wanted Kevin McGillis to represent him as well, but the guy took a pass. I have no idea if that's idle gossip, and I'm sure as hell not going to ask.

Instead, I shrug and attempt to keep the conversation light. "Don't worry about it, man. This is your year." Dylan had every intention of entering the draft last year until he was sidelined by the shoulder injury. Even though it's a lie, I throw out, "I overheard Coach Bauer say he felt it in his gut."

That comment does precisely what it's meant to. A reluctant smile tips the corners of his lips as one brow slinks upward. "He actually said that, huh?"

Not in so many words. "Sure did. And we all know that Coach's gut is never wrong."

I release a pent-up breath when he mutters, "I really hope not. I don't know what the hell I'll do if the NFL doesn't pan out for me."

"Hey, it's not like you haven't been working toward a degree."

Dylan will graduate in May. I have no idea what he majored in for the last four years. He's never talked about it. Hopefully, it's not some lame-ass crap that will end up being worthless in the real world.

There are athletes who have been allowed to cobble together bullshit classes in order to make up their own degree. It might not be basket weaving for idiots, but its damn close. I hope Dylan was more farsighted than that. I've seen my share of talented athletes whose futures look as bright and shiny as a newly minted penny, sustain an injury they can't come back from.

And then poof! all their dreams are flushed down the shitter.

That knowledge is always festering at the back of my mind. I'd like nothing more than to stick around for another year and earn my degree. Especially since athletic scholarships have paid my way for the last three years. Unfortunately, my family can't afford to keep limping along financially. They're the reason I'll cut out of here early and take my chances on the NFL draft. Once I'm done playing ball, I can always go back and finish up my degree. It'll just be on my own dime.

If there's been any takeaways from my family, it's that one day, everything can be moving along smoothly, and the next it can be turned upside down. I won't be one of those guys who blows his signing bonus and salary on partying, pussy, cars, and million-dollar houses.

Nope. I'll make sure my family has enough to live comfortably on, and the rest will go toward investments.

"Yeah, but working nine-to-five at a boring desk job isn't what I envisioned for my future." He gives me a bit of side-eye. "You know what I mean?"

"It doesn't have to be that way. There are other things out there. Maybe you need to take some time and explore the possibilities."

Dylan shrugs, looking uncomfortable with the direction of our conversation. "I don't know. My dad keeps harping on me to join his firm. If the NFL doesn't work out, I'll probably get sucked into that. I'll sit my ass behind a mahogany desk and talk about people's financial portfolios for the rest of my damn life."

It's on the tip of my tongue to argue with him, but I don't bother.

Dylan is in no frame of mind to hear what I have to say. I hope for his sake that it all works out the way he wants it to.

"It'll be fine, dude."

He flashes me a smile before throwing off the serious mood. "Hey, if Coach felt it in his gut, then it has to be true. Right?"

It takes everything I have inside not to wince.

CHAPTER 8

LIAM

As I push through the metal door of the house I grew up in, the screen whines on its hinges before slamming shut with a thud. It should have been replaced a couple of years ago. Then again, the same holds true for everything in this place.

Before my mother took off, our home looked worn but still well-loved. That's no longer the case. It's gotten a lot worse in the five years since she disappeared. Things that were shabby, now seem unkempt and forlorn.

A crushing weight settles on my shoulders as I step foot inside the living room. Even though I don't necessarily want to, I swing by at least once a week to make sure everything is running smoothly and nothing else has fallen to shit in my absence.

"Hey, son."

The corners of my lips hitch as my gaze settles on my dad. He looks the same as always. Maybe a little rougher around the edges. There are dark smudges under his eyes, as if he hasn't been sleeping well, and his complexion is ruddier than normal. I don't miss the beer can sitting off to the side on the dinged-up end table.

I hope the can is a leftover from the night before that didn't make it into the trash, but you never know. It might be barely past noon, but it's never too early to crack open a cold one on a Sunday morning.

"Hi, Dad." I settle on the frayed couch next to the brown corduroy-covered recliner he's parked in. It's one of the many pieces of furniture that my mom scavenged from the side of the road. "How's everything going?"

He shrugs before his watery blue gaze bounces to the television where they stay fastened. After a handful of silent moments that leave me fidgeting, I delve into the reason for my visit. Although, gauging from his silence, I have a damn good idea what he'll tell me. But still, I need to hear the words from him. I need to know where the situation stands.

"How did the interview go on Friday?" I ask.

When he jerks his shoulders for a second time, my stomach sinks further. That, along with the way he refuses to pull his gaze away from the hockey game playing out across the TV screen, is an indicator as to the direction this conversation will swerve. "It went all right, I guess."

Even though he says the words, I know they're a lie. His demeanor would be more upbeat if there was a snowball's chance in hell he would be offered the job. "They're looking for a welder with five years' experience."

That's good. My father has spent his entire adult life welding sheet metal.

I nod before pumping him for more information. "What did you end up telling them about Hansons?"

Hansons is the machine shop where Dad worked for fifteen years. Everything took a turn for the worse after Mom took off. Two years ago, shit really hit the fan, and he was axed. Ever since then, he's had a difficult time holding down a steady job. There have been a few gigs here and there, but nothing long lasting.

He presses his lips into a tight line, as if he doesn't want to say anything more on the subject. I release a steady breath and realize that something must have happened during the interview. Any glimmer of hope I'd been harboring dies a quick death. Even though I'd steeled myself for the outcome, disappointment surges through me. This isn't the first interview that hasn't gone his way.

I force myself to ask, "So what happened?" It would be a refreshing change if he would tell me how he fucked up the meeting instead of making me drag it out of him one word at a time.

A stilted silence follows that question before he tosses me a bread crumb of information. "Do you remember Eric Wexler?"

My brows pinch together as I rack my brain for an answer. The name sounds vaguely familiar, but I can't place where I know it from. I shake my head and wonder how this guy ties in with the job interview.

"He was my direct supervisor the last couple years I worked at Hansons."

Well shit. That's not good.

Dad's premature parting from Hansons was not one that could be described as amicable. Throughout his career, he had been a model employee, never having one HR problem. He fell apart after Mom walked away. I've never seen anyone shut down like that before. There was this vacantness about him that was frightening. After a few months, when it became glaringly apparent that she had no intention of returning, he started hitting the bottle a little too hard in the evenings.

More often than not, he'd show up to work the next morning still hung over from the night before. There were times when he'd drink so much, he'd end up passing out and wouldn't make it in the next day. No matter how much I tried to rouse his inebriated ass. It just wasn't going to happen.

I can't say his bosses weren't lenient with him.

At first, his supervisor would send him home in a cab and tell him to sleep it off. But there are only so many times that kind of shit will fly with an employer. When they realized this wasn't a passing stage, they issued an ultimatum—either enroll in a day treatment program to get the drinking and other issues under control or lose the job.

In the end, he chose the liquor.

Guess my father wasn't ready to quit drinking at that point. It was during that meeting with human resources that Dad became belligerent and was escorted off the premises by security. My guess is that urinating in front of everyone, from the owner of the company down to his direct supervisor, only solidified their decision to cut him loose.

Am I surprised the interview went south?

Nope.

But still…

It would have been nice for something to turn this shit situation around for us.

Unsure what to do or say, I drag my fingers through my hair.

From the bleak expression plastered across his face, it's obvious that he's embarrassed. It's only been within the last month or so that he's attempted to pull himself together. Most afternoons, he goes out and looks for work. He's thrown his application in for a couple of other jobs. Ones that aren't necessarily in his field. And he doesn't seem to be drinking quite as heavily as he was before.

It might not sound like much, but it's a small step in the right direction. I'm trying not to get my hopes up, but you have to start somewhere. Right?

That job would have gone a long way in helping him out of the vicious cycle he's been trapped in for the past five years. Unfortunately, what happened at Hansons follows him around like a stink he can't shake.

My shoulders collapse as I sit back against the couch. I don't know what to do anymore. And there aren't a lot of choices left either.

With those thoughts churning in my head, my gaze travels around the interior of the house. It's not any bigger than a shoebox with three cramped bedrooms. Now that I'm no longer living here, my brother has the room all to himself. Since Claire is the only girl, she's always had her own space. In addition to the bedrooms, there's a kitchen, a living/dining room combination, and one bathroom that we all share. There's no way this place is more than nine hundred square feet in size.

The unemployment checks Dad receives go toward the mortgage, food, and utilities. It doesn't cover anything else. There's no way in hell I could attend Barnett if I hadn't been offered a full ride. Cullum, my seventeen-year-old brother, quit playing sports so he could find a part-time job after school.

Except he doesn't just work part-time. Even though it's illegal, he works around forty hours a week. They pay him under the table in cash. Since he quit football and wrestling last year, there's no way he'll get an athletic scholarship to pay his way through school like I did. His grade point average is around a three point zero, and that's not high enough to receive an academic scholarship.

I rarely see Cullum when I stop by the house, which is probably for the best. He's surly anytime we come in contact. Trust me, I realize the situation sucks. But he doesn't have to take it out on me. I'm not the one who fucked up this family by walking away.

And then there's Claire. It's difficult to believe she's already a freshman in high school. As much as my sister has grown, she still struggles academically. Half the time, she barely scrapes by in her classes. What she needs is a tutor. Someone who can work one-on-one with her a couple times a week. Even though she's determined to succeed, academics have never come easy. It breaks my heart to watch her struggle. I've never seen anyone work so hard and get so little in the way of results. It's frustrating to stand by and watch.

But like most things, there isn't extra cash for something like that. There's barely enough money for the essentials, which is why I need to tell him what's going on. Dad doesn't know that I've already signed with an agent and have changed my plans. He wants me to stay in college and earn a degree before I move on to the pros. As ideal as that would be, it's not going to happen.

I clear my throat. "I've been giving a lot of thought to the upcoming draft, and I think I should enter it this year. There's no point in delaying the inevitable." Even though I don't tack on *because we need the money,* the words hang in the air.

His brow furrows, as if he doesn't understand why I'm bringing this up. "We already talked about this. You need to finish college first and get your degree."

My gaze bounces around the interior of our dilapidated house. What I see is all the improvements that could be made if I were to get picked up by a team this spring. It's all but a certainty. I've been scouted since I was a freshman in high school. I red-shirted my freshman year of college, which means I practiced with the team but didn't play in any of the games so I could retain four years of eligibility at the college level. I've only used up two. I could technically stay at Barnett for another two years if I wanted to get more experience under my belt.

With Cullum looking to attend college the following year, and my family barely scraping by financially, I don't see the point in waiting. Dad has been out of work for two years, and nothing has changed.

Claire needs more help than what the district is willing to provide. I've talked with the school about this. I can't get anywhere with her teachers. And her counselor is completely useless. They keep giving me the standard refrain that she's been tested and doesn't qualify for a learning disability. She's more of a gray area student, and guess what?

There isn't much help for a kid like that.

Those are the students who end up getting fucked by the system. They aren't needy enough to qualify for special education services, so they're left to their own devices. It's frustrating. My heart aches for Claire because she works so damn hard and there's nothing I can do to help her.

Doesn't my father see that entering the draft this spring is the only way to solve these issues? Doesn't he understand how much easier everything will be once I sign with an NFL team? Once I'm getting a fat paycheck?

"I can always go back to college and finish up later," I tell him. "It's not that big of a deal."

Sorrow and regret swirl through his eyes. The guy looks defeated. Beaten down by life. I can't even say that a good night's sleep would remedy the situation. In the five years Mom has been gone, the man has aged at least a decade.

It's sad to see. And it leaves me feeling helpless

With a sigh, he shakes his head. "I'm sorry, Liam. I never meant for any of this to get heaped on you or your brother." The moment those murmured words escape from his mouth, he gets sucked into the whirl of his thoughts, staring sightlessly out the grimy picture window to the tiny patch of front yard.

Heavy emotion turns the atmosphere oppressive. There's nothing I can say to change the past.

"It's okay, Dad. We're getting by. Somehow, we always manage to get by. Entering the draft this year is something that could really make a difference in our lives." I pause for a beat. "Don't you see that? The signing bonus alone will take care of everything. Cullum shouldn't be working all these hours." I gesture toward my sister's room. "Unless something is done and Claire gets the help she needs, she won't have the grades to get into college."

That's one of my biggest fears.

What happens then?

What the hell does she end up doing with her life?

Find some loser to shack up with before squeezing out three or four kids? Live in some run-down shithole like this?

No. My sister is way too good for that. She just needs a little help to make it through. Help I can provide by leaving college early and entering the draft.

Dad runs a hand through his already tousled hair. It looks as though it hasn't been brushed or combed in days. "There's an older boy from one of her classes who offered to tutor her."

I raise a brow. Yeah, that doesn't sound like a good idea. I don't trust any guy in high school. I can just imagine what he'd like to tutor her in. Guess I'll be having a little chat with my sister to see what's going on.

Claire is only fifteen years old and a freshman in high school, but she's beautiful. Tall and willowy with dark, shiny hair that falls down her slender back in a thick curtain. Last year, I brought her to a game and introduced her to a few of my teammates. A couple of them eyed her up when they didn't think I was paying attention.

You better believe I knocked a few heads together after that.

Fucking dumbasses.

The need to protect Claire rears up within me. My dad should be making sure nothing happens to her. At the very least, my brother should keep an eye on her. But Cullum is too damn busy keeping his own head above water to worry about anything or anyone else.

And I'm not around nearly enough to do it.

Another wave of suffocating pressure settles on my chest.

I lick my dry lips before going at my dad again like a battering ram. It's the only way out of this mess. "Entering the draft and turning pro has always been the goal. It's what the end game was going to be regardless of earning a degree. Who cares if it happens a year earlier than we anticipated?"

What's the point of prolonging the inevitable when my family needs the money now?

Except my father has it in his head that I need to be given that magic piece of paper from Barnett first. No one in my family has attended college, let alone actually graduated, so this is a big deal to him. And when I originally agreed to stick it out all four years and earn a degree in architecture, he was still working a job. At that point, we were scraping by. Money wasn't falling out of our asses by any means, but there was enough for the necessities.

That's no longer the case.

Dad's light blue gaze locks on mine. He appears more lucid than he has in a long time as he reminds sharply, "You promised to finish, Liam. You know it was important to your moth—"

Those words send my temper skyrocketing as I cut him off. "It doesn't really matter what Beverly wanted, now does it? She left us. Clearly, she didn't give enough of a crap to stick around." It's almost surprising just how painful those words are. I'd thought I was long past feeling anything where that woman was concerned. "She doesn't get a say in what decisions I make. She gave up that right when she walked out the door. Don't bring her into this conversation."

His red-rimmed eyes widen as his jaw goes slack before he slams it shut again. Dad's complexion turns even ruddier than before. For a moment, I feel like an asshole for voicing those vicious thoughts out loud. Except it's the truth, and he needs to get it through his thick skull that Mom isn't coming back.

When his gaze slinks toward the television in the corner, a reluctant pang of regret blooms in my chest, and I press my fingers against my eyes. I suck in a deep breath and attempt to settle everything rioting inside me. This behavior isn't like me. Normally, I don't get into it with my dad. And if I do, it certainly isn't over *her*. She's the one topic all of us avoid. If anything, I'm always trying to bolster the guy and get him back on track. Not tear him down.

What burns my ass the most is that we haven't heard one word from Beverly in all these years. Not one fucking word. She walked out on us and has never looked back.

No phone calls. No emails. Not even a lousy postcard sent from wherever the hell she ended up, letting us know she was alive.

I'll be damned if I give her any more thought than she's given us.

What pisses me off even more is that I'm taking the anger I have bottled up inside out on my dad. Sure, the man has problems. No one is going to argue that, but at least he stuck around.

I clear my throat. "I'm sorry. I know the plan had always been for me to finish college, but I'll be entering the draft this year. There isn't another way."

In response, he picks up the can of beer from the end table before giving it a little shake and lifting it to his lips.

Whatever is left, he swallows down.

My shoulders droop as I sink onto the couch and wonder when the hell I can get out of here.

CHAPTER 9

LIAM

"How old are these kids again?"

I shrug as we walk down the silent corridor. "Dunno. Second or third grade, I think."

We're on the hunt for room twelve.

"Any idea what we're supposed to talk about for thirty minutes?" The guy walking next to me yawns loudly, barely managing to cover his mouth.

I glance at him. He looks like he rolled out of bed ten minutes ago.

You're supposed to be representing here, dude. Get with the freaking program.

Jack Hillenger is a sophomore running back for the Bulldogs. He's great on the field but flies by the seat of his pants any other time. I'm the opposite. In my experience, shit gets fucked up if you don't go in with a plan. I always have an end game in mind. Half the time, it's the only thing that gets me through all the day-to-day bullshit.

An impatient sigh escapes from my lips as I ramble off a few topics. "The importance of athletics and reaching for your dreams. The discipline, dedication, and amount of hard work it takes to be a college athlete. How we balance sports with academics. The reality of how many players actually make it to the pros. Things of that nature."

Didn't Coach bother to tell him anything about what we're doing today?

His head bobs, as if my words are rolling around like marbles in the back of his brain. I'm beginning to wonder if that's all he's got rolling around up there.

"Sounds good." There's a pause. "You ever do this before?"

"Yup," I confirm, "but it was at a different school."

Last year, the public school district implemented a new program where representatives from each Barnett University athletic team would go to all of the elementary and middle schools in the city and speak about what it's like to play at the college level. They want to expose the kids to all of the different sports programs available, not just football.

Although, I won't lie, everyone is always excited to see the football players. They also want us to touch upon how many athletes actually go on to play professional sports. At this age, everyone thinks they're going to end up in the pros with a fifty-million-dollar contract.

My message last year was—aim for your dreams but have a realistic backup plan in place in case it doesn't work out. And if you really want to make something happen, you have to dedicate yourself to it. Greatness doesn't occur by accident. You have to actively pursue it. Every single day, you make the choice to practice instead of sitting on your ass, playing video games (minus the ass part). Contrary to popular belief, achieving your dreams has nothing to do with luck. It's all about hard work, commitment, and perseverance.

My aim is to inspire, but at the same time, keep it real.

"Cool." Jack shoots me an easy smile, as if he doesn't have a care in the world. I'm not going to lie, his blasé attitude is starting to chafe my ass. "You don't mind taking the lead on this, do you, bro?"

I almost shake my head. Jack has a lot to learn, which makes it impossible for me to resist fucking with him.

Instead of agreeing, I shoot him an innocent look along with a lazy smile of my own. "Nah," I say casually, "I had the pleasure of speaking last year. I thought you'd want the opportunity. I'll just stand back and jump in if you need some help along the way." I slap him on the back a couple of times. Hard enough to send him stumbling forward. "Consider this an initiation of sorts, *bro*."

It's almost hilarious the way his easy smile falls off his face. Not to mention satisfying.

His feet grind to a halt on the linoleum. "Dude, you better be fucking around with me."

My brows lower as I shoot him a look. "Watch your damn mouth, Hillenger. We're in a school."

He has the good grace to flush before his gaze darts around the empty hallway. When he realizes that his profanity has gone unnoticed, he drops his voice. "Are you being serious?" Perspiration pops out across his brow.

I don't bother to break my stride as I toss the response over my shoulder. "As a heart attack." Barely can I keep the evil grin from tipping up the corners of my lips. As far as I'm concerned, this is exactly what you get for assuming someone else is going to pick up your slack.

When we're separated by about twenty feet, Jack kicks it into gear before jogging toward me. Now his jaw is really flapping. You can almost see the panic that fills his wide eyes.

"But, but—" he stammers. Usually, Jack is one easy going son of a bitch.

Not so blasé anymore, are we?

I check my phone as we arrive at room twelve.

Right on time.

"But what, Hillenger?" I arch a brow before rapping my knuckles against the door. "Don't worry, man, I'm sure you'll be fine. Thirty minutes will fly right by. It'll be a piece of cake."

I didn't think it was possible for him to look anymore unnerved. I was wrong. The guy is sweating bullets.

"But—"

As he breaks into another sputtering rendition of *but*, the door cracks open a couple of inches, and a kid around the age of seven or eight peeks out at us. I feel like he's waiting for some sort of super-secret password before allowing us to enter. I ignore Jack, who is practically frothing at the mouth, and give the boy who stares up at us from behind a pair of wicked, black-framed glasses a cheerful smile.

"Hey, we're here from Barnett to speak with your class."

Those must be the magic words because the door swings wider, and I'm able to hear a voice in the background giving directions for cleanup. As I saunter in, Jack nips at my heels like a high-strung terrier. One that's going to get a swift kick in the ass if he doesn't pull it together.

"Dude," he whispers harshly, "there's no way I can speak for thirty solid minutes. I have absolutely no idea what to say for five." He hovers over my shoulder. "I'm going to make a total ass out of myself."

I give him a mock glare before saying, "Didn't we talk about this already? Ix-nay on the anguage-lay." I tilt my head toward the roomful of children who are watching us with owlish expressions on their eager faces. "Little ears are listening."

Jack glances around the classroom and loses what little color had been filling his normally ruddy cheeks. He looks on the verge of spewing his lunch all over the place. Bet that's not something these kids see every day.

I smirk. "Don't worry, it's all good. Just remember what we discussed in the hall."

"We didn't *discuss* anything other than a few talking points," he hisses.

Now it's my turn to look indifferent, which I do exceedingly well. My fingers drift to my chin as I ponder the comment. "Huh. Seems like you should have put a little more time and effort into this presentation." I pause for a beat. "Don't you think?"

His eyes narrow as he presses his lips together until they lose all color.

"Hello!"

As we swing toward the female voice, some strange memory pings in the back of my mind.

"Thank you so much—"

As our gazes collide, her voice skids to an abrupt halt. For one stunned moment, silence descends over the three of us before she quickly recovers.

"For, um, taking time out of your busy schedules to speak with us. The kids are so excited to hear about the football program at Barnett." She rips her startled gaze from mine before glancing at the students who sit quietly at their tables and stare expectantly.

Now that the initial shock has passed, a smile spreads across my face. An answering blush blooms in her cheeks as her gaze reluctantly skitters to mine. Unwilling to waste another moment, I thrust my hand in her direction. "We're happy to be here, thanks for having us. I'm Liam Garrison, by the way."

Indecision flickers across her face as she hesitates. It's almost as if I can hear the thoughts racing frantically through her head.

And I love it.

What's this guy doing here?

I never thought I'd see him again!

This is an absolute disaster!

$#@!*

Because clearly, she shouldn't be swearing around the kids. Even if it's in her head.

It takes everything I have inside not to chuckle gleefully at the current predicament. Good manners win out as she places her slim fingers in mine. I wrap my hand around her smaller one before giving it a gentle squeeze.

"Gia Monroe," she adds with a small frown.

I can't resist rubbing the pad of my thumb across her palm. As I do, something flares to life in her expressive blue eyes before she hastily yanks her hand away. She turns to Jack, who continues to stand sullenly at my side.

"And this is one of my teammates, Jack Hillenger," I say.

She reaches out and shakes his hand before pulling away. With her fingers clasped together in front of her, she warily backs away from us. Or maybe it's me she's attempting to distance herself from.

Yeah, that's not going to work, Ms. Monroe.

She clears her throat, looking shaken by the encounter. "Are you ready to begin?"

I flash her a dazzling smile along with a nod and wink before slapping Jack between the shoulder blades. "We're definitely ready to get this show on the road." It takes everything I have not to burst out laughing as I meet his gaze. "Aren't we, Jack?"

Other than to turn a little green around the gills, he doesn't utter a sound.

We trail after Gia as she makes her way to the front of the classroom. My gaze drops to the sway of her curvy hips. The woman definitely has one delicious backside. And just like that, I recall what if felt like to have those sun-kissed thighs locked around my waist.

Since my cock is starting to stir in my boxer-briefs and that's a definite no-no when talking with a bunch of eight-year-olds, I focus on the presentation we're moments away from giving. She introduces us to the class and asks them to show us their best second grade manners. Even though she seems to have pulled herself together again, I notice the slight tremble in her voice that belies her nerves.

Out of all the classrooms we could have ended up in, I can't believe I walked into hers.

This woman has been dominating my every waking thought for weeks. There was no way for me to track her down after the night we slept together. And now, here she is. Thrust into my life again. Almost as if some higher being with a wicked sense of humor has offered her up on a silver platter. There is no way in hell I'll allow her to slip through my fingers for a second time.

That's for damn sure.

When she turns the presentation over to us, I pause for a moment, hoping that my good buddy Jack is sweating his ass off, and has learned a valuable lesson. Although I won't hold my breath on that one.

I step forward and greet the kids with a smile. As I do, Jack's body collapses with relief. In no time at all, I launch into my schtick. I talk about growing up and participating in a wide variety of sports before figuring out that what I enjoyed playing most was football.

I tell them that showing up and playing hard on game day is about fifteen percent and dedicating yourself in practice and working on skills and conditioning is roughly eighty-five percent of the effort an athlete needs to put forth. I talk about the number of players we have on the Bulldogs football team, which is roughly a hundred, and how less than half will step foot on the field during a game. Out of all the guys playing college ball, less than one percent will make it to the pros. The rest will need to find other careers.

The entire time I speak, my gaze scans over the kids, making sure they're engaged and that I haven't lost their interest. Every so often, I glance at Gia, who stands ramrod straight at the back of the classroom. Her arms are folded tightly across her chest as a slight flush continues to sting her cheeks. Every time our gazes collide, hers skitters away.

Damn, but she's adorable.

She really is.

My memory of her from that night doesn't do her justice. She's a woman who can definitely rock the whole "hot teacher" vibe. My guess is that more than one of her students' fathers pop wood while sitting across the desk from her at conferences.

That night at O'Brien's, she wore something simple like jeans and a sweater. Today she's got on a cream-colored blouse that buttons up the front. The top one has been left undone, exposing a hint of flesh beneath. Even though she's covered up, I can see the soft curve of her breasts as the silky looking blouse molds to her body before getting tucked into a tight-fitting black skirt that hits above her knees. The outfit is topped off with a pair of black heels.

Her long, dark hair is piled high on top of her head with a few loose tendrils left to escape down her slender neck.

Yup, sexy as hell.

I keep an eye on the allotted amount of time we've been given for our presentation. Right around the thirty-minute mark, I wrap things up, knowing the kids will have a ton of questions. Now, whether or not these questions pertain to what I addressed remains to be seen.

For the first time in thirty minutes, I turn to my silent teammate. "Jack, is there anything you'd like to add?"

He surveys the crowd who, after a half an hour of listening to me yammer away, are still all eyes and ears. "Stay in school and say no to drugs."

I snort and shake my head. "Excellent advice. Now, are there any questions?"

Hands shoot up across the room. I point to a little guy with a mop of ginger-colored hair. "Yes, you."

He flashes me a grin, and I notice that his two front teeth are missing. "My dad says you're gonna turn pro, which will suck for the Dogs because you're the best quarterback they got." Then he adds, "The other guy had a crappy season."

A few giggles erupt from the kids as their eyes get all big and round like someone just swore a blue streak in front of them.

Before I can address the question, Gia gently rebukes the child. "Tommy—"

"But that's what my dad said, Ms. Monroe," he interrupts. "I'm not making it up!"

"I understand that," she says with a nod. "But is that appropriate language to use at school?"

He mulls over the question for a good ten seconds before shaking his head. "No. Sorry, Ms. Monroe." Even though he sounds properly chastised, a devilish glint lights up his dark blue eyes.

I have to bite my lower lip to stifle the grin from spreading across my face. These kids are seriously adorable. That being said, there's no way in hell I'd want to corral them all day long.

But still, they're kind of hilarious.

"Right now, my plan is to enter the draft. If I'm lucky, I'll get picked up by a team." Since I don't want this presentation to revolve around me, I try to keep my answer general. "Most of the guys I play with would like to turn pro. But the reality is that it won't work out for everyone. Either they aren't good enough to move up to the next level or they sustain a career-ending injury. So even if you think you want to play in the NFL, NHL, or MLB, it's still important to have a backup plan in place in case it doesn't work out."

Before anymore hands can shoot back up, Gia asks, "You spoke about the importance of having a backup plan, Mr. Garrison. What is your plan if playing professional football doesn't work out in the future?"

Since she's asking me a direct question, I allow my gaze to settle on her as if we're having a private conversation. "The entire time I've been playing ball at Barnett, I've also been working toward a degree. When I was in high school, I took a few CAD classes, and ended up enjoying them. If playing in the NFL doesn't work out, I plan to finish up my degree in architecture and hopefully design houses. Even if I end up turning pro, I still plan on pursuing architecture when I'm done playing football. Most NFL careers don't last more than five years. A lot of players who end up leaving a pro sport have a hard time moving on with their lives because they don't have anything to move on to."

Surprise flashes across her expression. It seems like my answer has thrown her off guard. When our gazes linger, I flash her a grin. She blinks, as if shaking herself out of a daydream, before quickly ripping her gaze from mine.

She might think I'm nothing more than a meathead jock, but it's an erroneous assumption. I've busted my ass the entire time I've been at Barnett. I've spent the last three years loading up on as many credits as I could. If I can't play football, then my scholarship disappears.

Unlike a lot of guys in my position, I've never taken school for granted. Without football, I wouldn't be receiving a free education.

After that, there are a few more questions. Most of which I allow Jack to field since I've done all of the talking. Even though our thirty minutes have officially run out, there are a dozen or so kids with their hands waving frantically in the air.

My attention stays pinned to Gia as she walks to the front of the room where Jack and I stand. "All right, boys and girls, we're going to wrap up our presentation because it's time for music." That announcement is met with groans.

When she raises her hands in a that's-enough gesture, her students quiet down. "I know you have more questions, but Ms. Jenson will wonder where we are if we don't get down to the music room on time. Can you please give Mr. Garrison and Mr. Hillenger a big thank you for taking time out of their busy schedules to speak with us?"

Somewhat in unison, all twenty-six kids say thank you, which leaves both of us grinning.

"All right, everyone, line up at the door."

As the kids bustle en masse to the exit, calling out exuberant good-byes to us, I take advantage of the chaos to speak privately with Gia.

After a moment, it becomes apparent that she's attempting to get away from me as she speed walks to where her students are lining up. She's about halfway there when I catch up to her.

"Well, well, well, *Ms. Monroe*," I say once I'm close enough, "so very nice to see you again."

Unable to avoid me, she spins around, still looking flustered by my presence.

Obviously, she hears the up-to-no-good tone riddled throughout my voice because another blush creeps into her cheeks. I can't imagine how warm they must feel, but I'd certainly love to find out. They've been on fire almost the entire time I've been here. Her gaze jerks nervously to Jack, who has been waylaid by a boy not more than five feet from where we stand. The kid's arms are flailing about wildly, as if he's drowning.

Gia clears her throat uncomfortably. "Yes, it certainly is."

It's almost adorable the way she's trying to act as if we haven't seen each other naked. That I didn't make her come a handful of times or have my mouth on her—

"Thank you so much for speaking with the class today," she continues stiffly.

My hand shoots out, wrapping loosely around her elbow so she can't scamper away.

"Mr. Garrison," she says, a slight wobble threading through her words, "I'm afraid that you'll have to excuse me. I need to get the children to music."

I drop my voice so only she can hear the soft words. "I'd like to see you again, *Gia*." Damn, but I love the way her name sounds rolling off my tongue.

The flush already staining her cheeks intensifies. She glances around before saying in a hushed tone, "For obvious reasons, I'm afraid that won't be possible."

All twenty-six kids are now at the door, waiting impatiently for their teacher to lead them to music.

When I don't release her, she whispers, "I really do have to go." There's a panicked look filling her eyes, as if she's desperate to escape from my evil clutches. "*Please.*"

Since it was never my intention to upset her, I release her arm before jerking my head in a nod. "All right."

Almost at once, she regains her equilibrium. A cool mask of indifference settles over her features. As if we're strangers and she never spent the night in my bed. Or I've never been wrapped up in the tight heat of her body. She takes another hasty step in retreat before her gaze latches on to Jack, as if he's a lifesaving device.

Relief floods through her raised voice. "Thank you, Mr. Hillenger, for speaking with us today. The children enjoyed hearing about the football program at Barnett and what it's like to be a college athlete."

Oblivious to the tension swirling around us, Jack gives her an easy-going smile before tipping his head in my direction. "Well, I really didn't do much. It was all Liam."

Damn straight it was.

Her gaze doesn't deviate from him as the corners of her lips lift slightly. "Nevertheless, we appreciate it. You made quite an impact on them." This time, when she glances at me, there's a distant yet polite look filling her eyes. "Thank you both again."

What I want is to wipe away that expressionless mask that has slipped over her features. She sure as hell didn't look like that when I was thrusting deep inside her body.

Far from it.

That image is enough to have the edges of my lips quirking upward. Something flashes in her eyes before being snuffed out.

Without another word, she walks to the door of the classroom and makes certain all the kids are lined up before heading into the hallway. Just as she disappears around the corner, her gaze flits to mine one last time.

They touch briefly, and then she's gone.

A few seconds tick by as I stare at the empty doorway, willing her to return so we can talk without twenty-six pairs of curious eyes watching us. There's not much I wouldn't give to get her alone right now. I'd like to remind her how good it felt when my mouth was coasting over her flesh. My fingers itch to tangle in that long mass of ebony-colored hair.

An image of her sitting astride me flashes through my mind. Her head had been thrown back. Her slim spine bowed. And generous breasts thrust forward. Her hair had been a wild tangle, spilling down her back in a heavy wave as she moaned out her pleasure.

Even thinking about it has my dick stiffening to a semi-erect state.

Interrupting the fantasy I've got rolling through my head, Jack asks, "What's the name of that old eighties song? 'Hot for Teacher'?" He aims a wolfish grin in my direction, appearing a hell of a lot more at ease than when we first walked through the door forty minutes ago. "What I wouldn't give to tap that a few times."

My temper ignites. "Show some freaking respect, dude. She's, like, a teacher."

"Yeah," he agrees with a leer, "a totally hot one."

I shake my head before shoving his beefy shoulder. "Come on, asshole, let's get out of here."

And just like that, my luck changes and things are looking up again.

CHAPTER 10

GIA

*A*fter dropping the kids off at music, I head back to my classroom on legs that feel as if they're made of Jell-O. The entire time I'm walking down the corridor, I'm sending up a little prayer that Liam Garrison will have permanently disappeared from my life the way he should have after the night I spent with him.

Holy mother of God.

I almost died when he turned around and my gaze collided with gunmetal-gray eyes. A strangled gurgle of laughter escapes from my parted lips as the memory crashes through my brain. For just a fraction of a second, I thought I had—for whatever reason—conjured him up in my mind.

All right, not for *whatever* reason. It's no secret that I've been thinking about him these past three weeks. After the night I spent in his bed, it would be difficult not to.

But still, I never thought I'd actually come face-to-face with him again. And yet, there he was, standing in my classroom. Waiting to speak with my kids.

If the wicked gleam filling his gorgeous eyes can be believed, then he remembers every dirty detail I confessed that night. Every single thing we did to one another.

I shake my head in an attempt to dislodge those erotic memories.

When I reach the open door of my classroom, I hesitate before forcing my legs into motion. One step, then another. If he's still hanging around, then I'll deal with him and get it over with. Air gets trapped at the back of my throat as another step carries me over the threshold. My heart beats a painful staccato against my breast as my gaze flies around the perfectly ordered classroom.

Empty.

My body wilts with relief.

Thank you, thank you, thank you.

I grab the doorframe and realize my fingers are trembling. I have to take a moment to inhale a deep breath before steadying myself.

Make that five deep breaths just to pull myself together again.

He's gone. I'll never have to see him again. It was nothing more than a fluke meeting. No big deal. He got the hint that nothing more is going to happen, and disappeared back to wherever he came from.

I almost wince.

Liam Garrison. First string quarterback for the Division I Barnett Bulldogs.

Good lord. I had a one-night stand with a college football player.

A boy.

No. As much as I want to emphasize the age difference, Liam Garrison is most definitely *not* a boy. He's all man. The things he did to my body…

A shiver works its way through me as those delicious memories flood through my head before settling in my core.

We are definitely *not* going to think about that right now.

"Hey, girl."

I jump about five feet as Harper strolls into my classroom through the short hallway/storage area that connects our second-grade rooms.

"How'd your program go? I had two women from the softball team. Highly informative actually—" As her gaze settles on my face, her voice dies. "Gia? What happened? Is something wrong?"

I shake my head, unsure where to begin. Harper knows I went

home with someone a couple of weeks ago. Naturally, she tried to pull all the juicy details from me, but I kept my lips tightly sealed.

When I fail to respond, the expression on her face floods with concern. "Gia, tell me what happened. Was there a problem with the guys who showed up for the presentation? Or is it a parent issue?" Her hands settle on her rounded hips. "You better start talking, or I'm calling the office and telling them you need a sub for the rest of the afternoon."

"One of the football players who showed up to speak with the class—"

I can't believe I actually slept with Liam Garrison.

Even though I didn't recognize him that night, I've heard the name. I would have to live under a rock not to know it. The university is right in our backyard. The whole town is crazy about Barnett football. I've even seen a few of my kids wearing red and white jerseys with Garrison stamped across the back above his number.

Which is four, by the way.

Even when his roommates mentioned his name, I still didn't connect the dots and put it all together. Why would I?

I don't follow football. I have no idea what any of the Barnett players look like. I've seen a few games over the years because Tyler insisted I watch them with him. But I don't understand the finer intricacies of the game. It's not like I paid attention to what was happening on the field. If my memory serves me correctly, I brought a stack of papers to grade.

Harper's brows knit together. "Go on." She gestures impatiently for me to continue. "One of the football players what?"

"It was the same guy I went home with a few weeks ago." I bite down on my lower lip as the truth tumbles out. "It was Liam Garrison."

Her eyes widen, looking as if they might pop out of their sockets. If the circumstances weren't so dire, and I wasn't feeling so blindsided by what transpired, her expression would be comical.

It's not often that my bestie is rendered speechless.

Laughter brims from her lips. "Oh, come on!" She glances

around to make sure we're still alone. Her voice drops as she steps closer. "There's no way you had a one-night stand with Liam Garrison!"

Disbelief isn't the reaction I was expecting.

"It was him. Liam Garrison, QB for the Barnett Bulldogs, that's who I—" Now it's my turn to glance around guiltily before whispering, "That's who I slept with."

My expression must convince her that I'm telling the truth because her breath catches as she shakes her head. "Liam Garrison! Oh my God, he's absolutely gorgeous! I had no idea he was the guy you left O'Brien's with."

"Obviously, I didn't either," I mutter. "Do you have any idea how embarrassing it was to see him again? Especially here! I almost died." The memory alone leaves me cringing.

Her eyes flood with sympathy as she nods. "I can imagine. Did he recognize you? I'm sure the guy gets around. I bet he takes girls home all the time."

I'm not sure if that comment is supposed to make me feel better or not. Until she mentioned it, I hadn't even considered he might be one of those manwhore athletes out to get laid by a different girl every weekend.

The thought makes me queasy.

I push it away before sighing. "He definitely recognized me."

She rapid-fires questions. "How do you know he remembered you? Did he mention anything about that night? Did you talk about it? Tell me everything."

"Thankfully, there wasn't much time for us to chat. I had to hustle the kids to music." I bite down on my lower lip before admitting, "He asked to see me again."

Her brows nearly hit the ceiling. "What did you say?"

For the first time since he sauntered into my classroom a little less than an hour ago, I feel like I finally have a firm grasp on the situation. "I said no, of course! There's no way I can see him again. I'm sure all he wants is a—"

"Repeat performance?" She waggles her brows.

I snort. "*Exactly*. And that was strictly a onetime thing. We both agreed."

"But it was a really good onetime thing, right?"

I press my lips together, unwilling to get into the nitty gritty details with her. The kids might be gone for their afternoon special, but still…this is hardly the time or place to talk about *that*. Plus, it's not in my nature to kiss and tell.

Although, if I'm being completely honest with myself… Yeah, it was good.

Better than good.

Okay, okay. It was amazing. Hands down, it was the best sex I've ever had in my life. If that was a ten, then the sex I've been having was probably a hard five.

If I'm being generous, a soft six.

But still, it was a onetime deal. It can't happen again. Liam Garrison is a high-profile Barnett University football player. He's still in college. He's probably twenty-two years old.

"So, that's it?"

And I'm closing in on thirty.

I slept with a man seven years younger than me.

Seven years!

That's a lot. Especially when one of you is twenty-two and the other is twenty-nine. It's like a Grand-Canyon size chasm.

I refocus my attention. "Yep, that's it."

She looks disappointed by my response.

Once I pick up the children from music, it's pretty much stack and pack time, which means that the kids clean up, stack their chairs on top of their desks, and pack up their backpacks before heading off for home.

After all of my students file out at the end of the day—and yes, they were still chattering about the football players who visited— I sit at my desk and decide what needs to come home with me for the night. There are spelling worksheets and math homework that need to be graded. I've discovered that if I don't take something home every night, it quickly turns into an avalanche of paperwork. It's better to stay on top of the situation rather than get buried beneath it.

Now that I've had more time to think about what happened earlier, everything in me has settled. As much as I hate the idea of being one of many—as Harper was kind enough to point out—I'm sure that's exactly what I was.

Just another Saturday night hookup from the bar.

Sure, he asked to see me again. But come on, I was an easy lay. The moment his lips slid over mine, I was putty in his hands. And then I was out the door before he woke up the next morning.

What college-aged guy wouldn't want to hit that again?

I push through the heavy glass door and tighten my coat around my body as I'm slapped with the chilly February air. It's almost half past four, and already the skies are darkening.

As I fish the keys out of my purse, someone calls my name.

Everything in me seizes with panic. Even though I've only heard that voice on two separate occasions, the deep timbre of it is all but burned into my brain. A chill scampers down my spine as my head whips around.

CHAPTER 11

LIAM

Gia's blue gaze widens as it collides with mine for the second time in the span of a few short hours. A satisfied smile tugs at the corners of my lips.

Looks like I've surprised her.

Again.

Oh, Ms. Monroe, did you really think I was going to let you slip through my fingers again? No way. Not after I've been thinking about you for three solid weeks. Ever since you warmed my bed with that hot little body of yours. We're not done just yet.

It's almost laughable the way her feet grind to a halt in the parking lot. Instead of closing the forty-foot distance between us, I lean against the seat of my bike. My legs are stretched out in front of me, as if I've got all the time in the world.

Even though my gaze never strays from hers, I take in every detail of her appearance. The ebony-colored hair, the delicate bone structure of her face, and the full lips that are in the shape of a cupid's bow. Not to mention, those gorgeous blue eyes that are framed by thick, sooty lashes. She can't be any more than five foot six or seven with a curvy build. Softly rounded hips, and breasts that are more than a handful.

I'll admit that my gaze detours to her breasts as I remember what it felt like to suck on her hard little nipples. She might be bundled up in a winter coat, but it doesn't take much to recall the pebbled feel of them against my tongue. The way they stiffened up as I sucked them into my mouth.

As my gaze swings up to hers again, a slight blush stains her cheeks, as if she realizes what illicit thoughts are rolling through my head.

Well, good. She might not want to be affected by me, but that doesn't mean she isn't. I can see it in the flare of her eyes. In the way her breath hitches as she stares at me.

Unable to hold myself back any longer, I straighten before swallowing up the distance between us. Our gazes stay locked as I stalk toward her. I have to crush the need that surges through me, demanding I take her in my arms. With the way she's watching me, I'm guessing that might be unwelcome at the moment, which is a shame. My fingers itch to wrap around her body again.

When I remain silent, she whispers, "What are you doing here?" Even though she attempts to keep her voice steady, a slight quiver threads its way through the richness of it.

I quirk a brow. "I think the answer to that is fairly obvious."

She shoots a quick glance around the parking lot. There are a few other teachers leaving for the day, but no one pays us any attention.

Her voice dips. "Liam—"

I love the way my name sounds sliding from her lips.

"You have to know nothing more can happen between us. The night we spent together…" Her tone turns hushed. "We agreed it was a onetime thing."

Maybe that's what the plan had been when I brought her back to my place, but everything has changed. After spending the last three weeks thinking about her, there's no way I'm walking away now that I've finally found her again.

I inch closer, wanting—no, needing—to catch the scent she's wearing. I remember the fragrance she'd been wrapped in that night. It had been something light and summery.

Her voice trembles. "I'm not going to sleep with you again, if that's what you were thinking."

All right, so maybe that's *exactly* what I'd been thinking, but that doesn't mean I can't change tactics on the fly. I wouldn't be the football player I am today if I couldn't assess the situation, think ahead a few steps, and rocket the ball to one of my teammates on the field. It's the nature of the beast, and I've learned throughout the years that life mimics football.

To a certain extent.

And right now, I see the play I was previously running isn't going to pan out the way I expected it to, which means it's time to switch things up.

I fold my arms across my chest. "Actually, I'd like to take you out."

Her brows furrow, as if I've thrown her for a loop. "Take me out?"

One side of my mouth hitches up.

I'm not going to lie, I'm more than aware it releases one of my dimples. Think of that as me pulling out the big guns and annihilating everything in my path. As far as females go, that is. For whatever reason, most chicks have a real thing for dimples. And I'm not above using them to press my advantage.

Her face softens before she narrows her eyes. "No, I don't think so. It's not a good idea."

Fine. I didn't want to do this, but she's not leaving me much in the way of options. I unleash the other one.

She blinks before the glare returns full force. "You're playing kind of dirty, aren't you?"

I suppress the urge to chuckle. She has no idea how dirty I can play when I'm going after something I want.

Instead of answering, I give her an innocent look. "I have no idea what you're talking about. I'm merely asking a pretty woman out to dinner. Last time I checked, that wasn't a crime."

The glare falls away. Sort of. She snorts, and I can't tell if she's reconsidering my offer or not.

When I walk away from this parking lot, I want to know that I'll see Gia Monroe again. That whatever this is simmering between us isn't over.

Her expression eases as she searches my eyes for an answer to a question she has yet to pose. As the moment draws out, everything in me tenses as I wait for her response.

Just when I think she might capitulate, she shakes her head. "No, I'm sorry. Us going out to dinner or doing anything together won't work."

"Tell me what the problem is," I cajole.

She nibbles at her bottom lip, as if unsure how to respond. My gaze drops to that pouty mouth. More than anything, I want to take her in my arms and sweep my lips across hers until she makes those throaty little moans that drove me so crazy. I don't realize that I've closed the distance between us until her palms flatten against my chest. It would be all too easy to plow through her feeble attempt to stop me, but I'm not going to do that.

When my gaze swings up to hers, her eyes are flared with panic. She's practically drowning in it. I don't understand what she's so frightened of.

"No! I-I can't do this with you." She draws away from me, as if I've burned the flesh of her palm, before retreating a step to create more distance between us. Then she straightens her shoulders. "I'm sorry, but the answer is no."

Unwilling to let her get away so easily, my hand shoots out, and my fingers wrap around her upper arm. Pure instinct drives me. I'm not consciously making decisions or weighing the consequences of my actions, which isn't like me. It's rare that I fly by the seat of my pants. But at the moment, I'm strictly operating on autopilot. I don't want her to slip away again.

Her breath catches as I reel her toward me. My fingers snake around her bicep. She's not flush against my body, even though that's exactly where I want her. There's a good twelve inches separating us.

In the back of my mind, I realize I shouldn't be manhandling her in this manner. Especially in the parking lot of her school. If I were thinking clearly, I'd let her go, and walk away without a second thought. There are plenty of chicks who are begging for a chance to warm my bed. I don't need to chase down a woman who wants nothing to do with me.

And yet…something won't allow me to walk away from her.

From *this*.

For three solid weeks, I've been trying to evict this woman from my head, and I haven't been able to do it. She refuses to budge.

When she doesn't resist, I tow her toward me until her warm breath can feather across my lips. The way her eyes flare and the panting little breaths that escape from her, drive me crazy. Memories of all the delicious things I did to that lovely mouth of hers explode in my brain.

"Liam," she pleads, "Please…"

The shiver that threads its way through her voice isn't fear. There's too much arousal stirring in her eyes. Even though she doesn't want to feel it, it's undeniably there, surging through her. Even though she's doing her damnedest to resist the attraction tugging at her, it's there.

My grip isn't one that is punishing. I'm merely holding her in place. The last thing I would ever do is deliberately intimidate a woman. I could never hurt one either. I have a younger sister who I'm protective of. I would wipe any guy off the face of this earth who dared to put his hands on her when she didn't want him to.

Hell, I'd kill any guy who put hands on her at all, considering she's only fifteen years old.

When it becomes apparent that words aren't going to get the job done, I drag her closer. Maybe what she needs is a reminder as to how good it felt between us. I've been dreaming of those full, sexy lips for almost three weeks. Every time I close my eyes at night, there she is, filling my dreams.

As my lips crash onto hers, her body stiffens, which is counterproductive to what I'm trying to accomplish. I change tactics and immediately soften the kiss, reining in the crushing need that runs rampant through me. Instead, I nibble at her lush lower lip before licking at the upper one. Her taste explodes in my mouth, and it goes straight to my cock.

Desire rushes through my veins as I sweep my tongue against the seam of her lips. She presses them tightly together, not allowing me entrance. A growl of frustration builds in my throat. The rumbling sound erupts from deep within my chest. I've never had a woman drive me so insane.

What is it about her?

I draw away enough to demand, "Open for me, Gia."

When I return to licking and nipping at her flesh, a whimper falls from her lips before she opens her mouth a fraction. It might not be much, but it's more than enough for me to slip inside. My tongue toys with hers before drawing it into my mouth. With a groan, she opens farther, giving me free rein to do as I please.

All I want is to hustle her back to my place and spread her out naked in my bed. I want to fuck this strange need out of my body until I'm able to think clearly. Until I can stop dwelling on her lush curves every moment of the day.

But that's not the way to go about this.

If I want her, I can't lead with my dick. I need to use my brain and reel her in nice and slow. She's not like the usual girls I jump into bed with. She's not throwing herself at me. Hell, she'd like nothing more than for me to disappear without a trace from her life. And damn if that notion doesn't have some primitive urge to conquer hurtling its way to the surface.

I really thought I was above all that Neanderthal bullshit.

Turns out I'm not.

Regret nearly swallows me whole as I pull away and rest my forehead against hers. Our breaths come out hard and fast. There's a dazed look filling her eyes, as if she has no idea what just happened.

I like that I can scramble her senses.

It takes effort to regain my equilibrium as I glance around the now empty parking lot. I realize she doesn't want anyone to see us together. Especially in such a compromising situation. Maybe I shouldn't have allowed myself to get so carried away.

Except I can't bring myself to regret it. I've been dreaming about her mouth for weeks. Now that it's swollen from my attention, my cock stiffens up.

"Let me take you out, Gia. Just one date." My lips quirk at the corners. "I promise to be a perfect gentleman."

Those words have the sexual haze clearing from her eyes. It makes me want to kiss her all over again just to put that glazed look back where it belongs. I want to kiss this woman into submission until she agrees to anything I say.

"I can't."

"It's just dinner," I coax patiently. "It doesn't have to be anything more."

Do I feel bad for feeding her a line?

Nope. Not even a little.

For a moment, Gia looks as though she might be turning the idea over in her mind. The way her body softens in my arms tells me she's tempted to explore whatever this is between us. When a regretful sigh escapes from her lips, I realize my kisses have done nothing to sway her to the dark side.

That's a shame.

"I'm sorry, Liam."

Why the hell is she fighting this?

The attraction between us is palpable.

Undeniable.

Unless…

My muscles stiffen. "Is there someone else? Are you in a relationship?"

Why didn't it occur to me sooner?

Just because she went home with me a few weeks ago doesn't mean she isn't involved with another dude. The realization pisses me off.

Her big blue eyes lock on mine as she shakes her head. I release the pent-up breath lodged painfully in my throat.

Thank fuck.

In all honesty, I'm not sure I could back off even if there was someone else in the picture. And that's totally messed up. I've never been into chicks who have attachments. I'm not that guy. The one who messes around with another man's woman. I believe in bro code.

But there's something about Gia.

Her tongue darts out to moisten her lips. "Just so you know, I wasn't involved with anyone the night I went home with you. But still, I can't do this." Her teeth sink into her lower lip. "You're in college, and I'm..." Her words trail off as we stare at one another.

"Not," I finish flatly.

"I've been out for eight years. We're in totally different places." She swallows thickly. "It's not going to work."

She won't go out with me because she thinks I'm too young?

That's complete horse shit.

Doesn't she feel the electricity pulsing between us?

It's all but eating me alive.

As my gaze scours hers, I realize the age difference is the problem.

I shift my weight as my fingers sink into her arms. "All I'm asking for is one dinner."

Regret flickers across her face as she shakes her head.

I suck in a breath before pressing my lips against hers one final time and then setting her free. There's nothing else I can do. I've already pushed the boundaries far more than I should have. It's not often I meet a woman I'm actually interested in pursuing. And now that I have, she won't give me the time of day.

Unconsciously, she mirrors my movements, drawing in a lungful of air and squaring her shoulders. With her attention locked on mine, she takes a step in retreat. When I don't eat up the distance between us, she takes another before giving me a bittersweet smile. "Bye, Liam."

Unable to force out the words, I jerk my head in acknowledgment.

I refuse to say goodbye. As far as I'm concerned, this isn't the end. This is me letting her walk away until I can devise a different plan to win her over. If there's anything positive that came out of this, it's that I know a lot more about her now than I did the last time she disappeared from my life.

Like her name and where she works.

I almost snort.

Hmm... That doesn't sound stalkerish at all.

CHAPTER 12

GIA

"Well, well, well... What do we have here?" Harper saunters into my classroom with a can of Diet Cherry Coke dangling from her fingertips and her lunch packed in a stylish hot-pink cooler. Unable to wait, I've already spread out the contents of my lunch on the horseshoe-shaped table I use when working in small groups with the kids.

I give her an I-don't-want-to-talk-about-it look, which she promptly dismisses.

"I see that you're not-so-secret admirer has sent you yet another gift." A sly grin spreads across her pretty face.

Instead of commenting, I focus my attention on twisting off the cap from my bottle of water.

When I remain silent, she forges ahead with another question. "So, that would make every day this week that you've received something?"

I don't know why she's bothering to ask. We both know the answer without me having to admit the truth. If she's attempting to make a point, I don't know what it is. She settles across from me before pulling out a small salad, sandwich, and bag of baked chips.

To answer her question, yes, Liam has had something delivered to the school office.

Every.

Single.

Day.

On Monday, it was a huge vase of flowers, which, in mid-February, is a lovely little reminder of what's to come a few months down the road when spring finally arrives. They continue to sit front and center on my desk. The kids went absolutely crazy over them. They took turns burying their noses in the bouquet and inhaling deeply. Gently, they touched the petals.

Tuesday was a cookie gram. There were all kinds of freshly baked cookies arranged in a pretty wicker basket. Sugar, chocolate chip (which he couldn't possibly know are my favorite), and snickerdoodle. Since there are a few kids in my class with allergies, I couldn't share them. But I did give about half to Harper and Sophie. The rest I took home and have been nibbling on.

Every time I put a cookie in my mouth, my thoughts turn to the handsome football player.

On Wednesday, he sent over a medium-sized gift-wrapped box. I'm reluctant to admit how my heart stuttered with excitement as I hustled down to the office to pick it up. Mrs. Banks, the secretary, eyed me with speculation before handing over the package. I think she wanted to keep it for herself.

And who could blame her?

It was beautifully wrapped. I should have realized how much trouble I was in when I couldn't set it aside and patiently wait until I was home to open it.

Since the kids were at recess for another fifteen minutes, I tore into the package like a kid on Christmas morning before pulling out a medium-sized, red and white jersey with Liam's last name and number embossed on the back.

Is it terrible that I've slept in the shirt the past two nights?

I think it might be.

As much as I'm trying to hold strong against the guy, he's beginning to wear me down.

On Thursday, he sent over a huge box of Barnett Bulldogs souvenirs for the kids in my class. Pencils, pens, visors, playing cards, stickers, tattoos, notepads, and autographed programs. It wasn't just football stuff either. There was paraphernalia from all of the other athletic teams, which was thoughtful since not all of the kids are into football.

Naturally, they went wild dividing up all the stuff.

And Friday...

I hate to admit that I'd spent all morning filled with anticipation for what today would bring. When I received the call around eleven that something else had arrived at the building, I dashed down to the front office as quickly as my kitten heels could carry me.

With my breath coming out in short pants, I glanced at a beaming Mrs. Banks, who gave me a knowing wink. "That was fast!" Then she handed over a card with a beautiful long-stemmed white rose. With a quick thank you, I hustled back to my classroom before ripping open the card.

Deep down, I knew what it would say before glancing at the neatly scrawled words.

Harper glances at the white rose on the table. A knowing grin curves her lips. "What are you going to do about this guy? Clearly, he doesn't give up easily."

I have to agree with her assessment regarding the situation. Liam Garrison will not go quietly into the night like I had assumed.

As I open my mouth to respond, Sophie rushes into the room with her bagged lunch in hand. "I didn't miss anything, did I? What did he send today?"

She has the look of a crazy person as her gaze darts all over the place. Her cheeks are flushed from speed walking to my room, which is located on the other side of the school from hers.

Her face softens and her feet grind to a halt when she spots the rose. She sucks in a breath before releasing a sigh, as if this is ten times better than any sappy, over-the-top, Hallmark movie during the holiday season.

"A rose? He sent one long-stemmed rose?" Just in case I missed it the first time, she releases a dramatic sigh before settling next to Harper. "That is so stinking romantic, I almost can't stand it."

It's painful to admit that I feel the same. The gesture is ridiculously romantic. I can't remember the last time a man sent me anything, let alone a week's worth of gifts.

Her gaze falls on the card as she sinks her teeth into her sandwich. With a mouthful of bread, cheese, and turkey, she asks, "What does the card say?"

I pick up the thick, white envelope and hold it out to Sophie. Her face lights up as she carefully pulls out the creamy card and stares down at it. Almost immediately, her whiskey-colored eyes swing up to mine.

"All it says is *Be ready at six o'clock.*"

Silence falls over the three of us before Sophie and Harper explode with questions.

"Oh my God, what are you going to do?"

"You're not actually going out with him, are you?"

I squeeze my eyes tight and whisper, "I don't know."

It seems pointless to start up something with Liam if I'm not willing to get involved with him. Under normal circumstances, I'm not one for casual sex. That's just not me. If I find someone I like, then exploring a relationship is the next logical step. I might be attracted to Liam, but our lives are in totally different places.

"Gia, you have to go out with him!" Sophie's eyes are bright and shiny, her enthusiasm high. It's been a while since I've seen her look this excited. I'm half-tempted to go out with Liam simply because she's so thrilled by the prospect. "He could have given up on you, but he hasn't."

The corners of my lips tip upward as I shake my head. "Persistence isn't a reason to go out with someone." I sigh, then add, "In fact, in some instances, it's actually a reason to call the cops for a restraining order."

Sophie rolls her eyes as Harper adds her two cents worth. "Why would you even bother? He's still in college. Guys his age aren't interested in real relationships. They're interested in straight-up sex."

When Sophie glares, Harper holds up her hands in a gesture of surrender. "Sorry, but we all know it's the truth. If you're okay with being a piece of ass on the side, then, by all means, go for it." She gives me a hard look. "But that's not you, G. You're a relationship kind of girl. You always have been."

Harper's comment is enough to have all of my previous giddiness deflating. She's right. Liam isn't interested in anything more than a good time. Why would he be? It wouldn't surprise me in the least to discover there were twenty girls he could text at the drop of a hat if he wants to get laid.

The last thing I need is to get wrapped up in someone like that.

When I remain silent, Harper's voice softens. "Look, G, I don't want to see you get hurt. That's all."

"I know." It takes effort to shake off the disappointment as I force a smile. "You're right. He's too young."

Sophie cuts in as her gaze bounces between the pair of us. "Oh, come on, he's not *that* young."

Harper's brows snap together. "Soph, he's like twenty-two." She points to me. "G is going to be thirty this year."

Sheesh.

I almost wince as she says that number out loud.

Sophie narrows her eyes at Harper before dismissing her. Once her gaze has settled on me, she says, "So what if he's a few years younger? Does it really matter?"

I don't know.

Maybe?

My attention locks on Harper. I want to hear her thoughts on the matter. Her comments have only reinforced what's been churning inside my head.

Always willing to play devil's advocate, Harper shrugs. "Okay, let's say for shits and giggles that they go out and end up having a great time. They're both into it. So, they go out again. And again. And then they start sleeping together. After a month or two, he gets bored and ends it." Her gaze snaps to mine. "No offense, G."

My lips flatten. "None taken."

As difficult as it is to admit, she's right. That guy had tricks up his sleeve I'd never seen before. Sure, it was great for me. But what did he get out of it?

"Then Gia is left trying to get over a twenty-two-year-old player she had no business getting involved with in the first place."

Well, when she puts it like that…

"You have no idea what's going to happen between them." Sophie's brows furrow as a look of exasperation settles over her features. She glances at me. "It's just dinner, right?"

When I jerk my head in a nod, she says, "Go out with the guy and see what happens. Thank him for all the thoughtful gifts he sent this week. See how the night goes and then take it from there."

I bite down on my lip before voicing another question. "What about Tyler?"

Sophie raises a brow, as if she's already dismissed my ex from her thoughts. "What about him?"

"The whole thing feels awkward," I mumble.

"You and Tyler broke up almost three months ago and, according to you, there's no chance you'll get back together again. Whether he understands that isn't your problem. There's no conflict of interest or whatever lame excuse you're trying to come up with to get out of this dinner." She inhales a deep breath before finishing with, "For once in your life, just go with it, Gia. Enjoy an evening out with a really hot guy. It doesn't have to be anything more than that."

My gaze slides reluctantly to Harper as she shakes her head. "There's too much to overcome here." She ticks off the reasons on her fingers. "He's way too young to consider getting serious with." Second finger. "He's still in college." Third finger. "He's a high-profile athlete, which means he's probably a player." Fourth finger. "He's turning pro, so who knows where he'll end up."

Leave it to Harper to bottom line everything.

My gaze bounces between my two best friends and their conflicting advice. How is it possible that I'm more confused than ever?

CHAPTER 13

GIA

It's quarter to six and Liam should be arriving in fifteen minutes. Even though I'm showered and have shaved to within an inch of my life, my hair is straightened, makeup is perfectly in place, and I'm dressed, I'm still not sure if I'll go through with this date.

I hate to sound like a broken record but...

What's the point?

We're either going to walk away at the end of the night and never see each other again or—

My brain shies away from considering the other possibility. I'm scared to death that this date will go well. What if we have a nice time?

What then?

The age difference between us feels insurmountable. If we were both older, and in the same place in life, it would be a different story.

But we're not.

If I've learned anything over the years, it's that relationships are hard. What's the point of investing time in one when we both know it's not going to work out in the end?

I spend the next fifteen minutes torturing myself with indecision.

Vacillating one way and then the other. It was sneaky of Liam not to give me his cell number. There's no way to contact him and call this off. When the doorbell rings at six, I'm a ball of nervous energy. It's ridiculous how much this guy affects me.

He's practically a kid, for goodness' sake. Barely out of his teens. And I'm a grown woman. I really need to start acting like one. I suck in a steadying breath before carefully expelling it from my lungs. Then I square my shoulders and force myself to the entryway.

I can do this.

I will politely thank him for all the thoughtful gifts before declining his dinner invitation. In less than ten minutes, he'll be gone, and I can get on with my evening. I'll make myself a can of soup and a grilled cheese sandwich before grading papers. Maybe I'll pour myself a glass of wine. Then I can hit the sack early. It's been a long week and I'm exhausted.

I almost wince at the image.

That sounds...seriously pathetic.

All I need is a dozen cats and I'll be set for impending spinsterhood.

I snap out of those depressing thoughts as the doorbell rings for a second time, and butterflies wing their way to life inside the confines of my belly. Every step I take feels as if I'm walking toward impending doom.

I'll reiterate that we can't get involved. I just need to stand firm. Maybe then he'll realize I won't change my mind anytime soon.

Instead of the bell ringing for a third time, he raps his knuckles against the thick wood as I wrap my fingers around the knob and pull it open.

Our gazes collide, and the breath gets sucked from my body. He looks seriously handsome. The two times I've seen Liam, his mahogany-colored hair had been styled into a fauxhawk. According to Harper, this is his signature look. After she told me that, I realized I've seen about half a dozen kids around school sporting the same hair style.

Instead of the fauxhawk I've become accustomed to, the longer part on top is combed back, away from his face. His gray gaze snaps and sizzles as it locks on mine. He's wearing a short, black leather jacket. Even though it's frigid outside, it hangs open, revealing a tan Henley paired with dark-wash jeans.

My mouth turns cottony.

How is this guy only in college?

No one has ever made me feel so weak in the knees. It's ridiculous. When I continue to ogle him like a star struck fan, his mouth hitches up in humor. It releases one of his dimples. Those damnable dimples will seriously be the death of me.

And he knows it too.

Which makes it even worse.

"Hey." His gaze slides over the length of me before bouncing up to skewer mine. "You look gorgeous."

My hand flutters over my skirt. I might not have been certain about going out tonight, but I still dressed for it. My short skirt hits just above the knee, and a form-fitting floral blouse hugs my curves. A pair of tall, black boots completes the outfit. It's a little upscale casual.

I clear my throat. "Thank you."

Tell him you can't go out with him.

Just get it over with!

I bite down on my lower lip, knowing exactly what I need to do. That means ending this as swiftly and painlessly as possible.

His eyes lose their humor as he cocks his head. The smile fades from his face. "Are you having second thoughts?"

Somehow, the serious expression is more devastating than the impish smile that released his dimples. How is that even possible?

I release the air that's wedged in my lungs, wanting to be truthful. "It-It's just that…going out," I stumble inarticulately over my words, which isn't like me at all, "won't change anything between us. You have to know that." It feels like I'm fighting an uphill battle. Every time he looks at me with his fathomless gray depths, my insides turn to mush.

He nods. "All right. If it won't change your mind, then let me take you out. If you still feel that way at the end of the evening, then I'll say goodnight, and you'll never see me again." He draws an imaginary X across the left side of his broad chest. "Cross my heart."

As we stand at the front door and stare at one another, I realize he's waiting for me to make a decision. Even though it's a terrible idea—trust me, I know it is—I feel myself capitulating.

What is it about Liam that turns my brain cells into a pile of mush?

There's no way to deny the attraction that hums between us. It's like a living, breathing entity. I've never experienced anything like it before.

But still...attraction isn't enough of a reason to get involved with someone.

When a handful of minutes slip by, he stretches out his hand. For a heartbeat, I stare at it before placing my fingers in his larger ones. With a slight tug, he reels me closer. It's exactly what he did in the school parking lot a week ago. And just like then, my heart skips a beat at the contact.

His gaze sears mine. "Let me take you out tonight. We'll have a nice dinner, get to know one another, then I'll take you home. How does that sound?"

Argh.

Why can't I say no?

As I nod, I realize how much I want this. I want to figure out Liam Garrison. Maybe then I won't feel this all-consuming attraction to him. Maybe I'll realize he's nothing more than a twenty-two-year-old college student—one I have nothing in common with.

Physical attraction is important, but there has to be more to it than that. A relationship won't last if there's not a firm foundation of shared interests.

"All right."

He tugs me closer before pressing his lips against the side of my face. "Nothing will happen that you don't want."

Yeah...that's kind of the problem, now isn't it?

At the moment, I'm not sure what I want to happen between us.

Or maybe I do.

Maybe I know *exactly* what I want.

CHAPTER 14

LIAM

*A*s soon as she opened the door and my gaze slid over her, my heart stuttered before beating in double time. And—if you can believe this—my palms broke out in a sweat.

I know, right?

Completely ridiculous.

I don't think a chick has ever tangled me up like this.

It only makes me realize how much I want her to give me a chance. I don't want this to end before it even begins. After sending her gifts all week long, hoping to ensnare her attention, or at the very least draw out her curiosity, I don't have any other tricks up my sleeve unless I want to scare her with some borderline creepy behavior.

Now that her hand is secured in mine, there's no way I'll let it go. I've been thinking about Gia since I saw her last Friday afternoon.

"Let me grab my purse and lock up before we go," she says.

Does that mean I have to relinquish her hand in order for that to happen?

Because she's staring at me like it does.

Fine, I'll let her go. But as soon as I hear the lock click into place, I'm stealing her hand again. I like the way her fingers feel enclosed in mine. The moment I release my grip, she steps farther into the house before grabbing a black bag off the coffee table in her living room.

As I follow her inside, I can't help but notice how nicely decorated her place is. Warm earthy paint colors, an overstuffed couch, and two armchairs. Framed artwork hangs on the walls. It's a far cry from the apartment I moved into with Sam and Roan, which looks exactly like what it is—a dude's place where no one gives a shit.

That includes the cleanliness of the bathroom, which is just plain gross. You know damn well I'm the only one cleaning the toilet. At times, it resembles a sketchy-looking Chia Pet.

Know what you won't find at our apartment?

Posters of half-naked girls with their tits hanging out tacked up on the walls. I think Ivy, Roan's girlfriend, and Violet, Sam's significant other, would rip them down before shoving them right up their—

"All right, I'm ready to go."

"Great." Quietly, I slip her fingers into my own. For a moment, I wait to see if she'll attempt to pull them free. When she doesn't, something settles inside me.

Once Gia locks up her house, we walk down the cement path to my car. It's an old Honda Accord that has seen better days. My guess is that those days were probably in the late nineties. When I was a kid, there was this guy down the block who liked taking apart and fixing up old vehicles to get them running again. Luckily for me, this one has a rebuilt engine. So even though it's old, it's reliable.

I hit the locks and open the door for her. As soon as she's secured inside, I hustle around the hood before sliding in next to her. With a turn of the key, the Honda roars to life. We pull away from the curb and wind through the quaint, tree-lined streets near her house. The yards are tidy and neat. There aren't toys and junk strewn about the front lawns. Or dogs chained up outside, left to bark incessantly. The cars parked in the driveways are mostly minivans and other family-friendly SUV's. It's a far cry from the neighborhood I grew up in.

"No motorcycle tonight?" she asks, breaking into my thoughts.

I glance in her direction and notice the way the material inches up her thighs. With a raised brow, I shoot back, "You're wearing a skirt."

A smile quirks her lips as her muscles relax and she sinks into the seat. "Guess I forgot about that when I was getting ready."

I throw another glance at her gorgeous legs. "I'm glad you did. You look nice." And those black, knee-high boots hugging her calves are definitely starting to give me ideas. Although, I'll keep those thoughts to myself for the time being. The last thing I want to do is scare her away.

"Thanks." She clears her throat before changing the subject. "Where are we headed?"

"I thought we could try the Mexican place downtown."

Her eyes light up, and I'm doubly glad I picked that restaurant for our date. "That sounds great! I haven't been there in a while."

"Neither have I."

Even though I don't eat out very often, I've stopped in a few times. I don't have a lot of extra money to piss away like some of my friends and teammates. There's no way I can hold a job during the school year with football. Plus, I usually take eighteen credit hours each semester. During the summer months, I work at my friend's auto garage. It's six days a week and all the overtime I can put in. Since he charges significantly less than other garages, he's always slammed with work. If I'm careful, I can usually bank enough money during the summer to last throughout the school year.

I blew some of my savings on the flowers and cookies I sent to Gia. It probably wasn't the smartest way to spend my cash, but it was a gamble I was willing to take. And since she's sitting in the car next to me, I'm glad I did.

The drive downtown takes about fifteen minutes. Another five and we have menus in front of us that we're both perusing. Although, I've been here enough times to know what I want to order.

As I hold the menu, my gaze continually slides to Gia, who is seated across from me. The first time I saw her at the bar almost a month ago, her hair was falling down her shoulders in thick, heavy waves. I still remember how soft and luxurious it felt as I tunneled my fingers through it, holding her firmly in place as she sucked my throbbing erection into her mouth.

That thought alone is enough to have my cock stiffening up.

When I saw her at the school, her hair had been pulled up into a tight bun at the top of her head. A few wispy tendrils had been left to curl down the elegant column of her neck. Her cream-colored blouse paired with a narrow black skirt was sexy as hell. It had me wanting to pull her hair free before stripping off every last stitch of clothing.

Tonight's hair style is different again. This time it's straight as a pin. Long and silky. Already my fingers itch to sift through the heavy curtain of it.

I can't decide which style I like better.

It takes another full minute before I become conscious of the fact that her attention has settled on me. I should probably feel embarrassed to be caught staring so blatantly.

I'm not.

I want this woman.

And I want her to know it.

I've never been one to play games. I don't have the time or energy for that crap. When I see something I want, I go after it. And I don't give up easily. Hell, I wouldn't be where I am today if I went with the flow. If I've learned anything in my twenty-two years, it's that you need to carve out your own destiny.

You can't allow others to dictate the path you blaze.

A blush suffuses Gia's cheeks as her gaze stays fastened on mine. The sexual tension ratchets up between us until my fingers bite into the plastic menu.

Her breath catches.

It's crazy what this woman does to me. There's no way in hell she doesn't feel the strange energy we generate.

Gia shifts nervously, almost as if she can feel the sharp edges of my desire, before blurting, "I meant what I said in the school parking lot —I'm not going to sleep with you." As soon as the words escape, she nips her bottom lip with her teeth as a blush continues to bloom in her cheeks. She sounds a little less sure of herself as she tacks on, "If you were thinking tonight would end with us screwing each other's brains out, it's not going to happen."

Hearing her give voice to those thoughts makes me want to leap across the table and maul her with my lips. My cock is throbbing almost painfully.

I force out the air that has become trapped in my throat before admitting softly, "I won't deny that I was hoping it would end that way, but it was never a forgone conclusion. I wanted to take you to dinner and get to know you better."

I'm trying to be honest with her.

Do I want to sleep with Gia again?

Hell yeah.

I'd be lying through my teeth if I didn't admit it.

But is that all I'm interested in?

Nope. Not by a long shot.

Her gaze drops to the menu as she says in a clipped tone, "You don't know anything about me. We slept together once. It was a hookup. Don't make it out to be anything more than that."

I nod. She's not wrong.

The night I took her home was a hookup, pure and simple. Neither of us were looking to jumpstart a relationship.

I settle against the chair as her comments circle through my brain.

"It might have started out that way, but I'm interested in more. Haven't I made that clear?" Before she can open her mouth to respond, I continue in the same lazy tone, "And I'm an observant guy. I've already figured out a number of things about you."

One skeptical brow rises as she stares at me from across the table. The challenging look she aims in my direction prompts me to say, "I know you teach second grade at North Hill Elementary. And, if you decided to go into education, then you must like children. No one in their right mind would agree to spend their entire day around kids if they didn't have an affinity for them. How am I doing so far?"

My words do exactly what they're meant to, which is bring a slight smile to her lips and a softening to her eyes. "All right, you caught me. I enjoy spending my time with kids. They make me laugh, and I like sharing new ideas with them. I love the innocent way they view the world. It's refreshing. As much as I teach them, I learn a lot from them in return. I have yet to have a boring day."

Gia might not realize it, but she's revealing a lot about herself, and there's not a damn thing I don't like so far.

"You obviously have good taste because your home is nicely decorated. It's both comfortable and welcoming."

The slight smile simmering around the edges of her lips reluctantly grows. "Thank you."

This one is a total shot in the dark, but I'm going for it because my instincts tell me I'm right on the money. "And you have a brother."

This sends her brows shooting up across her forehead in a comical manner. "Is that a guess or do you know for sure?"

"The guy from O'Brien's, the one who was playing with the band, he's your brother."

She tilts her head. "Why would you assume that?"

I shrug. "After a while, I realized you two looked alike. Same color eyes and stubborn set to your chin. Plus, he was protective of you."

Her tongue sweeps across her teeth. "You're right. That was my brother, Noah. He plays with The Renegades. That's why we were at O'Brien's that night."

I pick up my glass of water and take a sip. "I've heard them a few times before. They're pretty good. How long has he been performing?"

Her muscles loosen, and the tight smile turns a few shades warmer as I draw her out of her protective shell. "I can't remember a time when he didn't have a guitar in his hands. You know the way some people are with their phones? Almost like it's an extension of them?"

When I nod, she continues, "That's the way he's always been with his guitar. My parents bought him a Fender when he was nine years old, and he taught himself how to play. When he was thirteen, he got some kids together from school, and they started hanging out in our garage and playing music. It evolved from there. He's been with the same group of guys ever since."

My brows rise. "He's been playing with The Renegades since middle school?"

"Pretty much," she says with a nod. "Logan, their drummer, recently quit to go back to school, but yeah, the other three have been together since the beginning. Even as a kid, Noah realized that music was something he wanted to pursue. It was never a question."

Her words reverberate through my head. "I guess when you know something's right, you have to do everything in your power to make it happen."

She shifts and gravitates closer to me. "Is that how you feel about football? Did you always know it was something you wanted to pursue?"

That's not a question I have to think about. Football has always been a bright light in the darkness. Sometimes it feels like it's the only reason I made it out of where I came from.

"The first time I picked up a football, it felt natural. From a young age, I could understand the intricacies of the plays. I was able to think a few steps ahead. I've always loved everything about the game. The camaraderie and the sense of belonging. The strategy it takes to win. The challenge of it."

When everything was falling to hell around me, all I had to do was immerse myself in the game. I could block out the bullshit that was happening. For a few precious hours every day, I could escape.

Even before my mom took off, life wasn't picture perfect. We struggled. Finances were tight. It wasn't like we were living in the lap of luxury. Like most parents, mine fought. Mom was never happy. And she made no bones about hiding it from us. Nothing my father did was ever good enough. But still, I never thought she would pick up and leave. One day I came home from school and she was gone. She said her goodbyes in a short note we found propped up on the kitchen table.

That was it.

Then life got shittier for all of us.

Dad wasn't able to handle us on his own. Once he started to unravel, there was no stopping the downward spiral.

It takes a concerted effort to clear away the memories. "At the end of the day, as much as I love the game, that's all it is. *A game.* It's not one I'll be able to play for the rest of my life. To some extent, it's just a means to an end. I don't ever let myself forget that."

A thoughtful expression crosses her face, as if she's silently turning my words over in her head. It occurs to me that I've probably revealed a little too much. Since I don't want to delve into all my family bullshit, I gloss over it. "I have a seventeen-year-old brother and a fifteen-year-old sister. Making it to the pros means they won't have to worry about paying for college. I can take care of that for them."

Emotion flickers in her wide blue eyes.

I don't add that it also means there will be food on the table and new clothes when they outgrow their old ones, which they do at an alarming rate. It also means no more having to wait until the next check to buy a necessity. Or shopping with a couple of bucks at the local thrift store. And I sure as shit don't mention that I'll have enough money to get my father into a decent rehab program so he can finally sober up enough to function the way we need him to.

Entering the draft this year means that my brother can stop busting his ass for cash under the table and focus on school for a change. He hasn't done that since freshman year of high school. His biggest concern in life should be acing his tests and making the varsity wrestling team. He shouldn't have to worry about paying the electric bill and buying groceries for the next two weeks.

But I don't say any of that.

The last thing I want is Gia's pity.

As far as the draft is concerned, it's a done deal. It doesn't matter what Dad wants. My family can't afford to wait for me to finish up my degree. Everyone is stretched painfully thin. Something has to give, and entering the draft is the only factor I have control over. So that's what I'm going to do.

Her voice softens, as if she understands there's more to the story than what I've put out there. "That's a lot of pressure riding on you."

I shift in my seat and shrug. "Not really." She has no idea what my life has been like up to this point. Playing ball in the pros is easy. Sitting by helplessly and watching shit fall apart at home is the hard stuff. It's the stuff I can't do anything about.

People say money doesn't buy happiness, and to a certain extent, I'll agree with that sentiment. What I know is that life is a hell of a lot easier when you have the funds to take care of the crap that's always falling apart. Life is easier when your belly is full of nutritious food instead of continuously growling with hunger.

Anyone who says differently has never gone without.

I push those unwanted thoughts away before hoisting my lips into a grin. "See? I've already learned quite a bit about you. And this is only our first date."

A spark of humor ignites in her eyes. "Were you thinking there would be more?"

The teasing tone in her voice puts me at ease. So far, I think this night is going pretty well. In fact, it's going a hell of a lot better than I imagined. Although, that doesn't mean I'm going to push anything. Not until I'm a hundred percent sure she's into it.

All right, maybe eighty-five percent.

Eighty, at the very least.

CHAPTER 15

GIA

He gives my hand a gentle squeeze. "I had a really good time tonight."

Liam has had my fingers enclosed in his larger ones all evening. Someone needs to explain how it can feel so natural when this is the first time we've been out.

We slept together a month ago…

And then I fled the scene of the crime.

This should feel awkward. Oddly enough, it doesn't.

Liam is so open and affectionate. Kind of like it's no big deal. Even though I try not to, I can't help but compare him to my ex. Tyler was definitely not into public displays of affection. We never held hands when we were out and about. It's only now that I realize how much I like the feeling of my hand being buried in his larger one. The instant connection and intimacy it evokes.

Or maybe it's just Liam.

I don't know.

"Me too," I admit.

We're standing on the tiny covered front porch outside my house.

Tonight has been surprisingly…nice.

Better than nice, if I'm being honest with myself. I haven't thought about the difference in our ages since I opened the front door and saw him standing on the other side. And I'm not thinking about it now either. Not when he's staring at me so intently with those gunmetal eyes. Something deep inside me twists and turns, tying itself up into teeny tiny knots.

Trust me, no one is more shocked at how this evening has turned out than me. More surprising than that, Liam isn't the arrogant athlete I pegged him to be.

Is it terrible to admit I kind of wish he were?

It would make walking away so much easier if he were an immature twenty-two-year-old jerk.

Big sigh.

He's the furthest thing from it.

If I were smart, I'd thank him for a lovely evening—not to mention the gifts he sent—before telling him that there is zero point in pursuing a relationship.

As I blink out of those thoughts, I realize he's closer than he was a few seconds ago. His nearness has me drawing in a sharp breath. The intensity of his gaze skewers mine in place. Everything in me stills. I can only watch silently, unable to protest, as his hand comes up to caress the curve of my cheek. His gentle touch sends a shiver of need careening across my spine.

"I really hope we can do this again," he murmurs.

Put an end to this!

Instead, I remain silent as an internal debate is waged. I never expected to feel any kind of connection with Liam. It's not a secret that I'm physically attracted to the guy, but now—over the course of a few short hours—it somehow feels deeper.

Yes, he turns me on. Although, after tonight, it's more than just physical. He allowed me a small glimpse into his personal life, and now I want more.

"Do you really think that's a good idea?" At this point, I'm looking for any reason not to see him again.

He tugs on my hand, pulling me toward him until his arms can wind around me. Being wrapped up like this makes me remember how good it felt to have his solid weight pinning me to the mattress.

With his gaze locked on mine, he asks, "What makes it such a bad idea?" Before I can answer, he adds, "Let me remind you that you admitted to having a good time a few moments ago."

"I did," I reluctantly confess.

"What's the problem, then?" There's a pause. "I'm not seeing anyone else. And neither are you. We're both available and interested. Shouldn't that be enough for now?"

Even though I don't disagree with his logic, I can only shrug. "I guess it comes down to you being in college and me...well...*not*."

He shifts his weight. "Why is the age difference such a big deal to you?"

A burst of frustration explodes inside me as I shake my head. I'm having a difficult time articulating my feelings. And maybe part of the reason for that is because I'm so conflicted about it.

Deep down inside, I know this is wrong.

The problem is that after spending the evening with Liam, it doesn't necessarily feel as wrong as it should. At the restaurant, I didn't dwell on our ages. I simply enjoyed his company and the buzz of electricity that constantly zinged between us.

As I force the explanation from my mouth, it feels like a paper-thin attempt to shut down something that has the potential to be overpowering. "Right now, the difference feels huge. I'm twenty-nine, Liam. I'll be thirty in October. If I'd just graduated from college two or three years ago, it wouldn't be an issue. But that's not the case."

His chest rises and falls as he presses me against him. His strong, steady heartbeat shouldn't put me at ease. Nothing about this moment should feel right. "Are you telling me that this connection isn't worth exploring because you're a few years older than I am?

"It's more than just a few," I say with a snort.

He pulls away before his hand drifts to my cheek for a second time, cupping it. "Maybe I need to give you something to think about."

He closes the distance between us until his lips can lazily skate over mine. If I thought he would take what he wanted in a show of physical strength, I couldn't have been more wrong. The caress is all soft strokes that leave me wanting more. This kiss melts every qualm clamoring inside me like snow in the springtime.

It's all too easy to lose myself in the slow sensual slide of his lips as they move across mine. I don't realize my mouth has opened under the firm pressure until his tongue slips inside to play havoc with my own. A whimper of pleasure escapes from my lips only to get swallowed up by him.

This man puts all the other kisses I've experienced to shame.

Just when I think he'll delve deeper and take it further, he surprises me yet again by drawing away. I'm pretty sure there's a dazed look filling my eyes. His kisses have a strangely drugging effect on my senses.

Before I can string together a few coherent words, he presses a gentle kiss against my forehead. "I want you to think long and hard about all the roadblocks you keep throwing up, Gia. If this ends tonight, it'll be because you shut it down. Not me. I'm interested, and I haven't played any games with you. We can take this slow. One date at a time. It doesn't have to be anything more than that. You're the one in control here. And yeah, even though the sex was amazing, that's not what I'm after." His gaze burns into mine. "If this were solely about getting laid, there are a dozen girls I could call right now who would be more than happy to show up at my apartment—"

My eyes narrow. It's not that I don't believe him. I'm sure that's *exactly* the way it is. Liam doesn't have to chase girls. Not with his bad-boy looks or the position he plays. And then there's all the NFL hype that surrounds him. It's yet another reason I'm hesitant to get involved. I've heard enough talk from Tyler about what goes on with these college athletes. They're treated like demi-gods around campus and in town.

Do I necessarily want to get caught up in someone who has groupies constantly hanging around them? Begging for crumbs of attention? Willing to do anything these guys want?

I don't know.

Before I can respond, he shakes his head. "That's not me bragging.

I'm simply stating facts. All I want is the chance to explore this." He allows those words to hang in the air. "The ball is in your court, Gia. You need to decide if getting involved with me is something you're willing to take a chance on."

Surprised by the ultimatum, I nod.

"Give me your phone," he demands.

I yank my gaze from his and fish the phone out of my purse before handing it over. As he taps in the number, I can't help but suck oxygen into my lungs. My head is spinning.

This is crazy, right?

There's no way I should be considering another date with Liam.

And yet, that's exactly what I'm doing.

A handful of seconds later, he returns my cell. When I attempt to pluck the phone from his fingers, he holds on tight. Our gazes fasten as the cold night air swirls around us in the darkness.

"As much as I want to see you again, Gia, it has to be your decision. You're the one filled with doubts, not me. I've tried to show you the kind of guy I am. If that isn't enough to put your worries to rest, then there's nothing more I can do."

He presses one last kiss against my lips before retreating down the front porch steps and into the night.

CHAPTER 16

LIAM

I glance at the bottle in my hand. I know zilch about wine. The best I can hope for is that the dude at the liquor store didn't steer me in the wrong direction by recommending this particular brand.

As I reach out to ring the bell for a second time, Gia opens the door. The breath gets knocked from my lungs as our gazes collide. It's like this every damn time.

I take her in, from the top of her head to the tips of her toes. Tonight, she's left her inky black hair long and loose. It cascades in glossy waves past her shoulders. It reminds me of the first night I saw her at O'Brien's.

I'm considering the merits of dropping to my knees and thanking whoever designed the sweater she's wearing because it hugs her body in all the right places as it showcases the amazing curves of her breasts, making them look even softer than I remember.

It's probably not a good time to dwell on her pink-tipped nipples. Somehow, I doubt popping wood within the first few minutes of her opening the door will score me bonus points.

My gaze continues to coast over her before landing on the skintight leggings.

Holy hell.

That boner is getting more difficult to control. I focus my attention on her feet because they can't possibly be—

Yup. Cute as hell.

Even though it's nearly the end of February, and it's still frigid out, she's not wearing any socks or shoes. Her toenails are painted a rich blue that match her eyes perfectly.

This woman couldn't be sexier if she tried. I'd like nothing more than to chuck this bottle of wine over my shoulder and haul her into my arms before tearing every last shred of clothing from her.

If she's trying to drive me insane...mission accomplished.

I'm already there. And I haven't even crossed over the threshold yet.

My fingers are wrapped around the neck of the bottle so tightly, I'm half afraid it'll shatter.

When my gaze finally detours to hers again, there's a smirk curling the edges of her lips. One dark brow arches on her forehead as if she knows *exactly* what kind of illicit thoughts are running rampant through my brain.

"You look gorgeous." I thrust the bottle toward her, attempting to get things back on track. Not to mention my cock back under control where it belongs.

She reaches out and rescues the wine. "Thanks. It was thoughtful of you to bring something."

"I, ah, hope it's okay." I give her a slight shrug, feeling out of my element. "I'm not much of a wine connoisseur."

Now that the bottle is in her possession, she turns it over and peers at the label. "No, this is perfect." She blinks. "It's actually one of my favorites." Her brow furrows before smoothing out.

Apparently, I'll be heading back to the liquor store to personally thank that dude. He did me a solid.

She shakes her head, as if to clear it, before stepping aside. "Come in, it's cold out there."

I move into the house and find myself in the entryway. Her place might be small, but it feels homey and comfortable. Kind of like you want to kick off your shoes and cuddle up on the couch with a blanket. And totally make out. I probably shouldn't be thinking about kissing her already. I haven't even removed my jacket.

"Here, let me take your coat," she says, interrupting those thoughts.

It takes effort to rein in the smirk.

I peel off my black leather jacket and hand it over. She opens up a slim closet near the front door and hangs it up before turning back to me.

As a smile curves her lips, I can't help but admit how happy I am that she finally called and is willing to give this a shot. Willing to give *me* a shot. I might have told her the ball is in her court the last time we spoke, but I don't know if I could have actually stuck to it.

I'm not sure if I could have walked away.

Every day that passed without a word from her, left me feeling on edge. It's not my usual style. I've never chased after a chick before. This is new and uncharted territory for me.

"Thanks for inviting me over. I wasn't sure if you would call," I blurt.

She meets my stare head on. I can't help but like that about her.

"To be honest," she admits, "I almost didn't."

It might not be what I want to hear but I appreciate her leveling with me. I want to know exactly what I'm up against. "What changed your mind?"

As her gaze locks on mine, I know whatever she's about to reveal will be the unvarnished truth.

"After spending time with you Friday and getting to know more about you..." Her voice trails off. "You're not what I pegged you to be." Before I can fully relax, she tacks on, "But I need to take this slow. The age difference... I won't lie and say it doesn't bother me."

I quirk a brow. "But not enough to stop you from taking this further?"

"No," she says softly, "not enough for that."

"Good." A relieved grin splits my face. "I'm glad."

Her lips curve upward. It's not a full-out smile, but I'll take it.

For now.

"Me too."

A few moments tick by before she clears her throat. "I'm making a pesto salmon along with quinoa and a salad. I hope you're good with that?" She holds up the bottle of white that I picked up at the store. "This will go along perfectly with it."

"That sounds great." I rack my brain, trying to remember the last time a woman cooked dinner for me. It doesn't take long to come up with the answer.

Never.

So, this is definitely a novelty.

One I'm going to thoroughly enjoy.

Just as that thought rolls through my head, something rubs up against my leg. Brows drawing together, I glance down only to find a deep green gaze focused intently on me. The animal is sleek, black, and a little on the thin side.

"That's Tango," Gia says.

I hunker down and give him a good pet from head to tail. When he purrs, I stroke him a few more times.

"I take it you're not allergic?" she asks cautiously.

A strange tone fills her voice, and I glance up to meet her wary eyes.

"Nope. I like cats."

We actually had one growing up. His name was Sox. Like the baseball team. I'm sure my sister, Claire, would get a kick out of this little guy. She's a sucker for any furry four-legged creature.

A sigh of relief escapes from Gia before a smile moves across her face. She glances at the bottle in her hands. "Do you mind if I open this?"

"Nope, go right ahead." I straighten to my full height before trailing after her to the kitchen. As I do, I take in everything about her home. All the little details that reveal pieces of who this woman is. The framed art that hangs on the walls along with the knickknacks displayed on shelves. There are books scattered across the coffee table and framed photographs on end tables. Her house feels very much lived in.

Comfortable yet uncluttered.

Well kept.

Just like the living room, the kitchen is small and tidy. There's a round, white-painted table with two chairs pushed up by the far window that overlooks the backyard, and a fancy coffee maker on the counter along with a few cookbooks.

She uncorks the bottle with ease before pulling open a cabinet and grabbing two glasses. After pouring the clear contents, she hands me a long-stemmed glass. There's no way in hell I'm going to admit that I don't drink wine.

If we're drinking alcohol, it's beer. Now, it might be an import like Heineken, but it's still beer. And don't even talk to me about shots. I usually steer clear of that shit. I had a bad experience on one of my recruiting trips, and spent the next day puking out my guts. Of course, the guy I was staying with thought it was hilarious. I'm probably lucky I didn't die of alcohol poisoning.

Plus, with my dad and his issues…

I never acquired a taste for alcohol.

A smile tips the corners of her lips as she takes a sip, savoring the pale liquid on her tongue. That probably shouldn't be so hot, but I'll be damned if it isn't. When I continue to hold the glass in my hand, her smile morphs into more of a knowing grin.

"You're not much of a wine drinker, are you?" Before I can respond, she says, "I can get you something else, if you'd prefer."

"What? Are you kidding? I love wine." The lie slips easily from my tongue before I bring the glass to my lips and take a healthy gulp. Unlike Gia, there's no savoring. It goes straight down the hatch.

My insides all but revolt as it hits my belly.

Holy crap, that's awful.

Even though I attempt to keep my facial expression neutral, I'm pretty sure I grimace. A soft chuckle escapes from Gia before she nips the glass from my fingers and sets it by the sink.

"I'll take that, thank you very much. This is way too good to waste on a heathen such as yourself."

"What are you talking about? I love it." I point to the glass on the counter. "Give it back. I've never had such amazing wine before. It's, you know, fruity. And full. Full of…" I rack my brain for another adjective to describe the terrible taste lingering in my mouth. "Vigor." I want to grab the blue dishtowel hanging on the stove and swipe my tongue across it in an attempt to make it go away.

It's that bad.

"I've never heard anyone describe wine as full of vigor," she says with a laugh. "What, pray tell, does that mean?"

My lips twitch. It would appear that the jig is up. I shoot her a superior look. "Apparently, you don't know as much about wine as you thought you did. I hear vino described that way all the time."

A giggle escapes from her before she calls me out. "Liar." Gia moves across the room before opening the fridge and pulling out a green bottle of beer along with a water. "I'm afraid these are your only options."

Without a second thought, I nip the beer from her fingers. "Sold."

An easy grin lights up her pretty face as we stare at each other. The moment stretches and lengthens. When she blinks, the energy that had been gathering strength between us shatters.

She breaks eye contact, quickly moving away to peek in the oven. "The salmon should be ready in about fifteen minutes."

A small pot boils away on the stove. My guess is that it's the quinoa. Not that I would ever mention this, but I've never had that either.

"Should we sit in the living room?" she asks.

"Sure."

I follow her out of the kitchen before we settle in our respective corners. She's in an over-stuffed chair and I'm on the couch across from her. The laughter from moments ago is a thing of the past. It's obvious that her nerves have kicked in as she takes another sip of wine.

Before I can come up with anything to smooth over the tension that's sprung up between us, she clears her throat. "I know we've only been out once and this" –she gestures awkwardly between us— "isn't anything serious, but you should know I just got out of a three-year relationship." There's a pause. It's almost as if she has to force herself to continue. "I need to take this slow."

As much as I appreciate her candor, I hate the idea that she was involved in something so deep with another man. Three years. That's a long time. My most serious relationship lasted just shy of six months. And that was two years ago. The other ones have been more casual.

A few months here. A few weeks there. Nothing too deep.

"I'm sure what happened after O'Brien's," she starts, then glances away before continuing, "probably happens all the time for you."

Huh?

What the hell does that mean?

With a frown, I tilt my head. My tone comes out rougher than I intend. "Excuse me?"

Her gaze snaps to mine before she quickly drops it to the glass clasped tightly in her hand. "I just mean that you're in college." When I remain silent, her voice turns desperate. "And you're an athlete. A high profile one."

When I nod, relief floods her face.

"Ahh," I say, drawing out the sound. "Being an athlete automatically makes me a manwhore." I point a finger at her. "Got it."

Her eyes flare. "What? No! That's not what I meant."

I arch a brow before taking an unhurried pull from my bottle. My gaze stays locked on hers. "Isn't it?"

Her shoulders wobble before collapsing.

Yup, nailed it.

"All I meant was that I remember what it was like to be in college. People hook up, and it doesn't necessarily mean anything." She shifts on the chair before forcing out the rest. "But I was never much into that. What happened between us..." She gulps. "It's not something I normally do."

If there's any balm for accusing me of being a man slut, that would be it. I'm not going to lie, her softly spoken admission makes my cock twitch. I like knowing that I'm different.

Since we're coming clean regarding our sexual habits, I admit, "It might surprise you, but I don't usually sleep around either." That's not to say I haven't gone home with chicks in the past, but it's not something that happens all the time. I haven't made it my sole mission in life to nail all the ass I can. There have also been a few girlfriends sprinkled in along the way.

But mostly, I've been focused on my family, football, and school.

That doesn't leave a lot of time for extracurricular activities. The girls I've been with were well aware I wasn't looking for a hardcore relationship. It was more of a casual understanding of sorts. And when that situation inevitably ran its course, we parted ways as friends.

No reason not too, as far as I'm concerned. It certainly wasn't love. More like lust.

Although, for some reason, it feels different with Gia. I can't explain the hows or whys of it. I just know it is.

Does that scare the shit out of me?

Yeah, it does. Our timing couldn't be worse. The last thing I need is to get sidetracked from the upcoming draft. I have way too much riding on getting picked up by a team this spring. My family's financial future is riding on me making it to the pros.

You know what scares me even more than that?

Gia pulling the plug on whatever we have going here.

The way her eyes narrow tells me she thinks I'm trying to blow smoke up her ass. It just goes to show how little she knows about me. I'm not sure about the kinds of guys she's been with, but I'm more of a straight shooter. I don't have the time or wherewithal to run games on women. And furthermore, I don't have to. I could be out fucking a different girl every night of the week. Probably several. But the reality is that I'm not. It's not who I am. And Gia needs to realize that if this relationship is going to progress any further.

"Really?"

I shake my head. "Nope."

"I find that hard to believe."

"Why?"

She opens her mouth to say something before slamming it shut again and jerking her shoulders.

"Oh, come on," I coax, "just say it."

"Well" –she flicks her hand in my direction— "look at you."

Ummm, okay.

"Are you suggesting there's something wrong with the way I look?" Because I was kind of thinking she liked what she saw. It would be a real bummer if that turned out not to be the case.

"You know there isn't. You're completely gorgeous."

A smile of satisfaction curves my lips. "I'm glad you think so."

The way she rolls her big blue eyes is too damn cute. It makes me want to leap across the coffee table so I can finally get my hands on her. "You have to realize that women find you sexy."

I swear to God, my body gravitates toward her all on its own. "The only thing that matters is that *you* find me sexy."

She nips her bottom lip between her teeth before admitting, "I do."

"I find you sexy as hell too," I growl.

It's been a while since I've found myself this sexually attracted to a woman. Even though this is new, it makes me want to hang on tightly with both hands and never let go. For a long moment, we hold each other's gazes. The atmosphere surges with electricity until it feels as if my fingertips are buzzing with it. Her breath hitches as my heart rate spikes. My whole body feels like a tightly coiled spring waiting for—

The oven timer dings, and the glazed look clears from her eyes. The spell holding us paralyzed disintegrates. A flush fills her cheeks as she jumps to her feet.

"That would be the salmon." She retreats to the kitchen as she adds, "I should, um, get that."

I force out a long breath as a smile settles across my face. I can practically hear the thick tendrils of relief that weave their way through her voice.

She may not want *this*. But that doesn't mean she doesn't want *me*.

And since beggars can't be choosers, I'll take it.

All day long.

A few minutes later, we're settled at the dining room table and digging into our dinner. The quinoa is...interesting. All right, it's pretty good. Kind of like rice but it has a different texture. Gia has informed me that it's a superfood. It takes all of my willpower to slow down and not shovel the food into my mouth.

Even when I lived at home, meals weren't what one would call *homecooked.*

Mom made simple things like tacos, spaghetti, and tuna casserole. She didn't much care for being in the kitchen. And after she disappeared... Well, let's just say Dad wasn't exactly spending his time slaving away over a hot stove.

It was a lot of frozen, ready-made meals that could be shoved in the oven for an hour. Or boxes of noodles that you added to ground beef, which unfortunately raised the status of tacos and tuna casserole to five-star cuisine.

So, this? Yeah, I'm enjoying the hell out of it.

Gia sits back and watches me with a small smile simmering around the edges of her lips as I continue to wolf down my dinner.

Amusement flits across her face as she shakes her head. "I've never seen anyone eat like that before."

One brow hikes up. "Did I mention that it's delicious?" I can't help but scoop up another mouthful.

"Yes, several times." She laughs before admitting, "And here I was worried you might not like salmon." Her gaze drops to my plate. "Or quinoa."

I don't bother to mention that I've never had salmon before. It wasn't exactly standard fare at the Garrison household. If it wasn't ground chuck or chicken thighs that were snapped up on sale, it was too expensive for the likes of us.

"I love it."

"Here." She forks the rest onto my plate. "Take the last little bit." I should probably politely decline. Except, it's too damn good to refuse. And who knows when I'll enjoy another meal like this again.

Because I'm a quick learner, I realize getting her to talk about her job and the kids she teaches is probably the easiest way to lower her defenses.

As I open my mouth, the song "We Are Family" cuts through the air.

I can only shake my head in exasperation. Looks like Claire got a hold of my phone again. She thinks it's hilarious to change my ring-tones on the sly. Although, this one is pretty tame. The last time she changed one, it was to "Baby Got Back."

For Dylan.

I glance at my cell.

I'm tempted to silence it, but Claire wouldn't call unless something was up. Normally, she'll shoot me a text. There's no way I can send it to voicemail. "Sorry, I have to take this."

With a nod, Gia rises to her feet and grabs our plates before moving into the kitchen. My gaze stays glued to her ass as she leaves the room.

Hopefully, whatever is going on can be solved with a quick conversation. "Hey, Claire-bear, what's up?"

There's a moment of silence and then a ragged sniffle before her soft voice comes over the line. "Liam—"

The thick clog of tears that fills her voice has everything in me deflating as I realize my evening with Gia has just gone to shit. I hate when Claire cries. It usually means there's a problem at home, which more than likely involves my dad and brother. My voice drops. "What happened, Claire?"

She sucks in a shuddering breath before releasing it. "Cullum and Dad got into a huge fight and then Cullum took off. He was so angry." She gulps as fresh tears fill her voice. "He punched a hole through the wall. I've never seen him so mad."

I plow a hand through my hair in frustration. Since Cullum spends most of his time being pissed off, especially when he's at home, something must have happened with my father to set him off. "Any idea why they got into it?"

"No." She sniffles again. "Can you come home? Please?" Her tone lowers. "Dad's drinking again."

Fuck.

This isn't how I pictured tonight turning out.

I squeeze my eyes tightly shut. It's not a question I have to think about. As much as I want to stay here and spend the rest of the evening with Gia, I can't. My family has always been my number one priority. And that won't change anytime soon. "Yeah. I'll be there in about fifteen minutes, all right?"

"Thanks." Relief sweeps through her voice.

My sister understands that no matter what is going on, I'm only a phone call away. Most of the time, I can be home in under twenty minutes. It's yet another reason I chose to attend Barnett University. There's no way in hell I could have left my sister and brother to fend for themselves.

Even though Cullum can be a dick, I get it. I understand why he's so angry at the world. And I can't hold it against him. If I were in his position, I'd probably feel the same way. A wave of guilt crashes over me that I'm attending college and playing Division I football while Cullum is just trying to make it through high school. Not to mention, work his ass off to support our family. It's a shit position to be in.

I shove my phone into the pocket of my jeans as Gia makes her way back to the dining room where I'm standing. Or more accurately, pacing. I don't have any other choice but to cut the evening short.

Like everything else in my life, it is what it is.

"You have to leave?" she asks.

If there's a silver lining in this situation, it's that she looks disappointed by the notion that I have to take off early. It would be a lot worse if she were breathing a huge sigh of relief.

So, yeah…I guess we'll focus on the positive.

I can't say I don't feel the same way. Tonight has been enjoyable. And having a woman cook a nice dinner for me? I'm sure I'll sound like a Neanderthal for saying it, but I fucking loved it. I like knowing she made all this with me in mind.

And I like Gia. I want to spend more time getting to know her.

For obvious reasons, it won't be tonight.

I force out the air clogging my lungs and jerk my head in a nod. "That was my sister on the phone. There's a problem at home, and I need to head over there. I'm really sorry about bailing like this."

"Don't worry about it." She shrugs. "Things come up."

See? I knew she was a cool chick. I've been with plenty of girls who get bent around the axel if your entire world doesn't revolve around them. If you're smart, that little peek into their personality is when you cut bait and run. Who the hell needs that hassle?

But Gia isn't acting like that. As much as I want to stay, even for another fifteen minutes, I can't. My mind is already filling with the possible scenarios I might get stuck dealing with for the rest of the evening. So, there isn't time for me to—

"Any chance you want to come with?" Once the words have been released into the atmosphere, I blink in surprise. What the hell possessed me to throw the offer out there? It's like I suffered from a petit mal seizure and can't recall the past twenty seconds of my life.

Seriously, what the hell was I thinking?

I could roll up to the house and find a total shitshow. For all I know, Dad is wasted. Or my brother might have returned, and I'll have to break up a physical altercation.

Introducing Gia to my family is a terrible idea. Even under the best of circumstances, it's a total crapshoot as to what you'll get. The last thing I need is for her to see how fucked-up we are. I don't need any questions, pity, or judgments.

And there's no way for me to rescind the offer without looking like an asshole.

All right, don't panic.

If I'm lucky, she'll turn me down flat. There's no way she wants to tag along. It's way too early for something like that. Plus, she wants to take things slow. Meeting someone's family has "serious" stamped all over it. You do that a few months in. Maybe. Although, I've never brought a girl home to meet the fam.

She looks as thrown off by the invitation as I am to have tossed it out there.

As we speak, I can feel the situation nosediving, plummeting toward earth.

If Gia's smart—which clearly, she is—she'll shove my crazy ass out the door before changing both her cell number and place of employment.

I can't say that I'd blame her.

If some chick wanted to drag me to meet her folks after two dates and a seriously hot hookup, I'd run for the hills.

Yeah, there's no way in hell she's going to—

"Sure."

Wait. What?

"Really?" A more shocking turn of events, I couldn't have predicted.

She shrugs as her blue gaze pierces mine. "Why not?"

Why not, indeed?

Actually, I can think of about thirty reasons off the top of my head as to why this little jaunt is doomed for failure. And yet, I can't bring myself to retract the offer.

For better or worse, this is happening.

CHAPTER 17

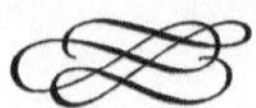

GIA

I'm ashamed to admit that I eavesdropped on Liam's conversation while cleaning up after dinner. The way he agreed to drop everything so he could take care of whatever was going on at his house only makes me respect him more. I don't know anything about his family situation, but my curiosity is piqued.

Whatever happens tonight, I'll come out of it with a clearer understanding of who Liam Garrison is. And maybe that's what I need at this point. A little clarity.

I sneak a quick peek at him as we drive. I'm not sure what it is about the dark-haired football player, but I'm drawn to him. Sometimes it feels like the more I discover, the more fascinated I become. He's not the guy I originally pegged him to be. There's an unexpected depth to him. An underlying seriousness.

On the surface, he seems like an easy-going, college-aged guy blessed with both good looks and amazing athleticism. Not that I know how he does in school, but so far, he strikes me as intelligent. You have to be fairly smart to go into architecture, right?

Plus, he actually has a realistic plan in place if the NFL doesn't work out.

How often do you hear *that*?

I'll admit it—I'm intrigued by everything I've learned thus far. Any woman with a beating pulse would be.

Liam hasn't said much since we left my house. He seems preoccupied with whatever is going on with his family. So, I haven't asked any questions. I'm willing to listen if he wants to talk, but I don't want to butt in where he doesn't necessarily want me.

Instead of filling the silence with mindless chatter, I stare out the passenger side window as we turn into an older residential neighborhood. This isn't an area of town I'm familiar with. Even in the darkness, under the illumination of streetlights, I can tell it's rundown.

The houses are small, rectangular ranches with single detached garages. Each is a carbon copy of the one next to it. A few of the residences have bedsheets hanging over the windows in place of curtains or shades. Chain link fences separate one tiny yard from another. Most of the cars parked in the driveways are old and rusted. There's an air of neglect to the area. Even in the darkness, it all looks a bit forlorn.

It's doubtful that daylight would improve the situation.

We make a few turns before pulling into a short drive. My nerves kick up a notch as I exit the car. Liam's gaze latches on to mine as he circles around the hood.

He looks—I don't know—self-conscious, maybe?

The last thing I want is for my presence to make him uncomfortable.

The urge to run my fingers through his spiked-up hair thrums through me. Although, given the circumstances, I get the feeling he wouldn't welcome the gesture. The need to offer comfort is so strong that I have to tighten my hands so I don't reach out and touch him.

"Bet you're wishing you'd passed on this, huh?" he mutters.

Maybe.

Maybe not.

That has yet to be determined.

What I do know is that I hate the tone coloring his voice. It's like a protective barrier falling into place between us. As if he's attempting to shield himself from my thoughts and judgments about where he comes from and who these people are. It makes my heart twist painfully under my breast.

In the blink of an eye, he reminds me of a past student who nearly tore my heart out my first year of teaching. That was when I thought I could singlehandedly swoop in and save every kid from life's bigger, more challenging problems. It was a bitter pill to swallow to realize that wasn't always possible.

Mistrust has seeped into Liam's gray eyes. Even in the darkness pooled around us, it shines clearly.

It might have taken me a while, but I've learned I can't change someone's circumstances. The only thing I can do is offer my support. I can hold their hand and walk beside them so they aren't alone.

I extend my hand to him. "I'm happy to be here with you, Liam. Whatever's going on, it's all right. Take care of your family and don't worry about me."

He blinks before reaching out for my fingers and clinging to them as if they're a lifeline. The tension filling his expression drains.

Silently, we walk up to the front stoop. Liam grasps the handle of the door and holds it open. As I step into the living room, my gaze lands on an older man sprawled out in a recliner. His dark hair is shot through with sparks of silver. I imagine that at one time, it was probably the same deep shade as Liam's. His eyes, though, are light blue. He's a big man but somehow looks shrunken. Beaten down.

His eyes widen when they land on me, as if I've walked into his house by mistake. Almost immediately, they shift to Liam, who has come in behind me. The heat of his larger body pressed against my back feels as if it's singeing me alive.

It's yet another reminder as to how physically aware of him I am. I'm not used to being so cognizant of another human being.

Every time we're together, the attraction grows, seeming to multiply.

A girl pokes her head around a corner from what I assume to be the kitchen. She, too, looks surprised by my sudden arrival.

When everyone remains silent, Liam clears his throat. There's an uncomfortable note tingeing his normally confident voice. Liam probably wishes he hadn't invited me to tag along, so he could deal with his family without a spectator watching from the sidelines.

"Dad, Claire, this is Gia." His hand rests on my shoulder. "We were having dinner together," he adds.

I keep a neutral smile glued in place as Claire inches her way into the living room. Even though I have no idea what will happen with Liam, I still want to make a good impression.

For some reason, it feels important.

The man in the recliner snaps into action. He rises to his feet before extending a hand to me. Except his fingers are still wrapped around a beer can. We both realize this at the same moment before he hastily sets the drink on the end table.

"It's, ah, nice to meet you, Gia. I'm Ray." The way his lips curl up at the edges reminds me a bit of his son.

"Thank you so much. I hope you don't mind that I've stopped over with Liam."

My words seem to do exactly what they're meant to and put him at ease. "No." His smile softens, becoming more natural. "We're happy to have you."

My gaze slides to Liam's sister. I overheard him call her Claire-Bear on the phone when they were talking. It's obvious he loves her a great deal. I could tell by the careful and patient way he spoke to her.

That night when I first saw Liam at O'Brien's, I was bowled over by how good looking he was. I'm just as stunned by his sister. She's gorgeous with dark, pin-straight hair that is similar in shade to Liam's and the same piercing gray eyes. She's tall with long, lean legs.

Even though she smiles, it's easy to see something is wrong. Only now am I wondering if it would have been better for everyone involved if I stayed home. Though it's much too late to do anything about it now. I'll have to suck it up and make the best of this situation.

"It's nice to meet you, Claire," I say.

Before she can respond, Liam cuts in. "Gia teaches second grade at North Hill Elementary."

Surprised, my gaze slices to his in question. I have no idea why he brought that up. It seems out of place. But then Claire's eyes brighten, and it becomes evident as to why Liam interjected that random piece of information into the conversation.

Her face lights up, making her even prettier than I first suspected. "Really? I want to be a teacher, too!"

Everything in me loosens as I smile.

"Claire." Liam's gaze holds hers. "Maybe you could take Gia into the kitchen. I bet she would answer any questions you have about teaching."

His sister looks thrilled by the prospect. Like I'm a minor celebrity interview she just landed. It's ridiculously sweet. I want to say *hey, it's not really that interesting*, but I don't. The last thing I want to do is dampen her enthusiasm. I remember feeling the same way when I first decided to pursue education as a career.

"Would you really?" Her brows rise.

"I'd be happy to answer any questions you might have."

When my gaze flickers to Liam, he gives me a grateful smile before tilting his head toward his father, who has reclaimed his spot on the recliner.

"I need to talk with Dad for a bit."

She nods before leading the way. Actually, it's a relief to escape from the living room and the oppressive energy.

Even though it's a Friday night, the small kitchen table is littered with schoolbooks. My gaze roams over the mess before bouncing to her. Most girls Claire's age would already be out the door with her friends.

"Wow," I say. "You must be really dedicated to stay in on a Friday night and work on homework."

The light shining in her eyes dims as she drops onto a chair, and I settle next to her. I don't remember if Liam told me what grade his sister is in. If I had to guess by the textbooks scattered across the table, I'd say middle school. One of the books splayed open is pre-algebra and most students take that course in eighth grade.

She sucks in a breath before releasing a long sigh. It's tinged with both sadness and frustration. "No, I just have a ton of homework this weekend. If I don't start it tonight, there's no way I'll finish on time. And I can't afford to get downgraded."

I'm unsure how to respond to that. Even though I don't work at a middle school, I'm certified by the state to teach kindergarten through eighth grade. During college, one of my student teaching placements was at a middle school, so I'm familiar with the curriculum and what standard practice is regarding homework. Spending two and a half days working on assignments seems excessive.

"What middle school do you attend?"

There are two in the city.

Her brows pinch together. "I'm in ninth grade at South Sentinel."

My gaze flickers to the books. I'm not mistaken about the math. It's definitely pre-algebra.

I smile in an effort to cover up my mistake. "I'm sorry, I didn't realize. It was just a guess." Again, I glance at all the work laid out on the table. "Do you always have so much?"

She presses her lips together before nodding. "Yeah. I have a hard time keeping up in school. At the end of the week, I always have a ton to bring home. As long as it's completed by Monday, most of my teachers won't downgrade me too much."

My eyes widen. "What needs to be completed?"

Her lower lip wedges between her teeth as she contemplates the array of paperwork. She shuffles around a few things before finding a small spiral notebook—an assignment notebook by the looks of it— and handing it to me. The entire page is filled with painstakingly neat handwriting. There's a laundry list of items that need to be completed.

My heart silently breaks as I scan each line.

Math pages 297-300. All the even numbered problems. Two physical science worksheets. Front and back. An outline of a book report for language arts. A map that needs to be colored in along with a study guide for chapter eighteen in US history.

No wonder she's not going out tonight. Or tomorrow. Possibly ever.

I'm overwhelmed just looking at this list. And I'm an adult.

"How much has already been completed?" Hopefully, at least one item can be crossed off the list.

Tears well in her eyes as she shakes her head before shrugging slender shoulders.

A pit settles at the bottom of my gut. I won't be able to sleep tonight if I don't do something to help her. I give Claire a reassuring smile, and immediately go into teacher mode.

"All right. Let's start out by organizing these papers. That should always be your first step. I think it'll help you feel better if we clear off some of this clutter and prioritize the tasks that need to be accomplished."

It takes a moment for the glassiness shining in her eyes to disappear as she eagerly agrees.

We go through the stack, throwing away old assignments and loose ends that Claire no longer needs. Then we create a pile for papers and books that aren't essential to what has to be accomplished over the weekend. After all of her subjects have been organized into tidy piles, we look through her planner and prioritize her assignments.

"What should we work on first? What can we do together that would be most helpful?"

"Math." It's not a question she has to think about.

I smile. "All right. Pull out a sheet of paper and your book, and let's get started."

Twenty-five minutes later, Liam joins us in the kitchen.

He takes in the scene before his gaze settles on mine. "What are you two up to?"

Even though every mathematical problem that we've tackled has been a struggle, Claire beams at him. "Gia is helping me with homework." Her face falls. "You're not leaving, are you?"

Indecision flickers over his handsome features as his gaze holds hers. In that moment, it's obvious how much he loves her. He's trying so hard to take care of this family. It seems like too much responsibility resting on his young shoulders.

"I was going to take Gia back to her place, squirt. It's getting late."

"Can you stay for ten more minutes? Please? I'm so bad at math, and that's what we're working on." Her voice continues to escalate, and I can understand why. Claire struggles to grasp the concepts. Even when that math is a full grade level behind where she should be.

I give him a small smile of reassurance. "I don't mind staying to finish up this page."

Surprise lights his eyes. "Are you sure?"

Honestly, I'm happy to help. Claire might struggle to comprehend arithmetic, but with one-on-one attention, she's slowly getting it. I hate to leave her when we're beginning to make progress. "It's not a problem."

He shoots me a skeptical look.

"Really," I say, "it's okay."

His gaze stays pinned to mine. "As long as you don't mind." He gestures toward the living room where he and his father have been quietly talking for half an hour. "I'll just hang out in the other room until you're finished."

It takes another forty-five minutes for us to wrap up one full page of math. Claire still has three more to do. I was hoping we could plow through two pages so at least half of it would be done. It can be a real mental boost to tick off completed assignments. Even though we've worked for over an hour, not much progress has been made. Although, I can only imagine how long it would have taken Claire to complete this much on her own.

Frustration surges through me, but it's not directed at her. "All right, Claire, I need to get going. You have everything organized and ready for tomorrow. I know you want to continue working, but I think you should take a break and go to bed early so you're clear headed and able to tackle a good portion of this tomorrow."

Doubt creeps into her eyes at the prospect of what still lies ahead. "If you think it'll help, then maybe I'll stop for tonight. Thanks so much for working with me."

My heart goes out to this young girl. Without someone sitting beside her, I'm not sure how she'll get all of this work completed by Monday.

The words tumble out of my mouth before I can think better of them. "Maybe your dad can bring you over tomorrow and we can work on some of this at my house. That way, if you have questions, I can help."

"Really?" Her voice fills with excitement.

Inviting Claire over wasn't something I consciously considered until this very moment. But I'm glad I did. This girl needs help, and I'm in a position to provide it.

"You would do that?"

"I have some stuff to do around the house, but other than that, I'm free. So, if you're interested in stopping by for a few hours, we can work on some of this together."

She jumps out of her chair. "That would be awesome! Let me ask Liam, though, because my dad doesn't have his license anymore so he can't drive me over."

I don't say anything to that bit of information as Claire flies into the living room where Liam is watching television with his father. In a rush of words that pour excitedly from her mouth, Claire tells her brother about my offer before begging him to drive her over to my house.

Liam studies me as if he doesn't understand why I'm doing this. I give him a small smile in return. "It's not a big deal. I don't have plans for tomorrow."

"Are you sure?"

"Positive. I have some papers to grade and lesson plans to go over for the following week, but I can do that while working with Claire."

His eyes bore into mine as he regards me silently. Claire steeples her hands in front of her before pleading with him. Her eagerness to receive assistance only makes me want to work with her more.

"You really want to do this?" he asks again.

"I wouldn't have offered if I didn't want to help." Claire needs help. Help that I can provide. So, yeah, I'm more than happy to offer my services.

"Okay." He nods. "What time were you thinking?"

"Does eleven work?"

After we agree on a time, Claire chatters excitedly about spending part of the day at my place.

Even though we've only just met, I pull her in for a quick hug before we take off. As we drive to my house, I notice Liam is just as pensive as he was on the ride over. Uncertainty crashes through me, and I wonder if he's annoyed that I offered to work with his sister.

"Thanks for what you're doing." His words are so soft and heartfelt, they tug at something deep inside me. "You have no idea how much it means to Claire." His gray depths pierce mine in the darkness. "And to me."

It's on the tip of my tongue to brush off his comments. But I don't. Can't.

The gratitude that shines brightly from his eyes, warms me from the inside out. "I'm happy to help."

Instead of responding, he reaches out and wraps his fingers around mine before giving them a squeeze. We fall into silence, simply sitting with our hands clasped as something indescribable blooms between us.

CHAPTER 18

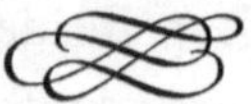

GIA

"Are you sure about this?" There's a crushed gravel quality to his voice. It's all low and rough. Almost gritty.

The thickness of it arrows straight down to my core before exploding upon impact.

"I'm sure," I murmur.

Even though I told myself I wouldn't do this, here I am—standing in the middle of my living room with my arms entwined around his neck and his hands cupping my ass.

When he gives my cheeks a hard squeeze, everything inside me riots painfully. Lust and longing clamor until every qualm that had been circling through my head when he first walked through my door earlier this evening is nothing more than a distant hum.

With deliberate strokes, he brushes his mouth across mine. "I don't want to rush you into something you're not ready for." The flintiness of his eyes slices through mine in the darkness.

I almost snort. If there's anyone rushing things around here, it's me. "You're not."

His hands drift from my backside before slipping beneath the hem of my sweater and gliding upward until they can mold to my breasts over the lacy cups of my bra.

When he pulls away from my mouth, I immediately feel the loss of him.

"Do you have any idea how many times I've thought about your breasts over the past month?"

I groan and arch into his palms when he tweaks and pulls at my nipples through the material.

Not a moment later, his mouth is back to devouring mine as his fingers play with my hard tips, driving me crazy. It's as if Liam has an intrinsic knowledge as to what will push me over the edge.

The need to feel his hard body surges through me as my hands slip under the soft cotton of his shirt before gliding over taut abdominals and rock-hard pectorals. The man must work out for hours each day to be so cut and chiseled. Before I realize it, I shove the fabric up and draw away enough for him to haul the shirt over his head and toss it to the couch.

Just when I think he'll delve back in, he grabs the hem of my sweater and teases it up my body before pulling it over my head. His gaze drops to my breasts. A worshipful light enters his eyes as he reaches around my back and unclasps my bra, allowing my breasts to spill free from their confines.

His gaze roams over my curves before he reaches out and cups me, palming the soft flesh in his hands. Back and forth, his thumbs strum my nipples as his gaze flicks to mine. "You're so fucking beautiful."

My fingers stroke over the wide expanse of his chest before whispering over flat male nipples. As I do, they stiffen into hard little points. A groan slides from his lips. The sound is so animalistic and raw that my panties flood with heat.

My hands glide down six-pack abs before coming to rest at the waistband of his jeans. I slant a look at him. Unbridled lust fire burns brightly in his eyes.

I don't think I could stop what's about to happen even if I wanted to. It feels like a barely contained fire moments away from blazing out of control.

And I want it. I want to be burned alive by the dancing flames.

A metal sound breaks the heavy silence of the room as I unsnap the button of his fly and lower the zipper. Anticipation bursts through me as I shove the denim down his hips and muscular thighs. When he's standing before me in nothing more than dark-blue boxer briefs that hug every delicious inch of him, I reach out, needing to cup the huge bulge beneath the cottony material.

A sigh flutters from both of our lips as I stroke my fingers over his hard length.

"Gia, you're killing me."

A hint of a smile plays around the corners of my lips as I slip my hand inside the waistband and caress his erection. Before I can recon-sider my actions, I drop to my knees. My gaze stays locked on his as I slide the material down his thighs until his cock springs free. Another long groan escapes from his lips.

With careful strokes, I run my fingers over the velvety head, unable to resist flicking my tongue out to taste him. It's nothing more than a fleeting touch over the bulbous tip. When a growl of approval rumbles up from his throat, I do it again. Only this time, the swipe is longer. My fingers glide over muscular thighs until they reach the hard planes of his rigidly held abdominals.

When my tongue flicks over him for a third time, his dick twitches at the contact. My hands trek downward until one can wrap around the solid length before stroking him from root to tip. The heat radi-ating off him nearly burns my fingers. I bring the crown to my lips before drawing the length inside my mouth. As I do, one hand continues to stroke his erection as the other cups his balls, gently massaging them.

His fingers sink into my hair, gripping my scalp as if he wants to hold me in place. The heavy breath that falls from him only ratchets up my own excitement.

I've never really enjoyed going down on a guy before. It was some-thing I did to give them pleasure. It never turned me on. But I don't feel that way with Liam. I want to watch him fall apart beneath my fingertips. I want him to lose control.

The growl that vibrates in his throat only spurs me on and propels me to take him deeper. My fingers work the steely length along with the two soft mounds of flesh.

"Gia," he groans, "that's just so… Fuck, baby. That's so good. I love the feel of your lips on me." His enjoyment only heightens my own.

It makes me feel powerful.

And sexy.

I've never felt like that before. Not from doing this. But like everything else with Liam, this too, is different.

As I work his firm flesh, I realize I actually want him to come in my mouth. I want him to shatter from the feel of my lips on the most sensitive part of him. So, I suck a bit harder, taking him deeper. My hands move faster, trying to coax a climax from his body.

"Baby, I'm going to come." Instead of his fingers sinking deeper into my hair, drawing me closer, he attempts to push me away. But I'm not having any of it. I want this to happen.

"Gia…"

His voice deepens, turning desperate, as if he's coming apart at the seams.

"Fuck, Gia!"

Even when his movements turn frantic, there's nothing he can do to stop this from happening. I won't release his cock until I get what I want.

After a long, shuddering moment, he groans in surrender. His body goes taut as he pulls me closer, holding me securely in place. His hips jerk as I suck and stroke him as the first salty spurts hit the back of my throat.

I draw him in deep and swallow it all down, wanting this to be the best damn blow job he's ever had. Liam's orgasm seems to go on forever, his grunts of pleasure washing over me. It's only when he softens in my mouth that I relax my touch. After releasing him, I give his head a kiss, nuzzling the velvety tip before glancing up to meet his sated gaze.

His eyes burn brightly with pure male satisfaction.

"Fuck, baby."

That's all he says.

It's all he has to say.

He reaches down and slides his arms around me before lifting me off my feet. My legs wrap around his waist as his hands slide over my backside. He carries me to the bedroom before laying me out on the queen-sized mattress. It's only then I realize I'm still wearing my black leggings. By this point, my panties are completely soaked.

From giving head.

And I love it.

Love that I could give him all that delicious pleasure while he simply stood there and accepted it.

He looms over me without a stitch of clothing. His fingers hover at the waistband of my leggings and panties before ripping them off with one swift motion that steals my breath away and has my desire intensifying.

His hands settle on either side of my shoulders, caging me in as he presses a kiss against each nipple before licking a path down the center of my rib cage. Once he reaches my pubic bone, my body feels like it will burn up with the need that pounds viciously through it.

With his fingers wrapped around my thighs, he carefully spreads them wide. For a long moment, he studies me. There's enough light filtering in through the windows that line the western wall of my bedroom. He massages my inner thighs before his fingers drift toward my center until they can touch the edges of my lower lips.

"Do you know how much I want to taste you?"

Air clogs my throat as anticipation brews inside me.

Liam lowers his head until his hot breath feathers against my flesh. Even though his hands are splayed wide across my inner thighs, holding me down, I attempt to wriggle closer. Instead of delving in, he takes his sweet damn time, pressing a kiss against my clit. The gentle caress has me arching into his touch, whimpering as a hot rush of pleasure spikes through my veins. The wait is driving me insane. I shift beneath him, needing so much more.

He raises his head until he can look at the most intimate part of me, so open and vulnerable to his hot gaze. The thought of him staring sends yet another thick shiver of need arrowing straight to my core.

"You really are beautiful, baby."

One hand leaves my thigh to stroke over my center. His touch is feather light as it dances across my soaked flesh.

"Did sucking my cock get you this wet?" he growls.

"Yes." The word is nothing more than a throaty groan as my body bows.

"Good."

His finger continues to drift over me until it feels very much like torture. Only then does he dip one digit inside me. A tidal wave of pleasure crashes over me as a moan escapes my lips.

"I'm going to fuck you nice and slow, until your pussy can't take another stroke of my cock. Until you explode around me."

Oh, God. Those words are so...*hot*.

It's almost shocking how much they turn me on.

With a deliberateness that makes me want to scream, his finger slides rhythmically from my body. "You're so fucking creamy."

He lowers his mouth to my flesh and takes a long swipe over my core. Pleasure explodes inside me. Not once does he cease his tender ministrations. With his fingers, he spreads my lower lips until he can nibble at my clit. There is almost an unbearable amount of sensation humming through my body. His touch sends everything spiraling out of control.

"Mmmm, you taste so damn good. I could eat you all night long."

His velvety softness dances over my clit before he sucks the tiny bundle of nerves into his mouth. I'm so close to shattering into a million broken pieces. The only thing I'm cognizant of is this man with his head buried between my thighs, his hot mouth roving over my flesh.

The pulse of all that pleasure as it unfolds inside me.

I've never felt anything like it before.

My muscles tighten in anticipation as my back arches off the mattress, trying to press closer. Just as I start to dive headfirst off the precipice, he backs away. The cool air of the room rushes over my flesh.

My eyelids fly open, and my gaze collides with his. A slow smile curves his lips.

Oh...that dirty, rot—

"Did you really think that I was going to give it to you so quickly?" He slants a dark brow at me before leaning down and pressing a kiss against my soaked flesh. "Sorry, sweetheart, I'm going to make you work for it."

I'm so close to splintering apart. My body trembles with the need to find its release. All I want is to feel the warm pressure of his mouth on me.

I grit my teeth as a mixture of pleasure-infused pain crashes inside me. "Liam." My tongue darts out to moisten my lips. "Please."

His chuckle is strained around the edges. "Please what, baby? What do you want?"

Arching my body toward him, I moan. "I want you to fuck me."

As soon as those words fall from my lips, he groans. "Do you want it with my soft tongue or hard cock?"

It's not a question I have to think about. "I need your cock."

I want his thick erection buried deep inside me, pummeling me senseless. I want him to take me the way he did before. No man has ever fucked me like that. There was something almost animalistic about it.

I never imagined I'd enjoy sex being a little bit rough.

Turns out that I do.

"Good choice."

I roll toward the bedside table before opening a slender drawer, pulling out a foil package, and tossing it to him. He catches it in mid-air before ripping the packet with his teeth. My gaze falls to his cock as he takes out the condom and sheathes himself with it.

Once he's back to kneeling between my spread thighs, his fingers wrap around his erection as he places it against my entrance. When he stills, not moving another inch, I grow restless beneath him. The tip of his dick nearly drives me into a frenzy. I want to feel him sliding deep inside me, filling me to the very brim.

Instead of giving me what I want, he doesn't move a muscle.

My gaze stays locked on his as I silently plead with him to give me the entire length.

I arch, needing to feel him buried deep inside my heat. When I attempt to get closer, he draws away so we're still touching but no more than that. The tip of his dick barely penetrates my soaked entrance. The throbbing in my core is almost unbearable.

"I decide how much you get," he growls. "Understand?"

I nod. At this point, I'll agree to anything. I just want his damn cock inside me.

My gaze fastens on the deliberate slide of his fingers against his firm flesh.

Why is that so damn sexy?

Just when I can't stand it another moment, he presses into my heat. It's only an inch, two at the most. I want to scream as pleasure explodes inside my core. A deep groan vibrates from his lips as he pulls out before thrusting forward again. This teasing continues until my fingers are twisting into the bed sheets.

Each shallow thrust has the intensity building inside me.

He never quickens his pace. Liam is in complete control, and he wants me to know that. I clench my muscles around him as he attempts to pull out.

A snarl rumbles up from within his chest. "Your pussy is like fucking nirvana."

He jerks his hips, gliding inside me again. His cock slides a bit deeper before stopping. Even though he barely moves a muscle, his breathing turns choppy. It matches the intensity of my own. My heart feels as if it will explode from my chest. I'm not sure how much more of this torture I can take.

His gaze stays fused to the place where we're intimately joined. "I love watching my cock disappear inside you."

When he draws out this time, he removes himself completely from my body before once again settling at my entrance. I've never been this drenched in my life. There were times with Tyler that I wouldn't get wet at all. And I would think, *well, that's just the way it is. What you read in books is complete crap.*

After this, I can't imagine ever going back to ho-hum sex again.

"How much do you want my dick, Gia?"

"So much. Please, I need you to fuck me." A shiver of need scampers down my spine.

"Good, because that's exactly what I'm going to do."

Air rushes from my lungs.

Thank God!

When he pulls out again, cool air hits my damp flesh.

Just as my mouth tumbles open, he commands, "Turn over."

The words don't immediately compute.

Turn over?

What for?

Before I can blink, his hand snakes out and gives the top of my pussy a little smack. It's really more of a tap but in the moment, it feels shocking. I've never had anyone hit me *there* before.

Okay, truth…I've never had anyone hit or spank me anywhere.

Ever.

"Turn over," he bites out, "so I can fuck you properly."

When I stare wide-eyed, he smacks my clit again. Only this time, it sends a lovely little thrill shooting through me. I can't stop the groan of pleasure as I arch my body.

"You like that, baby?" he asks gruffly. His voice sounds as if it's been dredged from the bottom of the ocean. His words are strung impossibly tight, as if he'll come at any moment.

Well, I didn't think I'd like it.

But, yeah… I suppose I do.

I should be appalled at myself.

I really should.

He slaps my heated flesh for a third time, hitting my clit at the perfect angle. It's as if he knows exactly where to strike to send the most pleasure rippling through my body.

"Sweetheart, I could slap that sweet little pussy of yours all night long, but I need to fuck you, and you definitely need to be fucked. Good and hard."

He's right.

I do.

My brain clicks back on, and I scramble up and over until I'm on all fours. When he kneels behind me, heat radiates off him in heavy, suffocating waves. Almost leisurely, he runs his hand over my left flank before giving my ass a sharp slap. I hiss out a breath before more pleasure floods through me.

His hand caresses the spot he just smacked. "You're so fucking perfect. Do you know that?"

I groan as his fingers find my drenched flesh, rubbing circles over my entrance before zeroing in on my clit.

Another moan of need escapes as he continues to play with me, wringing every last ounce of pleasure from me. It doesn't take long before I'm soaring high, perched on the edge of the precipice.

And Liam realizes it.

He knows exactly how much pleasure I can withstand without coming undone. It's sheer torture being with someone who has so much knowledge and control over their body.

And yours.

But I love it. Love the power he exerts.

"Liam, please… I need you." By this point, I'm practically sobbing. And I don't care. I've never begged a man for anything in my life. And this one? I would grovel at his feet.

"I know, baby." But still, he continues to stroke my delicate flesh. Every once in a while, his fingers will dip inside my heat. "I promise, Gia, I'll give you all of it. Every fucking thing you need." There's a pause, then he says, "Arch your back."

Without hesitation, I follow his instructions, bowing my body until I'm completely exposed.

"That's it," he groans. "So damn beautiful." His hands disappear only to be replaced by his lips and tongue. The velvetiness of his touch drifts over my shuddering softness. That's all it takes to get me there.

A few well-placed strokes and I'm hovering at the edge, sobbing with need.

All I want is for him to bury himself to the hilt inside me. One thrust, and I'd be there. But Liam refuses to do that. It's so frustrating, and yet… It's so amazing. The way he strokes me to the point of climax is the best damn feeling in the world. I want to teeter here forever.

Almost lazily, he continues to nibble at my flesh. His hands spread me farther apart. Under normal circumstances, I would feel self-conscious about being in such a vulnerable position, but I'm beyond that. I deepen the stretch, attempting to get closer.

I want to drive him deeper inside me. I'm nearly incoherent with the hot licks of need that continue to roll rampantly through my body.

It's crazy what this man does to me.

And I love it.

Sex has never felt this cataclysmic. It's like he's opened up a whole new world I never realized existed.

"Your pussy is delicious. I missed it."

I whimper as he laps at me, gorging himself until he decides he's had his fill.

"Are you ready for my cock, baby? Your pussy is so soft and wet. So ready for a good, hard fuck," he growls.

His gravelly voice, along with the firm thrust of his erection, are all it takes to push me over the edge. I scream out my pleasure as he pummels me from behind. The orgasm that has been building for almost thirty tortuous minutes explodes throughout my entire being, shattering everything I've ever known. His harsh groans reverberate in my ears as he spends himself inside my body before collapsing on top of me.

I'm exhausted.

Mentally. Physically. Emotionally.

I want to curl up and sleep for days. I feel so ridiculously sated, that it's almost a revelation.

Liam presses a kiss against my shoulder before rolling to the side and taking me with him. He repositions my limp form until I'm sprawled out across his chest.

"Fuck."

I can't help the gurgle of drained laughter that escapes from my lips.

That sums up the moment perfectly.

CHAPTER 19

LIAM

*A*n unexpected contentment fills me as I press her soft curves against my body.

Last night…

It was…well…it was pretty fucking amazing.

Hands down, the best sex I've ever had.

In my entire life.

And yes, I know I said that after the first time we were together, but this was like a hundred times better. It was crazy, almost unbelievably good.

What I really want to do is wake her up and take her all over again. But I won't, because I kept her up pretty late.

I don't know what it is about this woman that has pushed me over the edge. I really don't. After about ten minutes, Gia stirs in my arms before stretching her naked length against mine. The friction alone is enough to have me stiffening up.

"It's nice to actually wake up with you in my arms this time," I murmur. "No sneaking out at the crack of dawn."

With a chuckle, she relaxes against me. The sound is deep and throaty. It does funny things to my insides.

"It'd seemed like a good idea at the time."

I pull her close. "Just know it won't be so easy to shake me loose again."

Gia burrows against me. Her naked ass is flush against my growing hard-on. All I have to do is move a little more to the—

"You don't have to worry about that." Seriousness threads its way through her voice. "But I still need to take things slow." She glances over her shoulder, blue gaze locking on mine. "I don't want to complicate things any further than they already are."

"Are you having regrets?" My heart stutters painfully.

That would probably kill me. Last night was beyond amazing. Completely and utterly perfect. I don't think I've ever felt closer to another human being. And it wasn't just the physical, either. I've had sex before. Dozens of times. What happened last night meant way more.

She has to realize that.

We're way past the point of no return.

"No," she whispers, tongue darting out to moisten her lips. "Last night was...wonderful."

You're damned right it was.

"It's just that..." Emotion wavers in her voice. "Nothing has changed between us. The age difference..." She pauses before forcing out the rest. "It still bothers me."

Exasperation bursts inside me as I shake my head in frustration. "The difference in our ages doesn't mean a damn thing. You're making too much out of it."

"It matters to *me*. You're the younger guy in this situation. I get that it doesn't bother you."

After last night, I hate the direction this conversation has veered in. I don't want to do this with her right now. Playfully, I nip at her neck and lighten my tone. "It shouldn't matter to you either. We like each other, and we're attracted to one another. That's all that matters."

Gia sighs as I nibble my way over the curve of her shoulder. "I need to be sure about this."

"What you need to do is trust me, baby."

I've never been more certain about anything in my life. Not even football. This woman is fucking perfect. Last night only solidified that. The problem is that she needs to feel that way as well. I don't want her questioning what we could have. I don't want the age difference to be what keeps us apart.

The need to claim her pounds through me, and I twist toward the bedside table to grab another condom. After ripping into the package and sliding it over my rock-hard erection, I pull her backside against me. I lift her leg and slide my cock against her welcoming heat. Slowly, I stroke her pussy until a throaty moan falls from her lips.

"Are you really going to tell me that you're not sure about this?" I growl against her ear, giving her another deep stroke.

"Liam..."

My name falling from her lips is like a straight shot to the balls.

"What, baby?"

"You're not playing fair."

The chuckle I release is low and raspy. More than anything, I want to be buried deep inside her tight body. These teasing strokes are killing me.

"You're damned right I won't play fair. I've tried to be patient and give you time. I'm done with that. I want you, Gia. And I know you want me too."

Another stroke against her core has her widening her legs in silent invitation.

"You're right, I do. I just..." She gasps as I thrust rhythmically against her. "I need to take this slow. There's no reason we have to rush it, is there?"

Nope. We don't have to rush one damn thing. But at the same time, she needs to understand that she belongs to me.

This pussy belongs to me.

Unlike last time, I won't sit back and allow her to run.

"Do you think this is rushing? It seems pretty damn slow." I snake a hand around her rib cage before it settles over one breast. My fingers pluck at her pebbled nipple before sliding down her belly to play with her clit.

"Mmmm." Breathy little sounds of excitement fall from her lips as she writhes. "What are you doing to me, Liam?"

"Whatever you want me to," I murmur against her neck, meaning every single word.

What we did less than twelve short hours ago plays through my head.

Did I push her too hard, too fast?

"Did I hurt you last night?" The question is out of my mouth before I can rein it in again. That's the last thing I'd want to do.

Her body continues to rock against mine. Without breaking rhythm, she glances over her shoulder. The tentative stirring of an emotional connection swirls through me as our gazes stay locked. I've never felt anything like it before.

"No." She bites her lip as a blush stains her cheeks. "You didn't hurt me."

When she falls into silence, I blurt, "Did you like it?"

Her teeth nip at her lower lip as she glances away. "I've never done that before," she whispers.

I hate that she won't meet my eyes.

Is she embarrassed?

Shocked?

Disgusted?

Unable to withstand the disconnect, my hand skims over her belly and the valley between her breasts until I can wrap my fingers loosely around the delicate column of her throat. Her pulse kicks into overdrive. It's carefully that I rotate her chin until I can press a kiss against the corner of her lips.

"I don't want to do anything that makes you uncomfortable, Gia."

Her breath hitches.

The silence that stretches between us makes my heart riot. I need to know what's going on inside that beautiful head of hers. I want to know if I have to soften my touch with her. I'm not rough by any means, but I enjoy letting go and pushing the boundaries. There are times when I relish taking control and dominating a woman. I want to give her so much pleasure that she doesn't know what to do with herself. I want it to become almost too much for the confines of her flesh.

In order to do that, you need to be able to walk a fine line.

When I'm in control, pushing the limits, it's all about her pleasure and intensifying it. Magnifying what feels good so it's explosive. I want to be the drug careening through her body. It's about making her soar to uncharted heights before floating back to earth.

I like sex to be raw and honest. It's all about what feels good. There shouldn't be anything that holds you back from immersing yourself in the moment. There should be freedom to completely give yourself over to the pleasure coursing through your body without feeling ashamed or embarrassed. But in order for that to happen, there needs to be a certain level of trust. An openness between partners. Otherwise, it doesn't work.

For Gia, I would rein in that part of myself. It doesn't need to be that way, but there's an elemental wildness to lovemaking when it is. And it's something I enjoy.

"You didn't make me uncomfortable." She shifts against me as her voice drops. "I liked it. Everything you did... I wanted it."

Relief floods through me.

Gently, I stroke the length of her throat, all the while thrusting against her from behind. "Are you sure you liked it?" With a snarl, I add, "All of it?"

The blush spreads from her cheeks to her neck.

It's fucking adorable. It really is.

"Yes, I loved it," she answers truthfully.

"Good, because I enjoy playing with your body."

I don't want anything coming between us when we're in bed. If she's uncomfortable with something I've done, I need to know about it. My pleasure is only enhanced by hers.

"I like getting you worked up until you're practically sobbing. Until you're so desperate to come that it's the only thing you can think about."

"I've never orgasmed like that," she admits. "The guy I was with before...sex wasn't like that between us."

I shake my head. Sex should *always* be like that.

Hot.

Fun.

Mutually satisfying.

Pushing the limits to reach new pinnacles of pleasure.

Otherwise, what's the point?

"Whoever was stupid enough to let you go didn't understand what he had," I growl.

For a brief moment, a shadow clouds her blue eyes before she blinks it away. With my hard cock nestled exactly where I want it, I don't think too much more about it. When Gia spreads her legs wider, I thrust into her heat.

Any other questions flitting through my brain melt into nothingness as instinct takes over.

CHAPTER 20

LIAM

"Dude, where've you been? You're never around anymore." Dylan's gaze flicks to mine before arrowing to the television screen. "What? You think because it's the offseason, you can fuck around on me and I won't notice?"

I snort.

When I remain silent, he continues, unwilling to drop the conversation. "Seriously, where have you been hiding out?"

I run a hand over the top of my fauxhawk. The gesture is a reminder of how much Gia enjoys sliding her fingers through it. As soon as she breaks into my thoughts, need spikes through me.

It doesn't matter if I spent the night at her place, I'm already impatient to see her again. No matter how much time we spend together, it's never enough. I want more. Whatever this is coursing through me feels like an addiction. Even if all we do is sit on the couch together while she grades papers and I watch a little TV. Especially when there are sexy glasses perched on the bridge of her nose. I can't resist laying hands on her when she looks like that. Maybe one of these days she'll actually make it through an entire stack, but I can't imagine it happening anytime soon.

I'm like a walking boner around that woman. It's sad, really. I never realized what little control I have over my own body.

To answer Dylan's question—I've been at Gia's. I spend every bit of free time with her. I love waking up with her warm body nestled against mine.

Hands down, it's the best damn feeling in the world.

"I've been around." I'm leery of saying too much about our relationship. It's still new. Anything can happen.

Gia wants to take things slow, and I'm trying, I really am. I want to give her space. But at the same time, all I want to do is crowd her until she realizes that whatever this is between us is serious. This relationship feels more real than anything I've ever experienced.

"Everyone's meeting up at O'Brien's later. You know how I hate to sound like a whiny bitch, but it's been weeks since we hung out, dude. Your ass better be there tonight."

Gia and I are still in that stage where we spend a lot of time at her house. Once in a while, we go out to dinner or hit a movie.

I'm heading over to her place in a little bit to pick up Claire. They've been working together for three weeks. I've repeatedly told Gia she doesn't have to spend so much time helping my sister with her homework, but she insists it isn't a problem.

And Claire? Well, Claire adores her.

Gia can do no wrong in my sister's eyes.

I kind of feel the same way myself.

I shake my head. "I don't think I can make it. I've got shit going on."

"What shit?" Dylan keeps his gaze pinned to the seventy-inch television screen and the zombies he's intent on mowing down in a blaze of gunfire. "You've been gone an awful lot lately. You shacking up with someone?"

I drop onto the couch and glance at my phone. I've got an hour before I need to head over to Gia's. I'm taking her out for dinner after we drop Claire off. Us spending time together is pretty much a foregone conclusion. And I fucking love it.

One of the things I really like is that she isn't in college. Gia has other things going on. I like listening to her talk about her job. The stories she tells me about her kids are hilarious. It's nice to discuss something other than my classes, football, and the upcoming draft.

She's interested in politics, and what's happening in the world outside the Barnett bubble. I never realized how isolating it can be on campus. Not only does Gia take me out of that, but she makes me forget about the problems at home. When I'm with her, I don't have to think about any of it.

"Let me guess—this is about that girl."

I give him a sharp look because I haven't mentioned one damn word about Gia to these guys. "What girl? There's no girl." Technically, this is true. Gia isn't a girl.

Nope. She's most definitely a—

"Sure there is." His lips curl up at the corners and he gives me a who-the-hell-are-you-trying-to-fool look. "The one you've been secretly hanging out with."

Dylan doesn't even live here anymore. He moved into the apartment next to us with his girlfriend, Lexi. Although, when she's not around, you can usually find him rummaging through our cabinets or playing Xbox.

More than likely, both.

Someone needs to steal his damn key.

I snort.

Since I'm not sure how to respond, it's mostly for show.

"What the hell are you talking about?" Even I can hear the panicky timbre threading its way through my words. I clear my throat before dragging a hand over my hair.

His eyes narrow.

I probably shouldn't have done that. It's a nervous tic and everyone knows it. My muscles tense as I wait for him to call me out.

Instead, he chuckles, as if he knows every detail of my life, before shaking his head. "Dude. That's so sad. Why are you keeping her some dirty little secret? Is this just some chick you're banging on the down low? Too embarrassed to bring her around?"

His flippant words are like lighter fluid on dry kindling. Without thinking, I growl, "Hell no! It's not like that at all."

A smug smile slides across his face as he skewers me with a knowing look.

Damn.

Entrapment.

By Dylan Sullivan, no less.

The painful part of this conversation isn't me banging a chick on the sly, it's that he got me to admit it so freaking easily.

Rather than rub it in, which is odd, Dylan says instead, "So, now that we've established that there is, indeed, a chick, what's the deal with her?"

I release a steady puff of air from my lungs and turn the question over in my head. I don't have a problem bringing Gia around my friends. In fact, I've casually thrown out the suggestion a time or two in hopes she'd like to meet some of the people I hang with. Each time, my words have been met with hesitancy.

Or worse—silence.

It's the whole *you're still in college and I'm not* thing rearing its ugly head again.

I know Gia doesn't mean to do it, but there are times when *I'm* the one left feeling like a dirty little secret. I wish she would get over the age thing already. It's not like I'll be in college much longer.

"It's complicated," I mutter.

His gaze stays focused on the game as the sounds of gunfire ricochet off our walls. "How so?"

Sheesh.

Can't he take a hint and drop the subject? I don't want to discuss Gia with these guys. Even though we've grown closer and spend a ton of time together, I'm afraid to push for more of a commitment from her.

Because that's exactly what I want.

I suppose this is what one would call an ironic situation.

I've had more than my fair share of chicks try and lock me down. Not once have I ever wavered from telling them that it was casual or nothing at all. Now, here I am trying my damnedest to seduce this woman into a relationship, and she's having none of it.

She throws up roadblocks at every turn.

It's begrudgingly that I admit, "She's not in college." I pause before adding, "She's a little bit older."

Without glancing at me, Dylan holds out a fist. "Nice. A little cougar action. I like it."

Annoyed by his response, I leave him hanging. "For fuck's sake, it's not like that."

Unperturbed, he drops his hand. "All right, then, explain it to me."

What the hell? Are we seriously doing this right now?

I gnaw my bottom lip in contemplation. Part of me wants to talk to someone about this. I'm tired of holding it all in. Even though Sam Harper is one of my roommates, there's no way in hell I'm bringing this up with him. We're friends. All right, that might be overstating things a bit. We've been teammates for the last three years.

That's probably a more accurate description of our relationship. I think the dude is still pissed that I took his girlfriend out before they got together. To this day, he doesn't trust me around her, which I find hilarious.

Especially since Violet only has eyes for him.

And everyone, including myself, realizes it.

Fine, I'll admit it, every once in a while, I like to be a dick and fan the flames of his jealousy by pretending to hit on his girl. Obviously, I'm joking around, and if he weren't so consumed by her, he'd see it.

Violet doesn't take my antics seriously, which is nice. I enjoy teasing her.

And Roan is so busy getting ready for the NFL draft and trying to find time to see his girlfriend, Ivy. That's what I should be doing. No, not seeing his girlfriend but getting ready for the draft.

If I had any brains whatsoever, I'd steer clear of any female entanglements and focus all of my time and attention on my future. There's too much at stake, and the last thing I need is to get mind fucked.

Although, I think it's too late for that. My head has been full of Gia ever since I first laid eyes on her almost two months ago. Attempting to pull back now feels impossible.

More telling than that, I don't want to.

Dylan really wants to know what's going on?

Then I'll take a chance and dump all this on him. Hopefully, I won't regret this moment of weakness. The way my gut clenches tells me it's all but certain that I will.

"The woman I've been seeing," I say hesitantly, "she's an elementary school teacher. And the age difference between us..." I pause, wrapping my lips around the words. "It bothers her."

For a long moment, Dylan stays focused on the game. To the point that my brows draw together, and I wonder if he heard me. For fuck's sake, I just dropped a major bomb, and the dude can't be bothered to pay attention.

I knew this was a mistake.

"A teacher, huh? That's cool," he says.

Air leaks from my lungs as everything in me loosens.

He knifes another zombie in the temple and blood sprays everywhere.

With a cackle, he shouts, "Take that, you stupid motherfucker!"

"Yeah," I find myself saying, "she's really cool." Actually, Gia is way more than that, but there's no way I'm going to gush like a lovesick pussy. I'm more or less trying to ease into this uncomfortable conversation.

"You should bring her tonight."

I fold my arms behind my head and stare up at the ceiling. "I don't know, man. I'm not sure she's ready for that."

"What? You think we're going to embarrass you? Like we're a bunch of immature assholes?"

Nailed it.

That's exactly what I think.

"Um, you people *are* a bunch of immature assholes. I like this girl. I don't need you guys scaring her off."

His gaze shifts to me. "You've got my word that we'll be on our best behavior."

I snort.

Well, shit.

Now, I'm really screwed.

When he sees the dubious expression on my face, he says, "I'm totally serious, dude. Bring her along. It'll be fun."

As tempting as it is, I have no idea if Gia is ready for that. It's all about baby steps with this woman. Since I like her, I'm willing to go as slowly as she needs.

The last thing I want to do is fuck this up.

"I'll think about it," I tell him.

He nods, as if the situation is settled. "You do that, man."

CHAPTER 21

LIAM

After dropping my sister off at home, Gia and I head back to her place. For once, I don't have my mind on hustling her sweet ass into bed, which is a damn shame since her fingers are already stroking over me, working their way under my jacket and shirt until they're able to graze bare flesh.

I love the feel of her touch.

Before she can distract me, I blurt, "I was wondering if you wanted to head over to O'Brien's tonight and meet up with a few of my friends."

I give her a bit of side-eye to gauge her reaction. The way her fingers still against my abs has me tensing, wondering if maybe I made a mistake. My jaw locks as her blue gaze searches my face.

"Is that what you want to do?" she asks.

Tension settles over us.

"I thought it might be nice to meet up with some people." I shoot a quick glance in her direction before adding, "We never really do that, you know?"

We've been hanging out for a while now. Whatever this is between us seems to be moving in the right direction. At least in my mind, it is.

It occurs to me that maybe I'm the only one thinking along those lines.

I nod as her plump lower lip finds its way between her teeth. "It's just that..." Her words trail off into nothingness, as if she's unsure how to finish that thought.

My brows slide together. I hate that she's so reluctant to move this relationship forward. Maybe I've got this whole thing wrong. Maybe this is nothing more than two people screwing around. Not once has she suggested that I meet her friends. It's like she's afraid of worlds colliding or something like that.

"It's just what?" I bite out. Even I can hear the rough scrape in my voice.

Her fingers fall away as she sits back on the cloth seat. With her gaze trained on the windshield, she inhales a deep breath. "I don't know if I'm ready for that. If *we're* ready for that."

My fingers tighten around the steering wheel. The last thing I want to do is push Gia for more. I'm tired of forcing myself on her. But the flip side is that I'm tired of waiting around for her to open up and let me in. So far, that hasn't happened.

I'm beginning to wonder if it ever will.

Over the last three weeks, we've fallen into a comfortable pattern. When I finish up on campus, I head over to her place. By the time I get there, she usually has dinner ready and then we watch a little TV. We'll sit curled up on the couch, and she'll grade some papers. Then we make love before falling asleep in bed together. When she leaves for school around eight in the morning, I head back to my apartment.

Every once in a while, we go out to dinner.

We never run into anyone who knows either of us. We stay away from campus. I've been recognized a few times, but I try not to make a big deal out of it. I don't want that part of my life interfering with our relationship. So, I'll sign a couple autographs and snap a few pictures. That kind of thing. But I try to keep it lowkey.

I'm able to slip by unnoticed when I don't wear my hair in a faux-hawk, which has become my trademark look. When I'm out with Gia,

I keep my hair slicked back, away from my face. It's kind of funny that something so simple can do the trick.

Frustration bubbles up inside me. This conversation isn't going the way I'd hoped it would. Should I have expected it?

Probably.

"Look, I'm not trying to push you." Although, I think we both know that's what I'm doing. "But I'm tired of hiding this. I want you to meet my friends." I toss another look in her direction, surprised to find her wide gaze already locked on me. "And I want to get to know yours."

"I know," she murmurs. "But you agreed to take this slow. One step at a time."

Another shaft of disappointment slices through me. "You're right. And I meant every word, but I want to be more than the guy you fuck every night." In this moment, I hate myself for sounding like a needy bitch. All I'm doing is pushing Gia further away when all I want is to hold her close.

"Is that what you really think?" she asks, voice sounding stricken.

I jerk my shoulders, unsure what to believe. The emotions careening through me aren't something I've ever experienced before. I don't like it. Not one damn bit. No woman has ever tied me up into little knots.

"I like you, Liam." Her fingers slip over mine before she squeezes them. "You have to know this is more than sex."

Maybe that's the problem. I have no clue what I am to her or what any of this means. For all I know, she's just experimenting. Slumming it. Having a bit of fun with a guy who can get her off every damn time.

The thought makes me gut sick.

"Is it? I don't know, Gia." I glance at her as we drive toward her place. "You don't want me to meet your friends. You don't want to go anywhere where we might run into people you know. So, no, I guess I don't know what this is or how you feel about us."

Fucking Dylan.

I blame him for this. That's the last time I take advice from him. I should have let everything coast along. Status quo. But it's too late for that.

The words shoot from my mouth before I can rein them back in again. "Sometimes it feels like I'm your dirty little secret."

By this point, I'm practically frothing at the mouth.

If I looked in the mirror right now, I don't know if I'd recognize the person staring back at me. It's not a good feeling.

Actually, it's a shitty feeling.

Silence descends as she inhales a swift breath. A few uncomfortable moments tick by. It only amps up the stifling tension in the car.

"Is that really the way you feel?" she asks in a small voice.

I shrug.

To answer her question, yeah, that's exactly how I feel.

I'm good enough to screw, but not much else.

You know what?

Fuck this.

Until these thoughts were rocketing out of my mouth, I had no idea how much this bothered me. I thought I was fine cruising along, taking it day by day.

Most of my past relationships have been casual. I've never wanted to be tied down with expectations and commitments. I have enough of that bullshit with my family to invite more. And here I am acting like some clingy, desperate dude who's never had a girlfriend.

It pisses me off that I'm behaving in this manner.

I'm not this guy.

I've *never* been this guy.

By the time we pull up in front of her house, I'm irritated with myself, and yeah, with Gia for wanting to hide this relationship. Just like Dylan accused me of doing. This conversation has been a real eye opener.

And not a welcome one either.

What sucks is that I feel like I'm in a no-win situation.

I don't think I can continue seeing a woman who isn't willing to be involved in my life. And refuses to let me into hers. I need to know she can let go of the age difference. Instead, she's so hung up on it.

Doesn't she realize that no one else cares?

Is Gia really willing to throw away what we have because of it?

Maybe she is.

I don't know.

I thought I did, but obviously I was wrong.

Strangely enough, the thought of dialing this whole thing back and having nothing more than a sexual relationship with her won't work for me. I can't do it. Not with Gia.

This is such a fucked-up mess.

When I pull into her drive and don't turn off the engine, she wraps her arms tightly around her body.

"Are you going to come in?" she asks.

I shake my head. "No, I don't think so."

"You're that upset about this?" A mixture of surprise and disappointment swirls through her voice.

"Yeah, I am." My gaze stays locked on hers. "I've been honest about my feelings. You know I want more. This isn't some…" My voice falters before I clear it to get all the rioting emotion under control. "Whatever this is between us, it's not just sex. But I need to know you feel the same, that we're heading in the same direction." Even though I'm loath to say the words, I force them out. "Otherwise, there's no point in continuing this. I'm not in the market for a casual lay."

Color drains from her cheeks. "You said you'd give me more time."

I plow a hand roughly through my hair.

Guess I have my answer, now don't I?

"I'm sorry, Gia. I never meant to push, but I need more." I shrug, unsure what else there is to say.

I can't continue to spend time with her, make love to her every night, when I already feel myself falling. I can't allow myself to get fucked in the head by a woman who's looking for something casual. If it were any other female, this kind of situation would be a dream.

Hot sex without strings.

What guy in his right mind wouldn't want that?

Apparently, the answer to that is me.

"I don't know what to say," she whispers.

I jerk my head in a nod.

Even though it feels like everything fell to shit in the blink of an eye, I know that isn't the case. We avoided the minefield by not talking about it.

You can't do that forever.

I don't know, maybe it's better this way. Isn't it safer to cut Gia loose now before I become any more attached?

"I guess I should go." Tears flood her voice.

It takes effort to keep all the emotion swirling violently in me buried deep inside. I don't want her to see how much her rejection has destroyed me. I've made a big enough pussy out of myself for this woman. I'm done.

"Yeah, that's probably a good idea," I say gruffly.

"All right." Her fingers tremble as they wrap around the door handle and pull it open. Her gaze stays locked on mine the entire time. I have to fight myself not to lay hands on her.

But I don't.

Can't.

I need to let her go.

As she steps from the car, she sucks in a ragged breath before leaning down and searching out my gaze. Instead of looking at her, I stare out the windshield. I can't watch her walk away.

"Bye, Liam," she says brokenly.

"Take care of yourself, Gia."

Once she closes the door, I release a pent-up breath. Unable to help myself, my gaze fastens on her, tracking her movements up the cement path to the porch. She doesn't glance back at me. Not even when she slips inside the front door. For a moment, I sit frozen in place, stunned this relationship is over.

One heartbeat passes and then another. I slam my fists against the beat-up steering wheel. "Fuck!"

All I want to do is jump out of the vehicle and run after her. I want to pound on the front door until she opens it so I can yank her into my arms. I want to tell her that none of it matters. That we can carry on like we have been.

But I don't.

Because it matters.

More than I realized.

Even though it's the hardest thing I've ever done, I ignore what every instinct is screaming at me to do, and back the car out of the driveway before heading toward campus.

CHAPTER 22

LIAM

"Why are you all acting like such a sad bastard, Garrison? Someone run over your puppy?" Roan claps me on the back before sliding onto the seat next to me.

Instead of responding, I hoist the bottle of beer I've been working on for the last twenty minutes to my lips before taking a long swallow. Not that I thought it would, but it doesn't make the situation better. It doesn't dull the pain like I'd hoped. Even though it's been a few hours, the conversation—because I can't even say it was a fight—continues to churn in my head.

I've picked up my phone a dozen times and thought about apologizing for getting bent around the axel. It's not like she wasn't right—I told her I'd give her time, and we could take things slow.

But still…

I need more than what she's willing to give. Even though I didn't realize it before, these feelings have been brewing in me for a while.

When I remain silent, he lifts a brow.

I give him a tight shrug. "Nothing much. Just tired."

He nods in understanding. "Yeah, the schedule my trainer has me on is brutal. And the diet?" He raises the bottle to his lips. "Not supposed to be drinking either." His turquoise-colored eyes crinkle with humor. "I figure a beer every once in a while won't kill me. We all need to blow off steam."

Relieved to have something other than Gia to focus on, my thoughts turn to the upcoming draft. I can't afford to pay someone like Roan does, so I've been working with the team's athletic trainer. Since my ass always feels worked over from the regimen he put together, I have no complaints.

Roan leans back in his chair and takes another swig. "I can't believe I'm going to say this, but I'll be glad when the draft is over next month."

I understand where he's coming from. The football season might be done, but we're still putting in a handful of hours training each day. And then there's the stress of not knowing how everything will pan out.

Roan's girlfriend, Ivy, lives in Cincinnati, and they're doing the long-distance thing. He's on edge, wondering where he'll end up playing next season. They're hoping to be together by the summer.

So yeah, I get it.

With all the hype surrounding Roan, he'll likely go in the first round. Even back in high school, there was speculation about him turning pro. He's one hell of a wide receiver, and together, we make a great team out on the field. I'll miss playing ball with him next year.

I glance around the table crammed with teammates. I'll miss playing with a lot of these guys. They've become like brothers to me. Some more than others, but still…we all look out for each other.

As certain as I am about Roan getting picked up, I'm not sure what will happen with Dylan. Even though I would never say it to him, there's a good possibility he'll end up doing something else. What, I have no idea.

And then there's Sam.

He's not looking to turn pro. This was his last season playing college ball. I'm sure he'll miss it, but he's heading off to law school next fall. Even though we're not close, I trust him implicitly on the field. He's been my left tackle for the past two seasons. He's always taken care of my blindside. His presence allowed me to focus on the plays without worrying about being sacked.

Roan elbows me in the ribs, knocking me out of those maudlin thoughts. It's difficult to believe that a few short hours ago, I thought tonight would end up being a good one. I was planning on taking Gia out to dinner and then spending the rest of the evening at her place. Instead, I'm sitting in a shitty bar, moping about not playing ball with my team next season.

I think it might be time to head home before I actually cry in my beer.

"Hey, I could be wrong, but isn't that the chick who ran out on you a few months ago?"

My head jerks in the direction he's staring. The moment our gazes collide, her feet grind to a halt, as if she's unsure about being here. I rise to my feet before pushing my way through the thick crowd.

Once I reach her, she nervously tucks a loose strand of ebony-colored hair behind her ear and blurts, "I'm sorry, Liam."

Even though her words are barely more than a whisper, I hear them loud and clear over the music that pumps through the sound system.

Instead of responding, I haul her into my arms. The breath catches at the back of her throat right before my lips crash onto hers. Her arms twine around my neck as my hands stroke up her back, tugging her closer.

I'm ripped out of my Gia-haze by catcalls and whistles. A smile tilts her lips as she pulls away. We glance at the table my teammates are occupying. All of them are staring at us.

I shake my head as a smile creeps over my face. It doesn't take much to dismiss the noisy crew as I turn back to Gia and rest my forehead against hers. "I'm glad you're here."

Her gaze stays locked on mine. "I'm sorry about earlier. I never meant to hurt you."

"I'm sorry too."

We both fall silent amidst the chaos of the bar.

"I need you to be patient with me," she says.

"I know it doesn't seem like it, but I'm trying to give you time." I won't lie, it's difficult. I want to know this woman is mine. That's not something I've ever wanted before.

We untangle our bodies from one another before I slip her hand into mine. As we head to the table, all gazes are pinned to us. A few of the younger guys make noise.

Roan is the first to pipe up.

"Sweetheart, if his stalker-like tendencies start to scare you, just say the word" –he motions to Sam, who sits across from him— "and we'll drop him like first hour physics class."

I roll my eyes before sliding them toward Gia, attempting to gauge how she's taking all the attention. A tentative smile settles on her lips as I introduce her to my teammates. When I take a seat, Roan moves to an empty one so Gia can settle next to me.

I squeeze her hand, hoping to ease her nerves. When her attention bounces to me, I say, "Thanks for coming."

Gia has no idea how much this means to me. I want her to meet my friends and be involved in my life.

She leans toward me before whispering, "I really am sorry for earlier. I never meant to make you feel like I was hiding you or our relationship."

When I hike a brow, she has the good grace to duck her head before piercing me with her blue eyes. "I was never ashamed of you. I just want to take it slow. I want to be sure that whatever this is between us will last. That's all. I was being cautious. It has more to do with me than you."

I nod, accepting her explanation at face value. Just having her show up at O'Brien's feels like a huge victory. When I pulled away from her house earlier, I'd really thought we were finished. "We don't have to stay long."

"We can stay as long as you want."

Unable to resist the lure of her lips, I close the distance between us before pressing a kiss to her mouth. It's been more than a couple of hours since I've felt the warm slide of her lips beneath mine. I'm all but starving for them.

For her.

"All right, you two, enough of that!"

Uncaring of those around us, my gaze holds hers until a light blush crawls its way up her cheeks.

Damn, but I love when she does that. I'm beginning to realize that I love everything this woman does.

Everything except when she pushes me away.

But we're working on that.

Slowly but surely, we're working on it.

CHAPTER 23

GIA

*A*ll right, I'll admit it. I'm having a good time with Liam's friends.

I'm sure the two bottles of beer I've sucked down are helping with that. They've done an excellent job of loosening me up. The entire time we've been at the table, Liam's fingers have been threaded through mine. He's constantly playing or toying with them.

I can't say I don't like it. I love that he has this deep need to always touch me. I feel the same way. My attention fastens on him as he talks to one of his teammates across the table. I think the guy's name is Sam.

One positive to having Liam distracted by his friends is that I'm able to study him when he's unaware of my intense perusal. Have I mentioned how much I love when he wears his hair styled into a fauxhawk?

I was under the impression that it's his trademark look, but he doesn't always wear it like that. When he does, I have a hard time controlling myself. I love running my fingers over it.

It's sexy as hell.

Then again, so are the array of tattoos that decorate both his arms and chest.

I've spent hours tracing my fingers over the intricate patterns of swirling ink that mar his flesh. His left arm is composed of an elaborate design. Angels are surrounded by the sun and clouds. The names of his family reside there as well.

The other arm is decorated with skulls and a detailed clock that sits over a pyramid. There are blackbirds winging their way to life above it, almost as if they are attempting to fly away. Over the left side of his chest is a large cross made of wooden stakes held together in the middle by twine. The bottom of the stake looks as if it's piercing his flesh. Dark blood drips from the torn flesh.

I don't know what it is about that piece, but it tugs at something deep inside me. Too many times to count, I've curled up against his chest, fingers gliding over the artwork. I've never been attracted to men with tattoos. I can appreciate the art and the intricacy of them, but it's not like I've ever felt the need to have something inked permanently on my body. And yet, I love the different pieces that cover his muscular form. I love the meaning each one holds for him.

Earlier this evening, when we'd been in his car, and he asked if I'd come here with him, I felt broadsided. I've become used to the little bubble we've created around ourselves. It's comfortable. When we're alone, I don't have to think about the reasons we shouldn't be together. I can enjoy the moment. I don't dwell on the age difference. There aren't any reminders that he's still in college. Or entering the draft.

Maybe, deep down, I was worried his friends would think he's crazy for being with a woman so much older when he could be seeing a college-aged girl. Someone who isn't tied down with responsibilities. Someone who is carefree.

But none of them seem to care.

Or even notice.

There haven't been any strange looks aimed in my direction. Or sly jokes about him dating a cougar, which makes me wonder if I've placed too much emphasis on the age difference. Maybe Liam was right when he said that no one else gives a damn. Maybe I need to get over it and move on. What we have is too special to let something as unimportant as age get in the way of how we feel about each other.

It's only when Liam's fingers slip under my chin and lift it until his gaze can skewer mine that I realize I've spaced out. Silently, he leans forward and presses his lips to mine. That's all it takes for everything swirling through my head to stop.

The crowded bar fades away until it's just the two of us. When it's like that, nothing else matters.

"You gonna get up there or what?" he asks.

I blink because I have absolutely no idea what he's talking about.

With a grin, he jerks his head toward the front of the bar. I follow the movement until my gaze settles on the makeshift stage about thirty feet from where we're camped out.

"Karaoke," he says.

I almost laugh but stifle it at the last moment.

Oh.

Hell.

No.

My brother might have a great set of pipes and be musically inclined, but that doesn't mean I am. If he thinks I'll get up there in front of all these people, he's got a screw loose.

A grin tugs at his lips as he cocks his head. "You're not into karaoke?"

"I have no problem with other people getting up there and making a fool out of themselves, but I'm not doing it."

"So, you're drawing a firm line in the sand when it comes to karaoke?"

I snort.

"Are you saying there's nothing I can do to convince you to get up there and sing a duet with me?"

My eyes widen as I lean toward him and annunciate slowly, "Wild horses couldn't force me up there. Is that clear enough?"

"Have you ever done it before?"

"Yup. And after that mentally scarring performance, I promised myself I would never do it again."

He laughs. It's a sexy sound that rolls over me before arrowing straight down to my core where it settles. "Oh, come on, it couldn't have been *that* bad."

I shudder, remembering the incident. Sure, it may have been five years ago, but some things never fade from your memory. "Trust me, it was worse. *Much* worse."

He tugs me close before smacking a quick kiss against my lips.

"Then we'll just watch."

For the next hour, a long line of people climb up on the stage and belt out their songs. Most aren't great and they know it—they all but revel in the knowledge. It's fairly amusing. I don't think I've laughed this hard in a long time.

Once some of the football players lumber up there, it gets funnier. A few times, I actually find myself covering my eyes, embarrassed for them. Most can't hold a tune to save their lives, but they're up there, hamming it up the entire time.

I swear, the worse they are, the more fan adoration they receive.

Some of the more notable performances are "Purple Rain" by Prince, "I Want it That Way" by the Backstreet Boys, and "Fuck You" by CeeLo. Some guy decides to belt out "I Wanna Be Sedated" by the Ramones. Of course, "YMCA" by the Village People is a huge crowd pleaser, as is Dylan's rendition of "Roxanne" by The Police. The audience goes crazy when Roan jumps up on stage and sings Madonna's "Like a Virgin." And the way he struts his stuff is hilarious. Apparently, not one to be outshone, Dylan ambles back up there for an encore performance and sings "It's Raining Men" by The Weather Girls.

"Dude, you need to get up there!" someone shouts at Liam. "You always sing."

He does?

Eyes wide, I turn in surprise to the dark-haired guy at my side. This is the first I'm hearing about this. "You sing?"

He shrugs. "A little bit."

Before I can fire off any other questions, another guy yells from the far end of the table, "Get your ass up there, Garrison!"

When the entire table begins to chant, I can't help but laugh and encourage him as well. I'm curious if he can actually sing or, like a lot of his teammates, he'll just goof around.

His gaze slides to mine. "You don't mind?"

I shake my head. As long as he doesn't attempt to drag me with him, I don't mind at all.

Once he rises to his feet, everyone claps and whistles. Liam shakes his head before his gaze fastens on mine.

Just as I'm about to shoo him away, one of the guys at the table shouts, "Get the hell up there, Garrison." He shoots Liam a sly grin. "And don't worry about your girl. I'll take good care of her." He stares straight at me before giving his knee a pat. "Why don't you come park yourself here, sweetheart, until lover boy is finished." The grin on his face grows when his gaze bounces to Liam. "Although, I can't promise she'll want to leave once she's in my arms. You know how the ladies love me."

Liam snorts. "How about I beat the piss out of you now rather than later, Morrison?"

The guy chuckles in response. It's obvious Liam isn't taking him seriously, because a moment later, he gives me a wink before making his way to the stage.

A pretty blonde sitting on the other side of the table leans toward me as Liam talks to the person running the karaoke machine.

"Have you heard Liam sing before?"

I shake my head, still surprised by this hidden talent. "He never mentioned it."

"He's really good." She smiles before glancing around at all the random girls hanging out at our table. As I do the same, I realize how many of them there are. I hadn't been paying much attention before. "Oh, you can bet there will be some real panty flooding going on."

Thankfully, the music starts up so I don't have to respond to that comment. My gaze slices to Liam, only to find him staring at me.

Something in my belly hollows as the fast-paced chords of Jet's "Are You Gonna Be My Girl" pump through the sound system. Before he gets out a full verse, I understand what the girl across from me was talking about. I sit up a little straighter as my mouth tumbles open in shock.

Liam has the most amazing voice. It's smooth and soulful. His gaze cradles mine throughout the performance, as if I'm the only one in the packed bar.

Holy hell, who knew the guy could sing like that?

And the way he grips the microphone, holding it close to his lips the entire time might be the sexiest thing I've ever seen in my life. When he finishes the song and the last notes reverberate through the air, the crowd goes nuts. Girls scream, bouncing up and down on their toes. It wouldn't surprise me if he returned to the table with a couple pair of panties hanging off him.

Out of everyone up there tonight, Liam was by far the best. He has a beautiful voice. The girl sitting across the table was absolutely right—my underwear is completely soaked.

A smile simmers on his lips, as if he can tell how affected I am by his performance. Once he's settled next to me, he tugs me into his arms.

I didn't think it was possible for him to push me any further over the edge, but he does it by whispering, "So, you gonna be my girl or what?"

He draws away enough for our gazes to meet. Humor sparkles in his gray depths, but there's an underlying seriousness there as well. One that pulls at every fiber of my being.

I suck in a breath, finally giving myself permission to say what's already in my heart. "Yeah, I'm your girl."

As the quietly spoken admission tumbles from my lips, relief fills me, leaving me to feel lighter. I'm tired of denying what I feel for Liam.

I want this man.

I want to belong to him.

And I want him to belong to me.

Before I can blink, he drags me closer so his mouth can crash onto mine. I don't think twice about opening to him. It doesn't matter if we're in the middle of a crowded bar.

There's just Liam.

The man I've been trying so damn hard not to fall for.

The man I've been fighting my attraction for.

The man I've been fighting my feelings for.

It's been a losing battle since I first laid eyes on him.

I realize there are issues standing in our way, but if they don't matter to Liam, then maybe I need to just go with it and see where we end up.

The feel of his tongue stroking over mine has my muscles turning pliant against his hard body. There's something masterful about the way he touches me. As if he's spent years getting to know every single dip, curve, and nuance.

By the time I draw away, I'm breathless and ready to come in my panties from his kisses alone.

"I had no idea you could sing like that," I say, trying to find my bearings.

He grins. "I took choir throughout high school. I've always enjoyed singing."

"I guess if my brother needs backup for The Renegades, I'll pass your name along." I press a kiss against his lips. "You're really good, Liam. I'm impressed."

"I'm all right." He jerks his shoulders modestly. "It's just something I fool around with."

Is he kidding?

There are about twenty girls hanging back, waiting to maul him if he so much as gets up from the table. In fact, there's one in particular hovering five feet from us. She hasn't taken her gaze off him.

"Oh, come on, you're way better than that. You were..." My voice trails off, and I shake my head, feeling floored all over again. "Amazing."

A smile plays around the corners of his lips. "Maybe I'll break out my guitar and serenade you sometime."

And now I'm totally done for.

"You have a guitar?" My brows rise.

His grin broadens until both dimples are popping.

Gahhhh.

Could this guy be any sexier?

I glance around the table. Tonight has turned out to be really enjoyable. Meeting all of Liam's friends and teammates—getting to know them—has unexpectedly put everything into sharp focus. It's done the impossible and solidified all of my feelings regarding this man.

I want to be with Liam.

And for now, that's good enough. I'm done questioning it. I'm done looking for reasons to walk away. I don't want this relationship to end. And maybe, sometime down the road, it will. But I'm not going to focus on that right now.

"Do you want another beer, or should we take off?" he asks, lips hovering at my ear. His voice is low and a bit growly. The deep timbre of it arrows straight down to my clit, making it throb with awareness.

And he's got that look in his eyes...

The one that tells me we'll barely make it through the front door before he's tearing the clothes off my body. Even the thought is enough to have need spiraling through me.

"Let's just—"

I get two words out before he's shooting out of his chair and dragging me up with him. Goodbyes are hastily being made when a dark-haired guy shouts, "Next weekend, baby! It's the big one. We're gonna do it up right, Garrison!"

A few of the guys joke in agreement before adding in their own comments.

My questioning gaze lands on Liam. Instead of answering my silent inquiry, his lower jaw tightens and the sexy look filling his eyes disappears. His fingers tense around mine. Without answering, he pulls me away from the table.

We don't make it far before someone else shouts, "Where are we going for your birthday, dude?"

It's Liam's birthday?

How didn't I know this? Hurt and confusion bubble up inside me. "It's your birthday? Why didn't you say something?"

His gaze fastens on mine. There's an odd look filling his eyes.

Guilt, maybe?

What are they planning to do, hit a few strip clubs?

Is that why he didn't mention it?

Honestly, I wouldn't have cared.

Not really. I'm a big girl. I could have handled it. Now, if he was spending all his time in a club, then we'd have a problem.

Liam's gray gaze pins mine in place.

Before he can open his mouth, someone else cuts in loudly, "Hell yeah, it's his birthday! Garrison is finally turning twenty-one! Can you believe it? Twenty-one shots, dude! You have to down twenty-one freaking shots!" Since my attention hasn't deviated from his, I have no idea who is crowing the words. "You're going to be so wrecked!"

Everyone laughs. A few more comments are hurled in Liam's direction regarding how they'll have to drag his drunk ass home at the end of the night.

Air clogs in my throat, making it impossible to breathe.

Twenty-one.

Liam is turning…*twenty-one?*

No. That can't be right.

He's turning twenty-three. Or even twenty-two, for God's sake. Liam can't be…

There is no way that Liam Garrison is twenty years old. I have *not* been sleeping with a twenty-year-old for the last month.

His gaze clings to mine in the dark bar. Remorse seeps into his gray depths. The reality of the situation crashes over me like a tidal wave. All of a sudden, I feel sick to my stomach.

I'm not someone who is prone to swearing but…

Fuck!

This guy—the one I let into my bed, the one I've been falling for—is twenty years old.

He's a baby.

How did I not know how young he was?

My mouth opens. There are so many questions churning in my brain, but no sound comes out.

"All right, we gotta take off," Liam says, giving a quick wave to his friends before towing me away from the table. When my feet stay locked in place, he gives my hand a firm tug until I stumble into movement. He has a death grip on my fingers as he pulls me through the thick crowd.

"Yeah," someone yells after us, "I thought that song would do it for you!"

More rowdy laughter follows, but I don't turn around. I keep walking, needing to get out of the stifling darkness. Even when the cool night air slaps at my cheeks, my mind continues to spin. I'm almost dizzy with the sensation.

I knew he was young. It's been a *huge* issue for me to overcome. But I never imagined he was younger than I suspected.

There's a nine-year difference between us.

Nine years!

I almost wince as that number circles viciously through my head. Seven seemed bad enough. What the hell am I doing with someone who isn't even twenty-one years old?

He's practically a teenager. A little more than two years ago and he was nineteen years old. Three years ago, and he was still in high school.

Maybe it's ridiculous to think along those lines, but that knowledge makes me feel like a pervert. I shouldn't be dating, or sleeping with, or contemplating a future with someone who is so much younger than I am. I should be going out with a man closer to my own age.

What hurts most is that I was starting to fall for him. I'd finally come to this place where I could let the seven-year difference go.

But nine years?

Nine?

No, I can't do it. It's too much.

CHAPTER 24

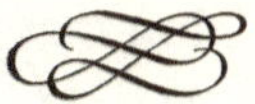

LIAM

*S*hit.

In hindsight, it probably would have been a good idea to have mentioned that I'm only twenty years old. At the very least, she should have heard it from me. Except, I knew it would cause problems. It's the reason I kept the information tightly under wraps. Like I have to give this woman another reason to break things off with me?

I don't think so. She's always had one foot out the door.

When Gia is wrapped up in my arms, everything is great. The difference in our ages is the last thing she's thinking about. But when we're apart?

That's when uncertainty bubbles up inside her like a geyser, and she allows all those outside forces to dictate our future.

It sucks.

As wrong as it might have seemed, I was trying to give her more time to come to grips with our ages before casually revealing that I wasn't twenty-two. She's broached the subject before, mentioning the seven-year age gap between us.

Yeah, it's not seven. More like eight and a half.

With my birthday right around the corner, I was hoping to let the whole thing slide. In fact, I wasn't going to tell her about it. I have zero interest in getting together with a huge group of guys and liquoring myself up until I'm tossing up my intestines. I've been hanging out at the bars and drinking for the last couple years. It's not that big of a deal.

Judging by her silence, my guess is that this new revelation is a big fucking problem.

I have no idea what to say at this point. Every time I open my mouth with a rational explanation that will make everything better, I end up slamming it shut again. Deep down, I realize that nothing will make the shocked expression on her face disappear.

Worse, she hasn't uttered a peep since we left the bar. But then again, neither have I. Part of me feels like I should apologize, but what exactly am I apologizing for?

Being twenty?

I never said I was older. But I also know she assumed I was a senior and therefore twenty-two.

Another few minutes creep by before Gia clears her throat. My gut is a tangle of knots just like it is before a big game.

"Why didn't you tell me the truth?"

Even though the question is asked quietly, it sounds deafening in the silence of the car. I almost wince at the shock and hurt riddled throughout her voice. My shoulders slump because we both know the answer.

Not wanting to make the situation any worse, I stick closely to the truth. "I knew it would bother you."

Gia doesn't glance in my direction as she stares mutely out the windshield. When she fails to follow up with another question—or even berate me—panic prickles at the bottom of my gut. Instead of yelling or hurtling accusations at me, she focuses her attention on the window, as if she can't bear to meet my gaze in the darkness.

I'm going to lose her.

"I wanted you to get to know me without our ages getting in the way," I blurt desperately. I swing into her driveway and throw the car into park. Only then does she swivel toward me.

"The entire time we've been together, this has been an issue for me. Seven years is a lot." Her tongue darts out to smudge her lips before she pushes out the rest. "And now it's nine."

"Eight and a half," I cut in. "You won't turn thirty until October."

Gia tilts her head as she holds my gaze in the darkness. "That doesn't make it better, Liam. Don't you see there's a huge difference between where we are in life?"

I reach out and snag her fingers. As soon as I claim them, something loosens inside me. When she doesn't pull away, a puff of relief escapes from my lips. The last thing I want is for her to put more distance between us.

Silently, she stares at our hands, as if seeing them for the first time.

"I'm still the same person I was last week and the week before that. Just because I'm a little younger than you originally thought has nothing to do with the kind of man I am."

"I know this will sound stupid, and maybe you won't understand where I'm coming from," she says as she glances away, "but it feels like I'm taking advantage of you."

She's right, that's stupid.

Although, I'm smart enough not to voice that opinion out loud.

In a tiny, infinitesimal way, I understand it.

Sort of.

Maybe.

Kind of.

But I also think what Gia is feeling is amplified by the fact that I'm still in college, and she's already settled in a career. I'm sure college feels like a long time ago to her. She's moved on from that phase of her life, but I'm still in it.

I want her to realize how ridiculous what she's saying is. "Exactly how are you taking advantage of me?" Barely am I able to get the words past my lips without snorting. "It's not like I was a virgin. I'm a twenty-year-old man, Gia. I've been in physical relationships."

When she refuses to meet my gaze, I slide my fingers beneath her chin and lift it until she has no other choice but to look at me. "You haven't taken advantage of me," I reiterate. "We both know I pursued you every step of the way."

"It's not your age or the amount of experience you have. It's just that being a teacher...it makes me feel—"

She shakes her head, as if frustrated by her inability to put her thoughts into words. "I don't know...*dirty*. Like I'm doing something wrong by having a relationship with someone your age."

"Gia," I say patiently, "I'm not a kid in high school. I'm almost twenty-one years old, and a junior in college."

Her eyes flare. "What?" she gasps. "I thought you were a senior! I thought you were graduating this spring and looking to turn pro." She groans. "The fact that you're still in college was bad enough."

I'm tempted to plow my hands through my hair. I'd really thought when she showed up at the bar that we had turned a corner in our relationship. But that doesn't appear to be the case. Everything I say makes the situation worse.

I'm a week shy of turning twenty-one. I'm a junior, who will be leaving college to play professional football. There is nothing I can do to change those facts.

"Three years ago, you were in high school, and I was teaching second grade! When you were seventeen, I was twenty-five." She gulps, growing more agitated. "Do you know how *wrong* that is?"

The scary thing is that she's completely serious. Her mind is spinning out of control. The fact that we couldn't have a relationship three years ago is freaking her out. But that's not where we are right now.

How does she not understand that?

I suck in a deep breath before deliberately expelling it from my lungs. "Gia, I'm not in high school." I say the words carefully, hoping she'll see reason and stop this nonsense. "We didn't get together three years ago. You need to focus on the here and now. The difference in our ages is irrelevant. If you like me, if you enjoy spending time with me, then it shouldn't matter that I'm eight and a half years younger than you are."

Before I can add anything else, what—I have no idea—she tugs her fingers from mine. Her voice comes out sounding strangled, as if she's barely hanging on by a thread. "I don't know if I can do this, Liam."

All I want is to pull her into my arms and never let go, but I don't make a move. I can't. It's like I'm fighting every instinct inside me. I've never wanted a woman more than I want this one. I've never taken my time and gotten to know someone the way I have Gia. I don't want to lose what we've been building together.

Not over something that shouldn't matter.

The difference in our ages shouldn't be what keeps us apart. Not if we like each other. Not if this relationship could turn into something long-term. Because that's how I've been looking at it. If we're going to have any chance of moving forward, then she needs to be all right with where I'm at in life.

"I can't change how old I am. And in a few months, I won't be in college. I'll be playing in the NFL."

She releases a mirthless laugh. "How does that make anything better? I don't know much about football or the draft, but I'm assuming you'll get picked up by a team and won't be living here anymore. You could end up anywhere in the country, right?" Her blue gaze bores into mine. "If anything, it only proves how much is stacked against us."

Fuck.

I want to slam my fist through something. I'll take physical pain over mental or emotional anguish any day of the week. Because right now, this hurts. Surprisingly more than I thought it would.

Steadily, I release all the pent-up breath wedged tightly in my chest before muttering, "I don't understand why our ages have to be such a big deal to you."

She's slipping through my fingers. It's like she's already decided that I'm not worth taking a chance on. That there's too much standing in our way. Too much to overcome. But still, I can't let her walk away without a fight.

Desperation has me reaching out, grasping her fingers. "I like you, Gia. No one has ever mattered to me the way you do. I know you think the age difference is an issue, but it doesn't have to be. In all the ways that count, we fit together. As far as the NFL goes, I have two months until the end of the semester. Let's focus on seeing if our relationship goes anywhere before we jump the gun. No matter what team picks me up, we can make it work. Plenty of people do."

As I run out of steam, I realize there is nothing more I can say to change her mind. If she walks away from me tonight, I'll know I've done everything I could to show her the kind of man I am and how much she means to me.

"I don't know," she whispers. "It feels like our ages are more of an issue than I originally thought. I'm practically nine years older than you are. That's huge." She shakes her head. "I'm already settled in my life and career, while yours is just taking off. You could end up anywhere. We're in such different places. And that won't change because you leave college and play professional football. If anything, it'll make it more difficult for us to have a relationship."

"Can't you see that the only thing standing in our way, is you?"

She works her lower lip between her teeth before admitting, "Maybe." Unable to hold my gaze, she squeezes her eyes shut. "I need time to figure this all out. Can you give me that?" Her voice dips. "Please?"

I want to laugh at the absurdity of her question. Do I have a choice in the matter?

Instead of responding, I say gruffly, "Come here."

Her breath catches at the back of her throat, as if she understands what the change in my tone means. As if she can sense my intentions. Instead of giving in to the command the way I know she wants to, she remains still. Gia must realize that if I get my hands on her, she'll end up succumbing to the attraction that simmers between us.

"I want to hold you," I coax. "At the very least, let me do that."

My gaze drops to her plump bottom lip as she nibbles at it. I can't deny I want to bite it as well. More than that, I need to hold her in my arms. I need to feel her warm body pressed against mine. I need to taste her on my lips.

All so I can prove to myself that this isn't over.

Not by a long shot.

Hesitantly, she scoots closer until I can snake my arms around her body. We sit wrapped up in one another for what feels like hours.

Everything about this woman speaks to something deep—something elemental—in me.

The last thing I want is to set her free.

Doesn't she see how well we mesh together? Isn't that what should matter? Not the difference in our ages. I hate to say it's just a number, but guess what? That's exactly what it is.

It's a fucking number.

Get over it.

Maybe I need to remind her how perfectly we fit together. How good it feels when I'm running my hands over her. Even though the physical is what attracted me to her in the first place, there is so much more to our relationship. What I feel for Gia runs deeper than that. I've been with enough women to know when it's nothing more than sexual attraction holding us together.

It's not like that with Gia. I enjoy spending time with her, talking to her, getting her take on things. I love how open her heart is. I can't explain how much all the time and effort she's put into helping Claire means to me.

Maybe it's a shitty move on my part, but I need to use whatever weapons I have in my arsenal to convince her that breaking up isn't an option. She needs to get her shit figured out and accept that the years standing between us don't mean a damn thing.

CHAPTER 25

GIA

I shouldn't be sitting here, wrapped up in Liam's arms as if I belong buried in their comforting strength. When we're together like this, I forget all the reasons why this is wrong. My head is so messed-up. Untangling myself from him is the last thing I want to do.

Part of me thinks I should pull the plug on this relationship and walk away before I get entrenched any deeper. Before I get hurt. But the other part wants to stay burrowed in his arms forever and forget about everything that eats at me during the cold light of day.

Somehow, we go from simply embracing to his mouth cruising over the bared column of my neck. The feel of his lips on my flesh makes my breath catch.

I must be out of my mind.

For goodness' sake, I told him I needed time to think about our relationship. I should definitely *not* be letting him lick and kiss my body. When his lips are on me, I find it impossible to hold a coherent thought in my head. His mouth is lethal. He understands the effect it has on me.

"Liam…"

"Yeah, baby, what do you want? Tell me what it is, and I'll give it to you. I'll give you anything."

Oh my God.

Who says that?

Worse than that, I know he means every word.

Whatever I want, he'll give me.

That thought sends a sizzle of heat straight to my core. It makes everything throb to life. I've never had anyone turn me on so completely.

Or so quickly.

With so very little effort.

Why is it so hard to wrap my brain around rational thought when he's licking and sucking at my flesh? Barely do I realize his hands have slid around to my front. Or that they've shoved my shirt up until it's over my head. As soon as the top disappears, he sinks his greedy fingers into the cups of my bra before carefully baring my breasts to the cool night air.

Before I can protest, he's stroking my nipples. Pulling and tweaking them until they're hard little points that ache for attention. Desire shoots to my clit, as if there's an invisible string connecting them.

An incoherent whimper escapes from my lips. Almost leisurely, as if he wants to take his sweet damn time, his mouth glides south. It skims down my chest until arriving at one stiff bud. His warm breath feathers over me, making my nipple tighten painfully. For one lazy moment, he hovers over the tip of my breast. Need claws at my insides as I wait for him to take me deep inside his mouth.

It's almost unbelievable how easily he can rouse my body to a fever pitch.

I've never connected to another human being on this kind of primal level. How am I supposed to walk away from him? From everything he makes me feel?

Unwilling to dwell on those disheartening thoughts, I push them aside and focus on the pleasure flooding every cell in my body. As he draws me into his mouth, his fingers toy with its twin while his other hand drifts down my rib cage and belly before flicking open the button of my jeans. A heartbeat later, his fingers delve into the front of them until he can push his way into my tight sheath.

My gasp morphs into a whimper of pleasure.

He draws away from my breast long enough to whisper, "That feel good? Do you like that?" Liam pumps his finger in and out of my wet heat until that movement is the only thing I'm cognizant of.

If a response falls from my lips, I have no idea what it is.

"I love touching you like this. You're so fucking wet." He nudges my inner thighs with his wrist. "Open for me, Gia." A growl escapes from him as he plays with my body. "You have no idea how much I want to bury my cock deep inside your pussy. Is that what you need? My hard cock filling you up? Proving to you that no one else will be able to make you feel what I do?"

Another unintelligible mouthful of words falls from my lips as he pistons his finger before pulling away enough to trace the blunt tip over my clit with enough pressure to leave me gasping. "Yes, I want that."

I want him more than I've ever wanted anything in my life.

Satisfied with my answer, he moves to my other nipple, drawing it into his mouth. I arch my back, attempting to get closer. As if we can somehow meld into one. He drives his fingers into my slick heat until an orgasm swirls inside me.

Even though I'm still wearing my jeans, I widen my legs, needing more. I want him inside me, filling me to the brim with his thick cock. I want him to fuck me until I can no longer think straight. He withdraws his fingers, swirling them over my drenched lower lips. The ache inside me is ferocious. I'm teetering on the brink of pleasure-infused pain.

His tongue flicks at my stiffened peak before he whispers harshly, "No one will ever be able to give you what I can."

I whimper in answer, knowing it's the truth. I need his mouth and hands on me, pushing me relentlessly toward climax.

Instead of doing that, his voice grows sharp. "Do you feel the way your body responds to me?" When I remain silent, he bites down on my nipple. It's hard enough to make me yelp, but not enough to hurt me or leave a mark upon my sensitive flesh. "Do you feel it, Gia?"

"Yes," I admit.

And I do.

"Has anyone ever made you feel like this?"

I shake my head.

I don't want to think about the questions he's forcing me to answer.

His teeth close over one taut bud, and yet he doesn't bite down. Not yet. "Gia," he growls.

"No," I whisper on a rising sob, "no one has ever made me feel like this. *Not ever.*"

And that's scary.

Tyler and I were together for three years, and the physical intimacy we shared was *nothing* like this. There's a strange, incomprehensible intensity with Liam. It pulls at us like opposite poles of a magnet. I've felt the lure of it since the beginning. Even when I tried to fight against the attraction, ignoring it, turning away from it, I couldn't. How is it possible for someone I've only just met to understand my needs so much better than the man I spent three years with?

It doesn't make sense.

It's almost as if Liam has an innate knowledge of me.

Of my body.

Of what I secretly crave.

Whatever this is between us, it shouldn't feel so perfect.

There's too much standing in our way for this to work out in the end. The difference in our ages, the direction of our lives... None of this should feel right. But I can't deny that it does. Not to myself. No matter how much I want to.

I jerk out of those thoughts when he yanks my jeans and panties down my thighs until they're bunched around my knees. With hasty movements, he slides one leg from the material.

"What—"

His heated gaze cuts to mine in the darkness. "I need to taste you. When you come, it'll be because my tongue is lashing your pussy, lapping up all the sweet nectar between your thighs. It'll be because my teeth are scraping against your clit."

I've never had anyone talk so dirty to me. Tyler didn't do much more than grunt a few times when he orgasmed. When Liam talks like this, my insides shudder with need. I could come from his words alone.

Even though we're sitting in his parked car, on the verge of having sex, not one word of protest leaves my lips. Worse than that, I'll scream if he stops what he's so intent upon doing. It's startling to realize how much I want his mouth on me.

My breath catches with anticipation as he spreads me wide. This wasn't something Tyler did very often. I was always left with the feeling he didn't enjoy it. And knowing that, having it constantly circle in the back of my mind, made me feel self-conscious and tense when he did put his mouth on me. It's much too intimate of an act to share with someone unless they enjoy it.

And Liam?

He *relishes* it.

The feral look that enters his eyes drives me wild.

He moves between my thighs, forcing them even wider before settling between them. Liquid heat slides through me as his hot breath feathers over my core. I've never felt this kind of anticipation thrum through me. That has everything to do with Liam and the connection forged between us.

He runs the flat of his tongue over my slit. At the first touch of his velvety softness, it feels as if I could splinter apart. Wave after devastating wave crashes over me. Euphoria infuses every fiber of my being. My hips lift off the worn seat, wanting only to inch closer to the pleasure he's so intent upon giving.

His hands settle against my inner thighs to keep me grounded to the seat. My back is wedged against the door. Barely do I feel the handle as it digs into my spine. His fingers splay across my naked flesh, forcing my legs wide.

I'm so far gone that I can only focus on the insatiable need pumping wildly through my veins.

This is what he does to me.

When Liam touches me like this, the difference in our ages no longer matters. I don't care about him entering the draft or all the women who throw themselves at him. I only care about the way he touches me and how I feel when I'm wrapped up in his arms. The way it feels when he's buried deep in my body, owning me the way no other man has before.

His tongue spears inside me before he uses the flat of it to lick over my shuddering softness. He backs away, nibbling at my clit. His tender ministrations have me moaning out my pleasure. My fingers dig into the seat, scrambling to find purchase, needing to ground myself in the present. I need something to steady me as euphoria ricochets through my body.

I'm on the cusp of splintering apart into a million crystalline pieces.

"Come for me, Gia. I want you to come right now. Just for me." He spears two fingers deep inside before sucking my throbbing clit into his mouth.

The sound of his voice is all it takes for me to careen over the edge. I scream out his name as my body shudders under his expert touch.

The entire time I float back to earth, he continues to lick me, running his tongue over my delicate flesh, as if he understands how exquisitely sensitive I am.

My thoughts are a scattered mess. They're everywhere and nowhere all at once. I force myself to dredge up our previous conversation but it's difficult. When it comes down to it, I have no idea if I can walk away from Liam.

From this.

From the way he makes me think and feel.

As my body calms, everything rushes back at me. I've never felt so torn. The concerns I have regarding our relationship aren't going to simply disappear.

In the end, I have no idea where that leaves me.

Or us.

CHAPTER 26

GIA

*a*s we settle on our stools in the darkened club, Sophie asks, "What time do the guys go on?"

I glance at the stage, catching sight of two members from The Renegades checking their equipment. "In about twenty minutes."

Even though it was short notice, I'm glad Noah called to let me know about their performance at one of the clubs downtown. If there's anything I could use, it's a girls' night with Sophie and Harper. All I've done for the past few days is go round and round in my head regarding my relationship with Liam. There's so much for us to overcome. What makes it worse is that I really like him.

When I climbed out of Liam's car Saturday night, all flushed from the orgasm he'd given me, I asked for time to think. As much as I wish the age difference weren't a big deal, it is. It's not like we're talking about a year or two.

It's nine years!

All right, eight and a half. Unfortunately, subtracting six months doesn't make it any better.

I'm scanning the area for my brother when Sophie hisses my name under her breath. I shoot her a quizzical look only to find her focused on something over my shoulder.

"Incoming," she squeaks. As I swivel around, my gaze locks on hazel eyes.

"Tyler!" I gasp. "What are you doing here?"

His gaze flits to my besties before refocusing on me. "I heard your brother's band was playing here tonight and thought I'd check it out."

"Really?" My brows rise.

His cheeks flush with color. I'm sure we're both recalling all the times I attempted to cajole him into going out. It's sheepishly that he adds, "I thought it might be a good idea to give his music more of a chance." He jerks his shoulders, as if he's unsure what more to say. "Plus, I thought you might show up." He clears his throat and shifts his weight. "And we could listen together."

Oh.

Well, damn.

I'm not interested in having another conversation about the state of our relationship.

Or lack thereof.

I came here tonight to have a nice evening out with my friends and to support my brother. If I'm being completely honest, I've been so tangled up over Liam, I haven't thought about Tyler in months.

"Tyler." I'm hyperaware of Harper and Sophie bearing witness to the scene playing out. "I came here to listen to my brother and—"

He must understand the uphill battle he's attempting to wage because he cuts me off. "I know. We don't have to talk about our relationship. I just thought if we ran into each other, we could enjoy the music. That's all, Gianna."

His use of my full name sets my nerves on edge. It's like a light switch being flicked on. My reaction is that quick. Honestly, if any other person did the same thing, it wouldn't bother me to this degree. But Tyler knows what I prefer.

And yet, he still insists on calling me it.

"Gia," I correct. The sharpness of my tone cuts through the music.

"Gia," he repeats hastily. "Sorry, old habits die hard."

That's precisely what I'm afraid of. It only solidifies my decision to move on from this relationship. Tyler won't change.

And you know what?

I don't want him to.

Not for me.

Even though I don't necessarily want to spend the rest of the evening with my ex, I find myself unable to send him away. In the awkward silence that follows, I hear the collective exhalation of my friends as I relent. "Okay, sure. You can join us."

Tyler beams before pulling up a stool. My heart sinks as he chats with Harper and Sophie before flagging down a waitress and ordering a scotch on the rocks.

That's when I realize it's going to be a long night.

CHAPTER 27

LIAM

This is the last place I should be.

Gia asked for space, and yet, here I am, forcing myself on her. No matter how hard I try, I can't stop thinking about the woman. She never mentioned coming to see her brother's band play, but I'm taking a chance that she might show up. Then I can pretend that running into one another is a coincidence.

Fuck. That sounds lame.

Seriously, I'm not that guy. I have *never* been that dude. The one who can't take no for an answer. The one who chases after a chick because she's no longer giving him the time of day.

I have no idea what it is about Gia that has me so twisted up. After nearly two months, I still can't figure it out. All I know is that she's unlike any other woman I've met before, and I don't want to lose her.

"What band is playing again?"

Roan nudges my shoulder as my gaze sifts through the mob of people in the darkened club. Who knew these guys were so popular? Unfortunately, the thick crowd makes it more difficult to locate Gia.

"The Renegades," I mutter.

They're in the middle of a set and people are gathered around the stage, dancing, or listening to the music. It's doubtful Gia is in the midst of all that chaos.

"Hmmm, they're not bad," he says. "Haven't we heard them at O'Brien's a couple of times?"

I'm only partly conscious of Roan shooting questions at me. I might have told him I was interested in checking out the local band that was playing here tonight. I failed to mention Gia in all this.

I almost shake my head at the desperate lengths I'm willing to go to. It makes me stop and reevaluate my plans. Maybe we should take off before I run into her and she figures out I'm stalking her.

Not really.

Well...sort of.

Fuck.

I'm on the verge of plowing my hands through my hair when I spot her across the club. She's perched at a high-top table, much like she was the first night I saw her at O'Brien's. It's not a conscious decision on my part. Before I realize it, I'm on the move, maneuvering through the thick press of bodies. This venue is more upscale than O'Brien's, that's for sure. Her brother's band must have a pretty decent following for them to land a gig here.

"Dude, where are you going?" Roan asks.

"I'll be right back." Not bothering to stop, I throw the words over my shoulder.

If Roan fires off a response, I don't catch it. All of my attention is centered on Gia. To a certain extent, this feels like déjà vu all over again.

Right before I arrive at her table, her gaze shifts to mine. She tenses before popping out of her seat like a tightly wound Jack-in-the-Box. Panic flares in her eyes.

Whatever reaction I was expecting, that wasn't it.

"Liam, what are you doing here?" There's a nervous edge to her question.

"That seems to be the standard refrain for the evening," her tall, auburn-haired friend says.

My gaze bounces to the woman before resettling on Gia.

I have no idea what that's supposed to mean.

Sure, I could go with the whole *what a coincidence, I was just out grabbing a beer* act. Up until now, that's exactly what I was going to do. But holding her alarmed gaze, I decide I don't want to play games with Gia. That's not the kind of relationship we have. She already thinks the age difference is an insurmountable issue. I don't need to prove she's right by using subterfuge.

Now that I'm standing before her, I realize that tracking her down was a mistake. I should have given her the time and space she asked for. Especially given the way she's staring at me. Kind of like a deer in headlights. As if she's at a complete loss for words.

"I thought you might be here to see your brother play." Even though the music is loud, my voice is pitched low. "I wanted to see how you were doing."

That statement has officially cemented my pathetic status.

"Oh." She bites her lip. "I was going to call you…" Her voice trails off as her gaze darts to the side. She tenses, and I'm struck with the realization that she isn't here by herself. I'm about to glance over my shoulder when a firm hand claps me on the back.

"Garrison? What are you doing here? Are you even twenty-one? Thought that was coming up in a few days," he says with a hearty chuckle. "Didn't they card you at the door?"

Coach Bauer?

I stare at him in confusion, attempting to play mental catch-up because I'm not sure what the hell is going on. It feels as if I've been plunged under water. Everything is strangely murky.

Is he passing by the table?

It's only when Coach takes up sentinel next to Gia that I awaken with a start and everything becomes appallingly clear. The only thing I can do is force a weak smile as emotion swims around in my cluttered mind. "Nah, they didn't bother to ask for ID."

With a grin, he shakes his head. "You can't go anywhere without getting recognized."

The fake smile stays plastered painfully across my face. "Nope."

As my gaze shifts to Gia, I can tell by the guilt flickering across her expression that Coach B isn't a random dude she met at the club. They know each other.

Is she seriously out on a date with him?

My mind races. I have to fight the urge to pull her aside so I can get to the bottom of what's going on. I mean, I thought we had something special.

And now she's out with someone else?

My fucking coach?

I see the exact moment he becomes aware of the suffocating tension that has settled uncomfortably over the three of us. His eyes narrow. "Do you two know each other?"

I stare at Gia, willing her to tackle this issue. Until I know what's going on between them, I'm not saying a word.

She forces a smile to her lips. "Actually, Liam was one of the football players who gave a wonderfully informative presentation to my class."

I wait for her to add the rest, because there's more to our relationship than that, but she remains silent.

Wow.

Guess I'm nothing more than a random athlete who spoke to her class a couple months ago.

It feels like I've been sucker punched.

Coach Bauer's body loosens as he flashes a smile. "Oh, right!" He claps me on the back again. "Garrison is the best quarterback in the conference. You should see the arm on this guy. And the girls go wild over him." He gives me a wink. "He can barely get around campus without all the groupies throwing themselves at his feet." Coach B shakes his head good naturedly. "Must get old after a while. Is that why you headed downtown? You were looking for a little action you had to work for?"

Gia's face pales, but she doesn't utter a word.

I'm so tempted to punch Coach. And that sucks. This guy has been one of my biggest supporters while I've been here at Barnett. He's more than just a coach.

"Nah, I came here strictly to listen to the band. They've played a few times at O'Brien's." I add, "King's here too."

Coach Bauer glances around but doesn't spot Roan. I'm wondering where the guy is as well. I need him to swoop in and save me before I do something I'll end up regretting.

"Knowing King, he's probably being mauled by the ladies." He smiles before shaking his head, as if we're just a couple of kooky kids looking to raise a little hell. "You ready to head back to the table, Gia?"

My gaze cuts to hers in question.

Not that I'm expecting her to say anything to clarify our relationship but... I don't know... Maybe that's exactly what I'm hoping for. That she'll tell Coach B that I'm more than an acquaintance. That I actually mean something to her.

But that doesn't happen.

Instead, she flashes him a weak smile before her gaze slides apologetically to mine. Her voice is soft, maybe even repentant, when she says, "It was nice running into you again, Liam."

I give her a brittle smile in return. There's nothing more I can say or do. "Yeah. Be sure to tell those little squirts I said hello."

"I'll do that," she says.

With his hand settled on the small of her back, Coach escorts Gia to the table where her friends wait. When Gia is a few feet from me, she throws a glance over her shoulder. Our eyes lock and hold for a split second before she turns away.

"What the hell was that all about?" Roan asks. "Why is Coach B with your girl?"

I shoot him a dark look. "I don't know." Even though I'm reluctant to admit the truth, I force it out. "I think they're together."

Roan releases a low whistle. Even over the pulsing beat of the music, it rings hollowly in my ears. "For real?"

"I think so," I admit.

"Your girl is out tonight with someone else and you didn't know about it?"

I stop and turn, my gaze boring into his. "Yeah, that pretty much sums up the situation."

His brows jerk together. "What are you going to do about it?"

I shake my head. "Not a damn thing."

As much as I want Gia, it turns out she's not my girl after all.

CHAPTER 28

LIAM

It's been five days since I ran into Gia and Coach at the club. Even though I've been tempted to reach out, to understand what the hell all this means, I have a pretty good idea. No one has ever accused me of being dense.

With measured movements, I force the weights above my chest before bringing them down again, counting the reps in my head. I try to focus on my lift instead of Gia, but it doesn't work.

Nothing I do evicts her from my brain.

I don't understand what happened. I was under the impression she was taking a few days to think about our relationship. Guess I didn't realize that meant dating other people in the interim.

"Hey, Garrison," Coach B says as he walks into the weight room. "You keeping up with your regimen?" He doesn't wait for a response. "Hard to believe the draft is right around the corner."

His chipper voice has me swearing a blue streak under my breath.

I've never had a problem with Coach Bauer. The dude is our offensive coordinator. He's damn good at what he does. Anytime you want to find him, there's a good chance he's somewhere on campus. All of the coaches have offices at the athletic center. If he's not camped out in his office, he's in the weight room, on the field, or working with the guys who need an extra push to reach their maximum potential. He spends a lot of time pouring over game film with players, trying to help them figure out where they're making mistakes.

There's not one guy on this team who doesn't love Coach B.

Including myself.

Since I realize there's no way to sidestep this conversation, I release a steady breath and place the bar on its holder. I sit up and grab a towel before wiping the sweat from my brow.

Truth be told, Coach Bauer has been one of the most instrumental men in my football career at Barnett. He's the one who scouted me when I was a freshman in high school. He checked in from time to time and encouraged me to play for the Bulldogs.

When I was in high school, he would finagle it so I could stand on the sidelines during games and feel the energy of a stadium that could hold forty thousand fans. It was an amazing experience, one of the few high points after my mom took off.

When he was able to recruit me in earnest, he stopped at the house and spoke with Dad about the bright future I had in front of me. I sat down with him during my junior year, and we discussed the recruitment offers pouring in from around the country. He helped me weigh the pros and cons of each program. He never made grandiose promises that he couldn't keep, the way some of the other coaches did.

So, yeah, Coach and I have a history.

A long standing one.

That being said, I fucking hate that he was out with Gia.

Even though I'm not really thinking about his question, the answer comes spilling out of my mouth. "Yup. Just trying to stay focused." This man has been my sounding board in all things football. I look up to him. I trust his advice. He's never steered me wrong.

He settles across from me on a padded bench. "Good. I'm glad to hear it, son. You're ready for the next step. I wouldn't tell you that unless I was sure. My gut tells me this is your year."

Even though there's nothing particularly funny at the moment, a smirk curls the edges of my lips. Coach and his gut feelings.

But here's the thing—I can't say there's been one time in the last seven years that he's been wrong. He doesn't utter those words unless he wholeheartedly believes them.

There aren't many people I trust, but he's one of them, which is why this situation is so fucked-up. Normally, he's the first person I talk to when I'm messed-up about something. And not just football either.

Not being able to go to him makes me feel lost.

"I hope so."

"You're not having second thoughts about this, are you?"

I draw in a breath and ponder the question. There are times when I worry that I'm not ready to play at the next level. Or that I'm rushing it because of my family's financial situation. Once you enter the draft, there's no way to go back and play at the college level if it doesn't work out.

It's a gamble, and I could be throwing away my football career.

He must sense his question has struck a chord in me. "Look, Liam, you've already dealt with more bullshit than some of these guys will experience in their entire lives. I also realize this decision isn't simply about you moving on to play professional ball. There's a lot more riding on the draft. But I want to assure you that not only is this the right decision for your family, it's the right one for you. In all the years I've spent coaching and working with young athletes, I've never seen a QB with more God-given ability. As far as I'm concerned, you're ready for this." He searches my eyes before adding, "You were born ready, Liam."

Some of the heaviness weighing me down seeps from my body. If there's one person who has been privy to the fucked-up mess that is my life, it's Coach Bauer.

In a way, he helped me pick up the pieces after Mom took off during my sophomore year of high school. He's the one who got me out of my head by letting me hang around with the team. He gave me a glimpse of what college would be like if I could keep focused on school and ball.

It would have been all too easy to stray.

To fall apart.

To shut down and say *screw it*.

He refused to let that happen. He stayed in touch and checked in regularly. I could set my clock by it. And that helped to keep me motivated. There were low points when I wasn't sure if I would make it through another day. And I would think, *if I can't do it for myself, then I'll do it for Coach Bauer*. I didn't want to let down the one person who believed in me.

This man has seen it all. He's been there every step of the way, which is why this is such a shit situation.

Even though I don't want to bring Gia up, I have to. I need to know what she is to him. Maybe then I can move on. "Ms. Monroe seemed nice."

His eyes brighten.

And my heart sinks.

"Yeah, she is." He falls silent, as if lost in thought. I grow fidgety as the quiet stretches between us. "We were together for three years."

Fuck. Fuck. Fuck.

Air gets trapped in my throat. I couldn't feel more blindsided. I want to plow my hands through my hair as everything Gia said clicks into place. Coach Bauer is the dude she was in a long-term relationship with. He's the one she broke up with four months ago.

He gives me a crooked smile. "We're not together, but I'm still trying to work things out with her."

Don't ask.

Don't fucking do it.

You don't want to know any more than you already do.

The words slide from my mouth before I can stop them. "Any luck with that?"

"I don't know," he admits. "I fucked up. I probably love my job a little too much." He gives me a self-deprecating smile. "I made her feel as if she didn't matter as much as football. I shouldn't have done that. I really love her. And I'm trying to show her how much she means to me." He shrugs. "Listen to me, sounding like an old man with my problems."

It takes a Herculean effort on my part to plaster a small smile on my face, as if what he confided is no big deal. Like I don't have a stake in whether or not he wins her back. "Nah, it's not like that at all."

"I bet the only girl problems you're having right now is too much pussy and not enough time to nail it all." He shakes his head as his grin grows. "You know it's only going to get worse when you make that jump to the NFL." He claps me on the shoulder. "You're one lucky son of a bitch, Garrison. You'll make us all proud. You know that, right?"

I give him another weak smile in response. I can't have this conversation with him, even though in the past, this is exactly how we bullshitted with one another. In some regards, the man is like a father figure or mentor to me. In others, he's like the older brother I never had. My guess is that he's around thirty-one or thirty-two. Certainly no older than that.

Have we sat around, shooting the shit, talking about all the available pussy there is on campus and how ridiculously easy it is to get laid?

Hell yeah.

It's how we relate to one another. Especially after delving into some of the deeper issues I have. It's always been a way to lighten the mood.

But Gia isn't a piece of ass I want to nail.

And, clearly, from listening to everything he revealed, she's not like that for him either.

CHAPTER 29

LIAM

"Hi, Dad," I greet. The front door slams behind me as I step into the living room. Even though it's the beginning of April, the weather is still frigid. My father doesn't keep the thermostat set any higher than sixty-four degrees, to keep the energy bill down.

Every little bit helps.

The corners of his mouth curl up as his gaze settles on me. "Hey, I didn't know you were dropping by today."

"I had some time and thought I'd see how everyone's doing." I settle on the couch and run a hand over my hair. The top has grown out, but I still have it shaved close on the sides.

Concern flickers in his eyes. "Anything going on that I need to know about?" My dad is always waiting for the other shoe to drop. Can't say I don't feel the same way most of the time. I don't think I've ever sat back and taken a breath.

I open my mouth to put him at ease when my brother stalks out of the kitchen. As soon as he sees me, he halts in his tracks. His lips flatten into a thin line as he pulls out his earbuds.

"What are you doing here?" He folds his arms across his chest before leaning his six-foot frame against the doorjamb. The pissed-off expression intensifies as we stare at one another.

His demeanor sets me on edge, and my muscles tense.

Believe it or not, our relationship wasn't always this contentious. We used to be close. Sure, we would wrestle around, and I'd pin his skinny ass to the floor until he cried uncle, but that's what brothers do, right?

It's not like I was a total asshole to the guy. If anyone dared to lay their hands on him, I beat their asses. There was an unwritten rule around school and our neighborhood that you didn't mess with any of the Garrisons.

Once upon a time, he respected me.

Looked up to me.

Did his best to emulate me.

Somewhere along the way, that stopped being the case.

I hate to pin all the bad shit that's happened to us on my mom, but that's when my relationship with Cullum went south. After she disappeared, he took it the hardest and became more withdrawn. And then, full of rage. Out of the three of us, my mother had a real soft spot for Cullum. I have no idea how she could leave him without a word.

Not to mention, Claire.

How could she leave her own daughter when she was ten years old? Claire, however, has been surprisingly resilient. Even in the crap situation our lives have turned out to be, she always puts on a good face. She's not one to dwell on the negative. In almost every way possible, she's the complete opposite of my brother—easy, light, and happy.

But Cullum?

He never got over our mother leaving.

To a certain extent, I get it. Shit's been hard around here. Can't he see I'm doing everything possible to get us back on track? Doesn't he understand what the end game is? Everything I do is for this family.

For us.

It's not like I'll bail on them as soon as I make it to the NFL. Hell, I could've taken off and never looked back with all the out-of-state college scholarships I was offered. These people, *my family*, they're the reason I stuck around.

"I stopped by to see how things are going." Even though he just walked into the room, his attitude has my hackles rising. My voice comes out more clipped than I intend it to. When he doesn't budge from the wall where he continues to glare, I arch a brow. "Is there something you wanted?"

"From you?" He glares at me like I'm gum on the sole of his shoe before shaking his head. "Nah, I'm good."

I grit my teeth. I'm tempted to snap at him, tell him to knock this shit off. Cullum might only be a junior in high school but he's big. I have no doubt he'll end up being even bigger than I am. The kid was made for football.

I'm tall but lean. I've got quick feet. And even quicker reflexes. Cullum played QB for awhile, but he wasn't the player I am. He was made for the offensive line. Center, to be exact. But he ended up quitting after freshman year so he could get a job after school. I have no idea if he misses football or regrets having to give it up.

He never talks about it.

At least, not to me.

In order to keep the fragile peace, I've learned to keep my mouth shut and not ask too many questions. It's easier that way. It's not like there's anything that can be done about the situation.

Instead of taking the bait, I remain silent.

"Let me guess," he muses, deep voice reverberating throughout the small room, "you're here to whine about finally getting your ass to the pros."

His words knock me off balance. I can only stare. I don't understand what this kid's problem is. It sure as shit isn't my fault that Mom left us. And yet, I seem to get the brunt of his anger.

It sucks.

Unsure how to respond, my gaze shifts to Dad. There has to be a what-the-fuck-is-his-problem expression on my face. But my father doesn't utter a sound as he drops his gaze.

After a few uncomfortable moments, Dad clears his throat. "You could always wait until next year and get your degree first. There's no rush, Liam."

Even though his comment isn't directed at Cullum, my brother explodes. "Jesus Christ, Pops, the guy has been sitting on his ass in college for almost three years. It's about damn time he got out there and started making some money! Why the hell am I the only one around here who can hold down a fucking job?"

Air hisses from my lungs.

Dad's face pales before blooming with mottled color. His mouth opens and closes, as if he's having a difficult time wrapping his mind around the words he wants to fire back. Years of alcohol abuse have dulled his thought process. Even though I know there are issues between the three of us, it still burns my ass to hear my seventeen-year-old brother talk so disrespectfully to him.

The guy will never win any awards for best father, but he's all we have. At least he's still here, right? He didn't take off like a certain someone else did. It's not a great situation by any means, but it's the hand we've been dealt.

"Watch your mouth, Cullum," I bark. I've had enough of him and his shitty attitude. We haven't been in the same room for five minutes and we're already at each other's throats.

His blue eyes ignite with fury as he shoves away from the door-jamb where he's been lounging before straightening to his full height. "Or what, Liam? You gonna beat the piss out of me? Is that what you're going to do?"

Who the hell does this punk kid think he is?

I jerk to my feet, popping off the worn couch. I can't wrap my mind around his bottled-up anger. "What the fuck is your problem?"

Laughter bubbles up from his throat. There's an ugly twist to his lips that I find unnerving. I shake my head as my eyes narrow. I'm at a complete loss as to who my brother has morphed into.

Is this the same happy-go-lucky kid who followed me around the playground? I can barely remember back that far. He's a different person than the one he was five years ago. If I could find my bitch of a mother, I would wring her neck for putting us through this.

"What the fuck is my problem? That's rich!" He shakes his head like I'm the butt of a joke.

I clench my hands.

"Seriously, dude? You have absolutely no fucking clue what's been going on around here." His eyes widen at the confused expression on my face. "What? You think because you pop in every once in a while that everything is under control?" His gaze cuts to my father. "Why don't you tell your *golden boy* everything you've been keeping from him?"

Even though I don't want to take my eyes off Cullum, they dart to my father. Guilt flashes across his face like he just got caught stealing. It's enough to make my gut clench.

All of a sudden, I don't want to know what my brother is talking about. I want to walk out the front door and never look back. Dealing with the constant bullshit is exhausting. Worse than that, it's never-ending.

I know it's bad when Dad's shoulders quake before collapsing as he avoids all eye contact.

Make that disastrous.

Even though my mouth is bone dry, I force myself to swallow down the thick nausea rolling around like a bowling ball in the pit of my gut.

Whatever is going on, I need to confront it head-on. There's no other way around it. "What's he talking about, Dad?"

Tension crackles and snaps in the air around us. Cullum radiates barely contained fury. He's on the verge of blowing.

When my father remains silent, it's all the incentive my brother needs to let loose. "All the money I've been busting my ass for, giving him so he can pay the mortgage every month, is gone. He hasn't sent one damn payment in for the last six months. We received a letter from the bank that they're foreclosing, and the house is going to auction. Since he's been hiding the mail and all the notices, we have two weeks to get our shit together and vacate the premises."

My jaw goes slack as his words echo hollowly throughout my head.

There's no fucking way what Cullum's saying is true. What the hell could he have been using all that money for? I do some quick mental math. That has to be at least four thousand dollars he pissed away.

When I fail to respond, Cullum pulls out a folded piece of paper from his back pocket before tossing it to me.

"He wasn't going to say one damn word about it." He turns furious blue eyes toward our father. "What the hell were you going to do, old man? Wait for the sheriff to change the locks and throw all our shit on the curb?"

I catch the crumpled letter in my hands before smoothing out the sheet. Is it too much to ask that Cullum is messing with me? I've never wanted anything more in my life. And that's saying a lot. As I scan the paragraphs, I suck in a ragged breath.

Cullum isn't lying.

"Dad…" My voice trails off. I have no idea what to say or where to start.

"Gambling," Cullum snaps.

My knees give out and I collapse onto the couch. A heavy silence falls over us as everything swirls through my head.

"Instead of looking for a job, he's been pissing away all the money I earn at one of those charity poker places they set up in the basement of restaurants." Cullum's upper lip curls into a snarl as he shakes his head. "Good job, *Dad*. Well done!"

It takes effort to force my gaze to my father. I can tell by the way he's folded in on himself that everything my brother has accused him of is true.

Even though my mind is reeling, I realize that losing my shit won't solve anything. Although, I certainly understand why Cullum is so full of rage. The kid works his ass off to earn money that goes to our family. He doesn't keep any of it for himself. Instead of using that to pay for a roof over our heads, our father blew it on nothing.

Disgust churns inside me as I focus on my brother. It's as if he's the only other adult in the room. "I'll fix this, Cullum," I promise solemnly. "Give me all the information and I'll call the bank this afternoon. I'll tell them about the draft." I plow my hands through my hair. "Maybe it'll buy us some time."

The anger that had been wafting off him in heavy waves drains away, leaving a gut-wrenching exhaustion to fill its place.

I think I've really fucked up here.

That's the only thought circling viciously through my head as I stare at my seventeen-year-old brother. The bone-weariness I find looking back at me doesn't resemble the boy I once knew. It's like I'm gazing into the beaten-down eyes of a stranger.

I don't know what I could have done differently to change what happened, but I should have been around more. I should have kept a better eye on things. I shouldn't have left everything to rest on Cullum's shoulders.

Unsure of my next step, I rise from the sofa. Being in this house makes me feel a thousand pounds heavier. I don't know…

Maybe that's why I stopped coming around so often.

There are times when it feels like no matter what happens in the future, nothing will ever change. I'll never claw my way out. All I know is that Mom walking out on us is the gift that keeps on giving.

Time after fucking time.

CHAPTER 30

GIA

"Ms. Monroe! Guess who I saw at the grocery store last night?"

I smile down at Aiden Gibson. He's practically vibrating with all his pent-up excitement. Kind of like an overeager puppy.

He's ridiculously adorable.

Then again, they all are.

With only two more months left of school, I'm amazed at how much my second graders have grown. Baby teeth have been lost with new adult teeth poking through in their place. They've shot up a handful of inches. Reading levels have been exceeded. Triple digit addition is no longer an impossible concept to grasp. And they've all learned how to treat one another respectfully.

My little second graders aren't so little anymore.

I can't help but look around and feel lucky to have been given such a great group of kids this year. As proud as I am, it's always bitter-sweet to hug them goodbye on the last day of school.

Nostalgia swirls through me as I refocus my attention on Aiden. With a grin, I tap my finger against my chin. "Let's see," I muse, "who could Aiden have seen at the grocery store?" As I continue to tap, his body quivers at a higher frequency. "Who could it have been? Obviously, it was someone who shops for groceries." I point to him. "Am I right? Is it someone who eats food?"

Aiden giggles before rolling his big brown eyes and throwing his arms wide. "Ms. Monroe! Of course it's someone who eats food! *Everyone* eats food! We need it to live!"

My smile broadens. He's such an animated kid. "Very true." When I've tortured him enough, I say, "All right, Aiden. Tell me who you saw last night while out shopping."

"Number four—Liam Garrison! The Bulldogs' quarterback who came to talk with us!" There's a brief pause. "Remember?"

"Oh." My pulse picks up its tempo. Thankfully, Aiden doesn't notice my surprise because he continues to talk a mile a minute.

"Yeah. We were both in the cereal aisle. He was getting a box of Cheerios and I was begging my mom for Cinnamon Toast Crunch." His grin becomes even wider. "But since he was getting Cheerios, I got them too. Now we eat the same cereal, Ms. Monroe—me and number four!"

It would be impossible not to smile at the sheer exuberance he exudes. Liam might not realize it, but he made a huge impact on these kids. They bring him up all the time or wear his jersey to school. I wonder if he has any idea how much they idolize him. What I can't deny is that, unlike a lot of athletes you hear about, he's totally worthy of their admiration.

Liam is a wonderful role model.

Those thoughts leave my heart aching with both sadness and regret.

I clear my throat. "Did you stop and say hello?"

He shoots me a look like I'm crazy. "Of course I did!"

"Did you remind him that he spoke to your class a few months ago?"

He beams at me as his chest puffs up with pride. "I didn't have to. He remembered without me even having to tell him! Can you believe that?"

I keep the smile glued firmly in place.

Yes, I can. Liam is a really nice guy. It wouldn't surprise me in the least if he stopped and spent five or ten minutes talking with Aiden in the grocery store even though he was probably running in to pick something up.

I haven't seen or spoken to Liam in two weeks. I have no idea how he celebrated his twenty-first birthday. As much as I wanted to reach out, I didn't know if I should. Instead, I sent him a brief text. Later that evening he responded with a thank you.

That was it.

And… Well, it's probably for the best that it ended there.

I blink and realize Aiden is still talking.

"He said that he's going to some kind of…" His dark brows pinch together as he tries to remember the word. "Some place where football players get picked." He shrugs his thin shoulders. "He said I could watch on TV."

I nod. "Yes, the NFL Draft is coming up. In a few weeks, Mr. Garrison will know what team he'll play for." My heart clenches. It's painful to realize that in two or three months, Liam will be gone.

Aiden flashes me a smile. One of his front teeth are missing. I almost shake my head because the kid has some serious adorableness going on. "I don't care who he plays for, I'll still cheer for him."

"That's exactly the way it should be," I agree.

"He said he'd come back and talk to us again. Is that okay with you, Ms. Monroe?"

Air clogs my throat as I force another smile. "Of course it is, but it sounds like Mr. Garrison is very busy right now." Plus, I can't imagine him showing up at the classroom or what it would feel like to see him again. Especially now that he knows Tyler and I were together. That thought is enough to leave me flinching.

"Nah. He said he could come anytime. You just have to tell him."

It's getting more difficult to hold the smile in place. "I'll have to check our calendar and see when we have some free time."

"Can we do that right now?" he asks impatiently.

"No, I'm afraid we can't." I force out a laugh before glancing at the digital clock on the wall. It's time to hustle the children off to physical education. Hopefully, when they return in forty minutes, Aiden will have forgotten about Liam visiting our class. "We need everyone to line up for gym. How about you help me with that by being line leader today since Chloe is absent."

His eyes light up. Although, not nearly as much as when he was talking about Liam.

He pumps his fist in the air. "Yes!"

Without any further instruction, he swings toward the kids and shouts that he gets to be the leader again and they need to be quiet and line up.

"Aiden," I chide, all the while trying to suppress a smile, "perhaps we can do that without yelling?"

He flashes me an exasperated look. "But they're being really loud, Ms. Monroe!"

"Yep." I sigh. "They are. What should we do to get everyone's attention?"

When he realizes the answer, he swings to his peers and raises his right hand in the air before making the shape of a V with two fingers. I give him a nod of approval and do the same. Within thirty seconds, the entire class falls silent. All of them have their hands raised with their fingers in the shape of a V.

Just like I said—they've come so far this year.

The rest of the day passes by in a blur, which isn't unusual. There is always so much learning to squeeze into each seven-hour day. Even though one hundred percent of my energy is directed toward what I'm teaching, in the back of my mind, Liam continues to linger.

At four o'clock, after the kids have been taken to their appropriate drop off spots, there's nothing to stop my thoughts from settling on the dark-haired football player. Memories of the stunned expression on his face when he realized that Tyler and I were together, swirl through my head.

The rap of knuckles on my classroom door startles me out of those thoughts. For a heartbeat, I wonder if I've managed to conjure Liam up.

"Hi. Do you have a moment to talk?"

CHAPTER 31

LIAM

"Hey, is everything okay?"

My gaze slices to Sam, who hovers at the threshold of my bedroom. Guess I hadn't realized I'd been staring off into space. There's a lot of shit on my plate, and it's hard not to feel overwhelmed.

I'm trying to work with the bank and buy more time, but given the fact that my father didn't bother to respond to their previous attempts to contact him, they're not exactly sympathetic to our plight. Maybe if I'd found out a little sooner, I could have done something about it. We have little more than a week until my family is supposed to be packed up and out of the only home we've ever known.

I don't understand what Dad had been thinking. And no amount of apologizing on his part makes the situation better.

I shake myself out of those thoughts and shove my hands through my hair. "Yeah, it's fine," I say with a shrug. "Just some home stuff." I almost laugh.

It's *always* home stuff.

It never gets better.

Doubt flickers across his expression as he jerks his head in a nod, as if he understands where I'm coming from. Sam and I may have been raised in the same town, but that's where the similarities end. He grew up on the west side, which is an older, wealthier section with row after row of rolling lawns and stately Victorians.

I grew up on the east side. It's blue collar, and more rundown. The small, single-story ranches are cookie cutter in design. Other than a slight variation in aluminum siding color and the condition they're in, you can't tell them apart. There is a definite air of desperation that hangs over the crappy chain-link-fenced yards that make up the neighborhood.

The heavy pressure of it settles over me every time I drive home. Most of the people who live there work tirelessly, but it's never enough to get ahead. Every once in a while, someone from the neighborhood will get out, but most don't. I think that's why Dad is so focused on me graduating from college. He sees it as my ticket out of a place that sucks you in like quicksand.

Sam may have attended public school just like I did, but his was one of the best in the state. Mine—not so much. South Sentinel has a rougher element that it draws from. Sam's father is a state senator, and mine is... Well, mine is a drunk who enjoys gambling away his seventeen-year-old son's hard-earned money playing charity poker.

Christ.

Strangely enough, we played football against one another in high school. Although, Sam was a year ahead of me. When he graduates at the end of this semester, he'll head off to law school. I assume he and his girlfriend, Violet, will work something out in regard to their relationship. I can't imagine Sam will let her go. He's crazy about that chick.

I can't blame him for that. Violet Winterfield is one hot girl. She's not like the groupies that constantly hang around, looking for ways to be...er...*useful*. Sam and Violet attended high school together. They were best friends and neighbors before their relationship took a turn for the romantic.

Thoughts of Violet are enough to have Gia pushing her way into my brain. I've tried my damnedest to forget about her. Especially after my talk with Coach. It had been a real mind-fuck to realize they'd been involved in a long-term relationship.

What other choice had there been but to back off?

Gia wanted space.

Well, she's got it.

The only contact was the text she sent on my birthday.

As tempted as I've been to reach out, I've resisted the urge. She was sleeping with one of my coaches. They practically lived together. And then there's the issue that he wants her back.

Even thinking about everything they shared for three years is enough to make me gut sick.

Sam steps hesitantly into my room. Actually, it's Dylan's old room I've taken over. When he moved out at the beginning of the year, I moved in since my roommate situation wasn't working out. "Do you want to talk about it?"

I blink, surprised to find him lurking in my doorway like a vampire. The guy looks uncomfortable. Kind of like he's next in line for a root canal.

Without Novocain.

In a back alley where someone set up shop roughly five minutes ago.

One side of my mouth hitches. There hasn't been much to smile about lately, but this does it for me. "Nah, it won't help."

Indecision flickers over his face before he mutters, "Want me to get Violet? Is it something she can help with?" It's like he's reluctantly offering up his girlfriend as a virgin sacrifice to someone intent upon devouring her.

All right, now I really can't help it, which is why I burst out laughing.

No, I mean it. I am *dying* right now.

The look on Sam's face...

That offer must have hurt like hell.

His expression goes from uncomfortable to annoyed in three

seconds flat. "Dude, it's not that funny. Actually, it's not funny at all," he grumbles. "What the hell is wrong with you, Garrison?"

I haul myself up from my sprawled-out position on the bed. My shoulders continue to shake with uncontrollable mirth. It's all together possible that I'm losing it.

"Okay, okay." I chuckle, sucking in a ragged breath. "I'm sorry. You're right, it's not funny." I'm so mentally and emotionally exhausted that his offer—for whatever reason—struck me the wrong way. There hasn't been much to laugh about this past week. Shit keeps piling up faster than I can clear it off.

My situation might not have changed, but it feels good to release some of my pent-up tension. "I appreciate the offer, I really do." A grin simmers around the edges of my lips as he narrows his eyes.

The guy is head over heels in love with his girlfriend, and he hates that I took her out before they got together. Hell, he hates it when I'm in the same room with her. Sam has the tendency to hover over Violet whenever I'm in the general vicinity.

That knowledge only makes me want to fuck with him more.

I hate to admit it, but it's an enjoyable pastime.

It's one I should probably knock the fuck off.

Even though I've never shared any of my personal bullshit with him, I find myself admitting, "There's stuff going on with my family." I suck in a breath and decide to purge it from my body. It can't hurt, right? "It looks like we might lose our house."

His brows shoot up his forehead as he frowns. "Seriously?"

"Yeah." All of my previous humor disappears as I give voice to the reality of the situation. "You're not the only one who likes to keep a low profile."

He scratches the light stubble covering his chin.

Sam doesn't want people connecting him to his father, and I don't want anyone to realize how fucked-up my home life is. As far as I'm concerned, it's no one else's business. There are a few select people who know about my situation. Who understand that without a full ride to Barnett, I wouldn't have been able to afford college. I can tick them off on one hand and have fingers leftover.

Coach.

And Gia.

As that thought pops into my brain, I realize she must have known that Tyler Bauer was my coach. Hell, he could have even mentioned me. My situation. They were together for three years.

Three fucking years.

I was still in high school when they got together.

This thing with Gia has really messed me up.

I liked her.

No, I *like* her.

I *still* like her.

No matter how much I try, I can't evict her from my head.

The entire time I've been negotiating with the bank, begging for an extension, for a few more months to find a solution, she's been there, gnawing away at the back of my brain.

I scrub a hand tiredly over my face as it hits me again like a Mack truck cruising along at ninety.

On top of everything that's happening, I'm trying to keep up with my workout regimen. I can't allow my life to go to hell. Playing professional football will be a whole new level. I need to be as physically and mentally prepared as I can.

The crushing weight that has been solely reserved for when I stopped home for an hour or two each week, is now a constant presence. It presses against the walls of my chest until I can't breathe.

And there's no one I can talk to about it either. The one man I used to confide in, share pieces of my life with, is the same one who is attempting to steal my girl.

At this point, I think she's already gone.

As I force out a steady breath, my lungs feel as if they're being squeezed to death. It's almost like there's a gigantic fist wrapped around them. Without making a conscious decision, everything consuming me pours out of my mouth in one long tirade.

And I do mean *everything*.

Mom leaving. Dad's drinking. His unemployment. The gambling

problem that has come to light. Cullum and the amount of time he's been working just to pay the bills. Gia. And finally, Coach.

When I finally run out of steam, thirty minutes has disappeared and Sam is parked on my desk chair, which has been swiveled toward the bed. He's staring at me with a dumbfounded expression on his face.

Actually, we're both staring at each other.

"Fuck, dude," he says with a shake of his head. "I had no idea."

I drag my fingers through my hair. "No one does." My gaze hardens, needing him to understand what I mean by that.

He stiffens, looking somewhat offended. "I won't say a word. I just…" His voice trails off. "I wish there was something I could do to help."

I shrug. I won't admit it out loud, but getting everything off my chest has me feeling surprisingly lighter. Maybe there's something to the whole talking-about-your-problems thing.

Although, I can't see it becoming a habit.

"I hate to say it," Sam says, "but there might not be anything else you can do about your house. After you get drafted and you start earning money, you'll be able to buy your family another home. At this point, your time might be better spent finding them an apartment until you can make that happen."

I inhale a deep breath and allow his words to settle inside me. "Yeah, maybe." I've been so hellbent on trying to save the house that I haven't allowed myself to consider any other alternatives. It's a relief to realize there are other options.

It's the place I grew up and lived in for more than twenty years, but has it really been any kind of home?

Whenever I walk through the front door, it feels like there's an elephant sitting on my chest. There's so much bad shit that went down inside those walls. Maybe a fresh start would be good for everyone. The more I think about it, the more the idea takes root inside my head. I have no idea what Dad, Cullum, or Claire will think about it.

I'm ashamed to admit that I tried to pull the whole don't-you-know-who-I-am card with the bank. Not only don't they know, they don't give a rat's ass. I'm dealing with a conglomerate. They don't know jack shit about their customers.

"It's worth considering," he says, breaking into my thoughts.

I nod. "I'll bring it up with my family. Honestly, we might not have a choice at this point. We've run out of time."

Sam draws his lower lip between his teeth before saying hesitantly, "I could make a call to my dad. He might be able to pull some strings."

As much as I appreciate the offer—and I do, especially considering Sam and I haven't always seen eye to eye—I don't want him to do that. Recently, Sam went through a shitload of problems when a shot of his naked ass went viral. From what I understand, his father flipped his damn lid. Sam hasn't mentioned much about it, but I know things aren't a hundred percent back to normal with his family.

"Nah, but thanks. I'll deal with it on my own." It feels good to unload on someone. And Sam has given me another avenue to explore that I've been too single-minded to think about.

With a jerk of his head, he nods in understanding. "I still can't believe you were dating Coach's ex."

That makes two of us.

"What are you going to do now?" he asks. "I mean…are you just going to give up on her?"

My gaze turns hard as I shift on the bed. "What am I supposed to do? That's Coach B's ex-girlfriend. The one," I remind, "he's still trying to get back together with."

Sam shakes his head. "Yeah, it's pretty messed-up."

That is the understatement of the century.

We stare at each other for a moment before he clears his throat. "Violet and I were planning to grab something to eat, you interested?"

My brows shoot up at the unexpected offer to hang out with his girlfriend. A slow grin spreads across my face. That's when I realize I won't be able to quit yanking his chain cold turkey. Old habits die hard. "How about I take her out myself?"

The edges of his lips lift fractionally. "Fuck off, dude. She was never into you. Not even a little."

This is the first time Sam has ever come out and acknowledged that I took Violet out to shoot pool before they got together.

That's got to mean something, right?

Progress of some sort.

Instead of being a complete dick with a flippant comment that would piss Sam off, I say, "Nope. It was always about you, man."

CHAPTER 32

GIA

’m not sure what I was thinking when I agreed to this.

All right, yes, I do.

I'd been thinking I had no business getting involved with a guy who is twenty years old and still in college. Someone who is leaving town in a few months and won't be looking back once he makes it to the NFL.

When I found Tyler standing in the doorway of my classroom, I had a moment of weakness and thought, *why not?* Maybe I need to give our relationship one last shot. We certainly weren't perfect, but I did love him. And Tyler is a good man.

I could do a lot worse.

That's exactly what my thought process had been forty minutes ago. It's also how I ended up in a restaurant, having dinner with Tyler. But somewhere in that span of time, from when I saw him at my door to us sitting at a table and waiting for our dinner to arrive, I realize deep down that it will never work.

Now that I'm here, and see the hopeful expression written across his earnest face as he tells me about all the ways he'll change if I give him another chance, I understand that Tyler could be the most perfect partner and give me everything I've ever dreamed of, but I still wouldn't be happy.

What I want has changed.

Who I want has changed.

"Gia, honey?"

He's making an effort to call me Gia. Not once has he slipped and said Gianna. The man is honestly trying. And yet, I can't do it.

With an apologetic smile, I resettle my attention on Tyler. "Sorry, what did you say?"

"I was saying that even though I really missed you, the time we've spent apart has turned out to be a positive thing. It forced me to re-evaluate what's important and what I want out of life." He leans against the table that separates us. "Where I want to focus my energies."

I gulp.

Judging from the intense look aimed in my direction, I assume those energies have something to do with me.

I can't allow this to continue.

He reaches across the table before ensnaring my hand in his own. A knot forms at the bottom of my belly. I want him to stop talking for one minute. He's being so honest, and instead of returning those feelings, I feel nothing for him.

"Tyler," I say, attempting to interrupt, but he continues to steamroll over me.

"You mean everything to me, Gia. I love you so much. I want you to give us another chance to make this work. I know we can be happy again."

Panic bubbles up inside me as I raise my voice. "Tyler, I think—"

The words die a quick, painful death as my gaze collides with gray eyes. A jolt of electricity slams through me as we stare for what feels like an eternity. In reality, it can't be more than a few heartbeats. I find myself caught in the crosshairs of those deep, fathomless depths.

I'm not sure what I expected to find in his eyes, but it wasn't the guarded expression he now wears. He looks at me as if we're nothing more than strangers. It takes everything I have inside not to jump up and rush toward him. That's exactly what every fiber of my being is screaming for me to do.

I don't give a damn about the nine years that separate us.

All right, I do. But not enough to let it stand in the way of what we found in each other.

Not that I needed any further illustration as to how I feel about these two men, but it only drives home the knowledge that I can never go back to Tyler. We will never be able to recapture what we once had.

Liam might have just turned twenty-one, but he's all man. He's already dealt with so much adversity. More than I can fathom. His life experiences aren't those of a normal college-aged guy.

From the first moment I saw him, there was something magnetic that drew me in. It's still there, pulsing beneath the surface.

It is an undeniable truth.

As I continue to stare, I realize that whatever this is between us is too powerful to fight. I'm sick to death of struggling against what I feel. I want to give us a chance. *A real chance.* One where I don't hold back everything I feel, afraid of being hurt or left behind.

"Gia?"

As I rip my gaze away from Liam, resolve strengthens inside me. I know what needs to be done. "I'm sorry, Tyler. I can't do this."

His brows snap together. "What? But I thought—"

"I know, and I apologize for that. It was never my intention to lead you on."

"I don't understand," he says, confusion flickering in his eyes. "Are you involved with someone else? Is that what's going on?"

I draw in a breath and force out the truth. "For the last couple months, I've been seeing another man. We're no longer together, but I liked him." I pause before adding, "A lot."

When he continues to stare in shock, I slide my hand from beneath his before covering his fingers and giving them a squeeze. "I don't want to hurt you. But you should know what's going on and where I'm at. Right now, I feel like I owe it to myself to explore this other relationship."

He rips his hand from mine, as if I've scalded his flesh, before collapsing against his chair. It's as if he's attempting to put as much distance between us as he can. "You don't want to work on our issues?"

My teeth sink into my lower lip as I shake my head. "No."

He releases a stunned breath. "I don't know what to say, Gia. I always thought you would give us another shot. We were together for three years." He shakes his head, as if he can't wrap his mind around the fact that our relationship is truly over. "You're really willing to throw all that away?"

"We've been broken up for five months. I've moved on." Even though it seems harsh, I add, "You need to do the same."

His eyes widen before he jerks to his feet and stares down at me. Not only is he hurt, he's been thrown off guard.

"If you end up changing your mind in a month or so," he bites out, "it'll be too late. I won't wait around for you to come to your senses."

"No," I agree, "you shouldn't."

His jaw tightens. Surprise clouds his expression as he nods. He digs out a few bills from his leather wallet before tossing them on the table and walking out.

For the first time since we broke up, I think Tyler truly understands that what we had is over. It's time to move on.

I release a pent-up breath and pick up my glass of water before downing half of it. I could use a glass of chardonnay, but this will have to do. It's only when I set the glass on the table that I realize my hand is shaking. I hate confrontations. I don't enjoy inflicting pain.

But it needed to be done.

As I gather up my purse, my gaze unconsciously drifts in the direction I last saw Liam. Since my attention had been solely focused on him, I have no idea if he's here with friends. Although, my guess is that he is. I add a few bills to Tyler's stack to cover our dinner before making my way to the back of the restaurant.

My feet grind to a halt when I spot Liam. He's sitting at a table, talking with a pretty blonde girl. Emotion wells up in my throat when I realize they're about the same age.

The two of them look as though they belong together.

Him so dark and edgy.

Her so sweet and fresh-faced.

For a heartbeat or two, I watch them. It's obvious by their easy banter that they're friends…or more. She flashes him a smile before they burst into laughter. From the angle I'm standing at, I can only see the two of them. It's entirely possible they're out on a date. Just as I've moved on from Tyler, Liam has moved on from me. Sorrow and regret squeeze my heart at the realization.

There's no way I can go over and interrupt their conversation.

How pathetic would that look?

Like I'm some desperate, older woman chasing after some hot college athlete. I cringe at the mental image I've painted in my mind.

The entire time we were together, Liam pushed for more, and I held him at arm's length because I was scared of getting involved with someone his age. Someone who was moving on to bigger and better things.

It was stupid on my part. And now that stupidity has cost me my relationship with Liam.

Decision made, I spin on my heels and head for the front entrance. I need to get out of here. As I push out through the glass door into the parking lot, a hand locks on my elbow before steering me off to the side. Goose bumps prickle along my skin. Everything in me seizes at Liam's proximity.

It's been weeks since we've seen one another or been this close.

"Did you know?" His voice is low and hard.

I wish to God I didn't understand the question.

When I fail to respond, he growls, "Did you know Bauer was my coach?"

My heart riots painfully against my chest.

We both know the answer to that question.

Of course I knew. How could I not?

I'd heard stories about Tyler's star quarterback for years. Before I came into the picture, Tyler recruited him to Barnett University. He would go on and on about how amazing this kid was and what a shitty home life he came from. Tyler saw so much resilience in him. So much hope for his future.

Say what you want about my ex, but he's always had a soft spot for Liam. I've never seen him take such interest in a player before. Liam didn't have all the advantages that some of these other kids did. And Tyler understood that. Right from the start, he wanted to help Liam in any way he could.

The dark-haired guy's eyes bore into mine as he silently waits for an answer.

I give a reluctant nod before my tongue darts out to moisten my dry lips. I attempt to steel myself, but my voice comes out on a tremble. "Yes, I knew Tyler was your coach."

His brows knit together. "Why didn't you tell me that Bauer was the guy you'd been dating for three years? Don't you think that would have made a difference to me?"

In hindsight, I should have told him that I'd been seeing someone who was involved so heavily in his life.

But at the time...

"I don't know. Tyler and I had been broken up for a few months. We weren't together when I met you."

"You mean when we hooked up at the bar?" he cuts in sharply. An accusatory tone weaves its way through his words.

"Yes. To be fair, we didn't exchange names. I had no idea who you were or that you even played football." I gulp before forcing out the rest. "I never planned on seeing you again after that night. You know that. We agreed on it."

His gaze searches mine before he jerks his head toward the dining area. "Are you two getting back together?" His hand is still wrapped around my elbow as he drags me closer. Before I can formulate a response, he admits, "I spoke with him after I saw you two at the club." There's a pause. "You realize that's what he wants, right?"

A lump forms in my throat, making it impossible to breathe. "Yes, that's what Tyler was hoping for."

Liam plows his free hand through his dark hair. "Tyler..."

"We aren't getting back together. I made it clear to him that we're over."

Emotion sharpens in his eyes. "Why would you do that? He told me himself that he's still in love with you. Why wouldn't you give him another chance?"

Unable to respond, I shake my head.

"Why?" Even though Liam is riddled with confusion, he's still angry with me. It vibrates through his deep voice. "Coach B is a good man. I've known him for seven years. He's the one who recruited me to Barnett and took me under his wing." He shakes his head as his voice dips with emotion. "He's like a father to me."

I gulp as understanding dawns. The sparks of resentment that flare to life in his eyes make so much more sense.

"Tyler is a good man," I tell him, "but I don't love him. I can't spend the rest of my life with him."

"Why is that?" He tilts his head. "Why don't you love him anymore?"

A tortured expression fills his beautiful eyes, and it nearly breaks my heart.

Even though Liam still wants me, he doesn't want to hurt the one man in his life who has been there for him. The one man he can count on when there haven't been many who have proven to be worthy of his trust.

"Tyler and I aren't right for one another," I admit.

His fingers feather along my cheek until he can cradle the side of my face in the warm palm of his hand. I close my eyes and inhale the woodsy scent of his aftershave.

Only now do I realize that this is the closest I will ever come to being with him again. If I have any conscience whatsoever, I'll let Liam go. I'll walk away in order for their relationship to remain intact. Liam needs him in his life.

I remember all the stories of how Tyler would take the high schooler out to eat so he could buy him a proper meal. Or how they would sit down and discuss what Liam's future could look like if he remained focused. Or how devastated Liam was when his mother abandoned him and his family. How everything fell onto his ill-equipped shoulders.

As much as it breaks my heart to let him go, I can't take the one person Liam counts on away from him. I refuse to be that selfish. Even though it's the hardest thing I've ever had to do, I force myself to retreat until his hand drifts from the side of my face.

"There aren't any other reasons." The lie is painful as I force it from my lips.

Fresh anguish flares to life in his eyes before being snuffed out.

He nods before retreating a step. A muscle tics in his tightly clenched jaw. The gray in his eyes looks more like the dead of winter than liquid metal. I've never seen them so desolate.

Emotionless.

"Good to know," he bites out.

I straighten my shoulders and clasp my purse, as if the death grip alone can stave off the pain blooming throughout my body. As if it will prevent me from reaching out and grabbing hold of him.

Even though it feels as if I've been gutted, I say, "You should probably get back to your friend."

I need him to leave before I end up doing something I'll regret. When he doesn't budge, my gaze stays locked on his as I carefully back away. I'm so scared that he'll reach out and grab hold of me.

If he lays one finger on me, I'll crumble. Right here in the parking lot. There is only so much heartache I can withstand. I'm dangerously close to splintering apart. It won't take much to give in to the need pounding through me that wants so desperately to be unleashed.

Thankfully, there are no last-ditch attempts to keep me close or change my mind.

He lets me go.

It's the right thing to do. Even though it doesn't feel like it. I won't take Tyler away from him.

But still, he doesn't leave. Anger and disappointment brew in his gray depths. A struggle being waged inside them.

He doesn't want to let go.

I don't want to either.

But I can't hold on.

The grief thrashing around in my chest is on the verge of exploding. I turn away, darting to my car before sliding onto the seat and starting up the engine. Unable to stop myself, I glance in the rearview mirror only to find Liam standing rooted in place as I pull out of the parking lot.

I hate that the last image I'll have of him will be one full of anger and sorrow.

That's not the Liam I've gotten to know over the last few months. The one I've been falling for.

What hurts the most is that I'm the one who put it there.

CHAPTER 33

LIAM

My gaze travels around the new apartment my family moved into. It might not be much, but it's the best we could come up with on short notice. Hell, we were lucky to snag one with three bedrooms.

So, there's that, at least.

No one is happy about the move. Both Cullum and Claire have been uncharacteristically quiet about it. They understand there wasn't much choice in the matter.

And Dad?

He's been silent for obvious reasons.

It feels like I let everyone down by not being able to buy us more time with the bank and save our home. The only positive is that we have a plan moving forward. My brother will continue to work until I start earning a paycheck. As soon as that happens, he'll quit his job and focus on school. I'll handle the bills from now on until my father has completed an outpatient treatment program and can be trusted to deal with that responsibility again.

Whenever that is.

It sucks everything had to fall completely to shit. I'd thought we were at least keeping our heads above water. Turns out that wasn't the case. It makes me wonder how I could have been so blind.

Everything in my life is in a state of flux. If I dwell on it, anxiety rushes in, threatening to suck me under. The move my family was forced to make. The NFL Draft. Completing junior year. Dad's treatment program. All the bills. Claire's grades in school.

There's a lot going on. I need to stay focused and on top of it.

As excited as I am about my future in the NFL, I'd be lying if I didn't admit I'm nervous as hell. Once I get drafted, I'll leave. I have no idea who I'll be playing for. My agent has thrown out a few teams that have expressed interest. I've spoken with the general managers on the phone. But still, the future remains murky.

I'm scared to leave my family. I'm scared Dad will fall back into drinking and gambling. He needs to man up and take control of his life again so Cullum can be the kid he was meant to be from the beginning.

I release a steady breath and remind myself to take it one day at a time.

That's become my mantra.

I glance around and realize I haven't seen my sister yet. I figured she was sleeping late since it's Saturday morning, but there hasn't been any sound or movement from her room.

"Where's Claire?" I ask.

Dad is parked in his recliner. It was the one piece of furniture we opted not to get rid of. A lot of stuff ended up going to Goodwill since the apartment is smaller in square footage than our house. Even though it was hard to go through everything—especially Mom's personal belongings that she left behind—it turned out to be cathartic. It was like saying goodbye to a painful past and hello to a hopefully brighter future.

He rips his gaze away from the television screen. "Your sister is with Gia. You know they work together on Saturday mornings."

My breath catches at the back of my throat at the mention of her name. It's always like that when people ask about her.

It takes a moment to wrap my mind around his response. "They're still doing that?"

I had no idea Gia was still tutoring Claire. Maybe I shouldn't be so surprised. Gia enjoys working with kids. Especially ones who need extra help. She's so empathetic and kindhearted. They're just a couple of the qualities that drew me to her.

What does surprise me is that Claire hasn't mentioned it. I see her several times a week now. Ever since the bottom dropped out, I've made a point to be here more. I want to make sure Dad is attending treatment every damn day.

"I'll tell you, that woman has been a real saving grace." He drags himself out of the recliner before ambling over to the table and flipping through a thick stack of papers. Once he finds what he's been searching for, he hands me the folded sheet. For a heartbeat, I stare at it.

My gut clenches.

The last time I held a slip of paper like this in my hands, my whole damn world fell apart. I don't need to be thrown for anymore loops. I hold my breath as I unfold the sheet and glance at it.

It's a progress report.

For Claire.

And…well, it's actually pretty amazing.

It's not straight A's, but it's a hell of a lot better than what her report cards have been in the past. It's a mixture of B's and C's with one A thrown in. Her last report was mostly C's with a D in math and a B in foods.

I'm so damn proud of her that I want to frame this progress report. It only reconfirms that Claire has the ability along with the sheer determination to be successful. I always knew if she could get a little one-on-one attention, she would blossom.

And that's exactly what happened.

"That Gia… Don't let her go, son. She's one of the good ones."

My father has never been one to dole out advice. Especially regarding the opposite sex. Ever since Mom took off, he doesn't seem cognizant of what's going on. To hear him praise the woman I'm no longer seeing is like an unexpected punch to the gut.

Pent-up agitation surges in me as I scrub a hand roughly over my face. I have no idea how to respond. There's been so much other crap going on, I haven't bothered to mention that Gia and I are no longer together.

Unaware of the sudden change in my mood, he proceeds to rub salt in the wound by adding, "I don't know what Claire would do without her."

Honestly, I feel the same. These last few weeks have sucked. We might not have been seeing each other for long, but she left an indelible mark on my soul. Almost harshly, I remind myself that she made her choice. Maybe she's not seeing Coach, but she sure as hell doesn't want to be with me either.

Thank God I've had so much other shit to contend with, or I'd probably find myself at her door, begging her to give me another chance. You'd think after three solid weeks, I'd have moved on. It's not like there aren't enough chicks on campus clamoring for my attention. I should be able to distract myself with one of them.

But nope.

I don't know what it is about Gia. No matter how many times I've tried to evict her from my head and heart, she refuses to budge. It's frustrating as hell. I can't lose myself in someone else when she's all I can think about.

Even though I'm not looking forward to leaving my family behind, I think it'll be good for me to get the hell out of this place. It might be the only way I can move on from her.

My family isn't the only one who needs a fresh start.

I need one as well.

CHAPTER 34

GIA

"*D*oes that explanation help you understand the problem better?"

Claire nods before scribbling down the answer in her notebook. Once done, she glances up. Her expression is oddly pensive. "Why can't Mr. Schmidt explain it like that? The way he teaches is so confusing. It doesn't make sense to me."

A smile of encouragement touches my lips. "I know it might seem that way, but mathematics can be difficult to teach. The concepts aren't always easy to grasp or understand, and that makes it challenging."

I give Claire a little pat on the back. I'm so proud of the progress she's made. I've never seen anyone work so hard to comprehend one problem. She's so determined. Over the last two months, what I've learned is that Claire doesn't give up easily.

"Look how well you're doing! I think you can accomplish anything you set your mind to."

She beams. Claire is like a flower that has grown and bloomed under positive reinforcement.

Her gaze is full of gratitude. "Without your help, there's no way I would be doing this well. My dad was really happy about my last progress report. All my teachers keep telling me that I'm doing a great job and to keep up the hard work." She falls silent before adding, "Someday, I hope I can be just as good of a teacher as you are."

Thick emotion gathers in my chest. "Thank you, sweetie. That means a lot to me. Don't ever forget that the success you're finding is all yours. You're the one putting in the hard work." I close the distance between us, as if I'm about to share a secret with her. "You know what I've discovered?"

With her gaze pinned to mine, she shakes her head.

"That if you can take your struggles and turn them into something positive, that's when you can be great at whatever you set out to accomplish. If being a teacher is what you end up doing, you'll be amazing because you've been a student who knows what it feels like to struggle. Understanding that not all kids move at the same pace and have the same strengths is what makes a good teacher an outstanding one. I want you to remember that. Our failures don't have to define us. If you can turn them into something positive—something that helps others in the process—then it makes the struggle worthwhile. You'll be able to look back on what you overcame and see how it changed you for the better."

I straighten when she beams.

"All right," I say, "let's get back to work. I need to drop you off in about an hour, and I know we have more to get through."

Claire pouts, and I laugh before ruffling her dark hair. "I know, I know. But I have a few errands to run this afternoon."

For the next hour, Claire finishes up her math and science. Over the last couple of weeks, we've found a system that works well and streamlined her homework process. It takes half the time it used to. An added benefit is that Claire's confidence has skyrocketed with all the success she's having in school. Instead of giving up at the first sign of trouble, she's able to implement strategies to help figure out tough problems.

After the run in with Liam at the restaurant, I wasn't sure if I should continue tutoring Claire. I took a few days to mull it over. In the end, I decided that helping Claire may have been born out of my relationship with Liam, but it evolved into its own entity.

Instead of Liam bringing his sister to my house like before, I started picking Claire up myself. A few weeks ago, right before her family moved, she told me about everything that happened and how they lost the house. As much as I longed to reach out to Liam, to offer my support, I didn't feel like it was my place.

I didn't want to open up any old wounds.

For either of us.

Over the weeks, Claire has come to realize that something happened with Liam because neither of us mention him anymore. She might only be fifteen years old, but Claire seems to understand the finer nuances of relationships.

That's why it takes me by surprise when she asks on the drive to her apartment, "Is there any chance you and Liam will get back together?"

My gaze cuts to hers before slicing back to the ribbon of road stretched out in front of me. "Umm." I stall before answering honestly, "I don't think so."

"How come?"

My fingers bite into the steering wheel. I give her another sidelong glance, only to find her staring at me. I release a steady breath and do my best to answer that difficult question. "We're just in different places right now."

"But you still like him?"

"Of course," I say without hesitation. "Your brother is a wonderful guy." After everything he's been through, everything he's trying to do for his family, how could I possibly think otherwise?

He might be eight and a half years younger than I am, but he's more mature than a lot of guys my age or even older. If I didn't know he was twenty when we met, I would have thought he was older.

Actually, I *did* think he was older. He carries himself like a man who has already had the weight of the world resting on his shoulders.

"He's great," she says enthusiastically. "The absolute best." Her expression falls as her teeth sink into her lower lip.

I reach over and give her hand a squeeze. "Just because Liam and I aren't together doesn't mean you and I can't be friends. Or that I won't continue to help you with schoolwork." My gaze flickers to her. "You know that, right?"

Her lips bow into a smile. "I know. It's just—"

There's a loud noise and then a strange whapping sound that comes from the back end of the car. I've never had a flat tire, but I'm guessing that's what happened. The vehicle seems to be veering to the right.

Claire's eyes grow round as they fill with fear. "What happened?"

"I think there's a flat. It's not a big deal." Calmly, I steer the car to the side of the road. "I'm going to pull over and take a look. All right?"

Her brows pinch together. "Are we going to call someone to fix it?"

Thankfully, it's still early. I'm not overly concerned about sitting on the side of the road until assistance arrives. "Maybe. Let me see what's going on and then we'll figure it out from there. I don't want you to worry."

I pull over and set the car in park. Then I turn off the engine and exit the vehicle, walking around to the back of my Chevy Malibu.

My heart sinks as I inspect the back right tire.

Totally flat.

There's a spare in the trunk, but I have no idea how to change a flat. Thank goodness I have a car service that will take care of it.

Claire sticks her head out the window to see what's going on. Concern clouds her pretty features. "Is it a flat tire?"

I sigh. "Yup."

"Okay." She ducks back inside the vehicle as I hunker down to take a closer look. It's not like I can see anything protruding from the rubber. I straighten to my full height and walk back to the front of the car before opening the driver's side door to grab my phone. Hopefully, we won't have to wait long for help to arrive.

"Yeah, we're pulled over on the side of the road." She glances out the front window toward the streetlight up ahead. "It's right before the intersection of Maple and Fourth. Umm-hmm. Yeah, we will. Okay. See you soon. Bye."

For a moment, I wonder who she's talking to.

Before I can ask, she says, "Liam is on his way. He said we should stay in the car and that he'll be here in ten minutes."

"What?" My heartbeat hitches at the thought of coming face-to-face with him again. When I'm finally able to find my voice, I whisper, "Why did you call him?"

Seeing him today will hurt. I wish she wouldn't have done that.

She blinks. "He knows how to change a flat tire." Confusion laces her voice. Claire doesn't understand how much I still care about her brother.

I clear my throat. "I pay for a service to take care of things like this. They would have come and changed the flat for us. It wouldn't have been a problem."

She arches a brow. "I bet they won't be here in ten minutes."

Well, she's probably right about that. I'm sure we would have been sitting here for at least an hour before they showed up. I should be grateful that Claire had the foresight to call Liam, and that he's willing to drop whatever he's doing to help us.

But still…

When I continue to stare, she flashes an overly bright smile at me. With a sinking heart, I slide into the car, realizing there's nothing I can do about the situation.

True to his word, Liam pulls his Honda Accord behind us in less than ten minutes. Nerves careen down my spine as my gaze stays glued to the rearview mirror. My gut clenches as he unfolds himself from the car and swallows up the distance between us.

My gaze licks over him, noticing the way his hair his styled in its trademark fauxhawk. Memories of running my fingers over the top of it crash over me. For one brief heartbeat, I squeeze my eyes tight and try to still all of the emotion that riots painfully in my chest. When it feels like I have everything under control, I open my eyes and exit the vehicle.

I raise my hand to give him an awkward wave in greeting before shoving it into the pocket of my coat. The temptation to step into the protective circle of his arms thrums through me. But I can't do that.

Deep down, I realize how dangerous it would be to lay my hands on him. The weeks that have slid past have done nothing to diminish my feelings. They're still there, stronger than ever.

I clear my throat along with those thoughts. "Thanks for coming. I was going to call my car service to repair the tire."

His gray gaze locks on mine, holding it captive until my knees turn weak. "It's not a big deal. I'll have it changed in no time and you can be on your way."

I shift my weight, wishing this were easier. "Thank you. I appreciate you getting here so quickly."

Emotion flickers in his gaze. Silence stretches between us, and I wonder if he'll address the strange situation we now find ourselves in. Instead, he says, "Is there a spare in the trunk?"

Air rushes from my lungs. "Yes!" I back away to the front of the car. "I'll pop open the trunk."

His attention stays focused on me as he nods.

I have no idea what he's thinking. Is he happy to see me or does it no longer matter?

My fingers tremble as I lean inside the driver's side door and hit the button that will release the trunk. While I do that, Liam walks back to his car to grab his tools. Within minutes, he's got the spare tire on the ground and the back end of my car jacked up.

I forgot that Liam spent his summers working for a friend who owns a garage. As I stand by and watch, it's clear he knows what he's doing. This isn't the first tire he's changed. His movements are precise and economical, like a well-rehearsed show. After jacking up the car, he loosens the lug nuts, pops off the tire, and puts the spare in place.

Before I know it, my car is once again drivable. He secures the flat tire in the trunk before wiping the grease from his hands with an old towel.

"Thank you. I really appreciate you dropping everything to get here so quickly."

When he glances at me, his gaze pins mine in place, making it difficult—if not impossible—to suck in full breaths of air. "I told you before that it wasn't a problem." He points to the newly changed tire.

"You need to get the old one fixed. You can't drive around indefinitely on a spare."

My brows draw together at this information. "Oh?" I've never had to use a spare tire before. I assumed it was the same as a regular one.

Unconsciously, my attention drops to his wide hands as he continues to wipe them. I can't help but remember what they felt like coasting over my body. How he would—

"A spare should only be used for a short period of time until you either fix the old tire or buy a replacement. From what I can tell, it looks like you ran over a nail. I would take it to a shop and have them plug the hole. It should be fine after that."

My gaze jerks to his. Heat floods my cheeks. The thoughts running rampant through my head aren't ones I should be having.

Especially right now.

"Yeah," I say vaguely, appreciative of his advice since I know next to nothing about cars, except how to drive them. "I'll do that."

What I really need to do is get away from him. I'm seconds, maybe milliseconds, away from throwing myself at him.

"Do you have a place where you can take it?"

"Ummm, I don't know if the garage I use also repairs tires. I'll call them on Monday and figure it out."

His brows draw together, as if he doesn't like my answer. "I'll give my friend a call. He usually works on the weekends. I bet he wouldn't mind plugging it if he's at the shop. After I talk with him, I'll let you know."

Alarm bells ring in my brain.

That doesn't necessarily seem like a good idea.

I shake my head in response.

"Gia, you can't drive around on a donut," he growls. "The sooner you get it fixed, the safer you'll be."

Yeah, I get that, but I can't spend any more time alone with him. Not when I still have feelings for him. His presence has sent every one of them hurtling unwantedly to the surface. If I'd thought I was over him, that notion has been proven to be a misconception. I'm no closer to being over Liam than I was before.

I'm appreciative of everything he's trying to do. I really am. But I'm also someone who understands their limitations.

"I'll get it taken care of on my own," I say.

The glint in his eyes hardens. "I'm calling my friend. I don't want to worry about you breaking down again."

When I open my mouth to argue, he cuts me off. "I'm calling my friend."

I press my lips together.

He gentles his tone. "It's not a big deal. Just let me do this for you. All right?"

Only now do I realize this isn't an argument I can win. I jerk my head in a nod before glancing at Claire, who is in no way trying to disguise the fact that she's plastered against the window, watching us. "I should probably get going. I need to drop Claire off."

"I can take her back with me. You shouldn't be driving any farther than you have to."

"Okay, well...thank you."

"It's not a problem, Gia," he mutters. "It's the least I can do for all the help you've given Claire." There's a beat of silence before he adds, "I didn't know you two were still working together."

I hate how tentative this exchange feels. I wish it could go back to being as easy as it once was, but that's not possible. I have to keep the barriers firmly in place. Once they crumble, I won't have the strength to erect them again. I won't have the wherewithal to do anything other than give in to the sexual energy that crackles in the air. Even though it's tamped down— restrained—it claws at the edges, trying to break free.

"My relationship with you has nothing to do with Claire."

He nods, as if understanding the unspoken words and feelings that sit between us. "I just wanted to thank you for continuing to work with her. My dad showed me Claire's last progress report." Both his eyes and voice soften. The love he has for his family tugs at my heartstrings. There is nothing he wouldn't do for them. "Her grades haven't looked like that since elementary school. It's all because you've taken the time to work with her, to help her be successful." He glances toward the car before those liquid gray pools spear mine. "You've really helped to rebuild her confidence."

My muscles relax. Discussing the situation with Claire brings a genuine smile to my lips. How can it not? "Nope." I shake my head, giving credit where it's due. "It's all her. Claire did this. She just needed help getting organized and figuring out a system that worked for her."

When he takes a step closer, my heart thumps in response to his proximity. The attraction I feel for this man is so much more than physical. It may have started out that way, but it's grown into something deeper.

"You're the one who's taken the time to work with her every Saturday."

"I enjoy every minute we spend together," I say earnestly. "She's a sweet girl who wants to do well. It makes helping her a pleasure."

His voice drops. "There hasn't been a woman in her life since my mom left. I know she enjoys the time you spend with her. Thanks for not stopping the tutoring when things ended between us."

"I wouldn't have done that to her."

He inches closer, until there's no more than a foot of space separating us. My breath catches as he reaches out, picking up a long strand of hair before playing with it. "I know."

Unconsciously, I sway toward him. I long to feel his arms slide around me, holding me tightly against him. I miss the way his lips would feather over mine. I blink, jerking out of those dangerous thoughts before catching myself. As I retreat a step, my hair slides from his fingers.

"I'll text you after I speak with my friend, and let you know about the tire."

The notion of spending any more time with Liam now seems disastrous. I'd convinced myself that I'd put him—and what we had together—behind me. But that's not true. Him playing with the ends of my hair had me wanting to step into his warm embrace.

And that can't be allowed to happen.

My tongue darts out to moisten my lips. "I'll figure it out on my own, Liam. It's just a tire. It won't be a problem."

He shakes his head, as if the decision isn't mine to make. "No, we'll get the situation taken care of tomorrow. Most garages aren't open on Sundays, so it'll have to wait until sometime during the week. You work until four o'clock every day. It'll be difficult to get your car into a mechanic until next Saturday. We can get it done tomorrow and then you won't have to be concerned about it." He points to his chest. "And I won't have to worry about you ending up with a flat along the side of the road."

A stubborn light enters his eyes as we stare at each other.

My shoulders waver before slumping as I nod in agreement. "Fine. I'll wait to hear from you."

My heart rate spikes as he swallows up the distance between us again. I've never met anyone who is so capable of scrambling my senses.

His hand rises until he can stroke my cheek. "I've missed you, Gia. I miss every damn thing about you. The way your body curves against mine when we sleep. How your heartbeat quickens when I touch you. The way your breath catches and our eyes lock the moment I enter your body." He shakes his head before whispering hoarsely, "I miss all of it."

I squeeze my eyes shut to block out his words.

And their meaning.

I want to forget how good we were together. How right it felt to be with him. I want to forget everything he's capable of making me feel. The way he awakened all of my senses, showing me things I couldn't have imagined.

"Look at me, Gia," he rasps. "Tell me you don't feel it."

I force my eyes open.

Of course I feel the same way.

What good will it do to admit the truth? It'll only cause more pain and heartache. Even from this brief encounter, I feel ripped apart. Gutted. It's like I'm right back at square one.

His fingers strum my cheekbone. The urge to melt into his touch is powerful. I want to wrap my arms around him and never let go.

"I hate this," he admits.

"It's for the best."

"How can you say that?" His voice turns rough.

"There is too much standing in our way. Too much that will, in the end, tear us apart." When he opens his mouth to respond, I cut him off. "Please, Liam, I can't do this again." It's too painful.

His jaw clenches as anger flashes in his stormy gray eyes. "Just tell me you're over this, over *me*, and I'll walk away. I promise you'll never hear one damn word from me again." There's a pause. "All you have to do is say it."

Even though my heart is fracturing all over again, I open my mouth to tell him exactly that, but no sound comes out.

His hands settle on my shoulders before he hauls me against him. "Tell me, Gia," he growls against my ear. "Tell me there's no fucking hope left."

I shake my head as tears sting my eyes. If I were a stronger person—a better person—I would force out the response he so desperately needs to hear, but I can't.

I can't do it.

I can't lie to him.

Not when every emotion coursing through him brims in his eyes. Not when I could drown in those fathomless pools if only I'd allow myself to fall.

"Even though I can't tell you what you need to hear, nothing has changed. Just because we want each other doesn't mean we can be together." That's as close to the truth as I can get without lying to him.

His fingers curl, biting into my shoulders. Even through my coat, I feel the pressure of them. A small whimper escapes as he holds me in place.

His touch doesn't bruise my skin, only my heart.

"You know damn well there isn't a reason for us to be apart. You're doing what you've done from the beginning and throwing up roadblocks."

I bite down on my lip and whisper one word. "Tyler."

Emotion falters in his eyes. It's there and gone within seconds, but I still catch sight of it. Air leaks from my lungs. It only strengthens my resolve to do what's best for both of us.

"You need him in your life," I force myself to say. "I won't be the one to steal that from you."

"What I need is *you*," he growls, eyes flashing with bitterness.

I shake my head before untangling myself from him.

As much as I don't want to do this, I have to.

There's no other way.

CHAPTER 35

LIAM

I drop Claire off at the apartment and stop in briefly to make sure everything is running smoothly before picking up a few bills that need to be paid. After seeing Gia again—and touching her—I have all this unwanted energy careening through my system. And it's messing with my head.

It took every ounce of self-restraint not to haul that woman into my arms and kiss the hell out of her. To get her to admit that we're perfect for one another and that all the obstacles standing in our way don't matter.

Nothing matters if she's not in my life.

After more than a month, I want her just as much, if not more, than I did before. The moment she stepped out of the car was like a punch to the gut, knocking the wind from my body. I've tried to stay away from her.

To forget her.

I really have. But I'm done with that.

I can't do it anymore.

The need to expel some of this energy from my body pounds through me, so I head over to the athletic center on campus to lift weights. Maybe run a few miles on the treadmill. I need to clear my head, or I'll end up jumping back into my car and driving over to her place.

And I don't want to do that.

Not with the way I'm feeling.

I texted Gia after I reached the apartment to make sure she made it home safely. I probably should have followed her back to her place, but I could tell she needed space. I know she's conflicted. I saw it brimming in her wide blue eyes. The way they licked over me was like a physical caress. One that will forever be burned into my soul.

For the time being, I'll have to content myself with the knowledge that I secured her agreement to meet tomorrow.

After entering the athletic center, I check in at the front desk and head to the weight room. As I pass by the football offices, I notice Coach B's door partway open and soft light pouring through the crack.

Even though we have a room specifically designed for watching game film, he's going through highlight video in his office. His feet are kicked up on a desk littered with papers. His eyes are focused on the forty-inch screen.

I shift my weight before rapping my knuckles against the wooden doorframe. He swings around. As his gaze collides with mine, a smile lights up his face.

I didn't realize I needed to speak with him about Gia until I was standing outside his office. I need to come clean about our relationship. It's the only way Gia and I will be able to move forward.

Coach has always been there for me. Not only did he guide me through the process of applying to Barnett, but he helped steer me in the right direction once I was a freshman on campus.

I owe him a huge debt of gratitude.

I know I do. But it can't be at the expense of my relationship with Gia.

"Hey, what are you doing here on a Saturday afternoon? You got nothing better going on?"

I raise a brow and volley the question back at him. "I could ask you the same thing."

His grin broadens. We both know he practically lives here. His life revolves around this job. There's even a small sofa shoved up against the far wall. I've caught the dude sacked out on it a few times.

He shrugs. "Just looking over some high school game film. Got my eye on a QB. Miller is going to need another backup." He gives me a wink before adding, "I found one with a good arm, but he's no Liam Garrison, that's for sure."

Pride fills his voice. He's been telling me since the end of last season that I need to enter the draft and elevate my game. That I'm ready for the next step.

As much as I wish his opinion didn't matter, it does. It's been that way for the last seven years. I have no idea how he'll react when I tell him about my relationship with his ex-girlfriend. Something like that has the potential to destroy everything. And yet, knowing that— knowing what this man means to me—I have to go through with it.

It no longer feels like a choice.

He points to the chair parked on the other side of the desk. I've probably sat my ass in it a hundred times over the course of the last three years. "Go ahead, take a load off."

Once I've settled in, he takes a long look at me. His expression changes, becoming sober. All of the good-natured humor dancing in his eyes vanishes. "Is there something on your mind, son?"

Like I said before, Coach knows me well. He can tell when there's a problem. No matter how hard I try to hide it.

I draw in a breath and realize there won't be any more chit chat. We're delving straight into this. I've never been one for small talk. Not when something is eating at me.

"Spill it, Garrison. It's plain as day that something is going on." He straightens on his chair. "You're not having second thoughts about the draft, are you? It's next weekend." His brows slam together, and I watch as he compiles a quick mental list of all the reasons this is the right move to make.

"Nah, it's nothing like that." If only it were that simple. What I have to tell him isn't easy. I have no idea how to wrap my lips around the words, let alone push them out.

His voice drops. "More trouble at home?"

I shake my head, knowing I can't continue to sit here and avoid the issue. I need to man up and tell him what's going on. "No, everything's good there."

"Then what is it?" He rolls his chair closer as his gaze locks on mine. "If there's a problem, tell me what it is. We'll get it solved." A slightly crooked smile lifts his lips. "We always do."

This is so much harder than I imagined. Frustration pounds through me as I plow my fingers through my hair and glance away. My gaze falls on one of the team photos that line the wall of his office. This one in particular was taken my freshman year. My rookie season. I almost shake my head. We all look like babies. It's hard to believe that Roan, Sam, Dylan, and I will leave Barnett in May before moving on with our lives.

"Liam?"

I don't realize I've become lost in my thoughts until my gaze snaps back to him. And I remember the reason I'm sitting in his office. The statement tumbles from my mouth before I can stop it. For better or worse, it's out there.

"I didn't realize that Gia Monroe was your ex-girlfriend."

His brows slide together. Whatever he thought I was going to say, that wasn't it.

"Okay," he draws out the response, attempting to wrap his mind around the reason I'm bringing this up.

When he says nothing further, I continue. "We met at O'Brien's a few weeks before I gave the presentation to her class. Her brother's band was playing a gig there."

His eyes narrow as his voice turns guarded. It's as if he already has a sneaking suspicion as to the direction this conversation has swerved in. "Where you going with this, Liam?"

"After I ran into her again at the elementary school, I talked her into going out with me."

His lower jaw goes slack. "You were in her classroom at the beginning of February, right?"

I can almost see him mentally tripping back in time, re-examining everything in a new light. "She mentioned there was someone else she'd been seeing," he mutters. All the little pieces that hadn't made sense earlier, now fit perfectly together. "When I ran into you at the club last month, were you there to see her?"

I jerk my head, refusing to lie. "Yeah."

"I can't believe this!" His voice cracks like thunder throughout the small office. "All this time, I've been trying to win her back and she's been fucking around with you!"

I straighten up in my seat. "Coach, it wasn't like that."

He stares at me from across the desk like he doesn't know who the hell I am. "Did you know?" When I remain silent, he grits out, "Did you know we had spent three years together?"

I shake my head. "I thought you were out on a date or something like that. It wasn't until we had the convo in the weight room that I realized you two had been involved in a relationship. And then I backed off."

A heavy silence falls over us as he runs his hand through his hair before leaning back in his chair and staring up at the ceiling. This sucks. Coach and I have always been tight. Not once in all these years has he ever been pissed at me.

I'm wondering if I should leave when he asks, "Are you two together now?"

"No." Even though he's angry, I have to finish this. I can't walk away from his office without laying it all out on the table. "Gia thinks there's too much of an age difference between us." Those words have his gaze sliding to mine. "And she doesn't want to get in the middle of our relationship."

I fidget uneasily on my chair, and realize he's trying to rein in his anger. The internal struggle is written all over his face. I've dropped a major bomb on the guy.

"But you like her?"

It doesn't sound much like a question. I think he already knows the answer. I wouldn't be here, in his office, telling him what happened with his ex-girlfriend if I didn't have strong feelings for her. I wouldn't risk my relationship with him if Gia didn't matter more than anything else.

"Yeah, I do."

His voice grows quiet. "And she cares about you?"

I shrug. "I think so."

He shakes his head. "This is really fucked-up."

Can't deny that. "Yeah."

The flames of his fury—the ones that had been burning so brightly minutes ago—have died down. I've never known Coach Bauer to be a hot head. Out of all the football coaches, he's the most levelheaded and even keeled. That doesn't mean he's not going to get in your face and yell. But if he does, it's warranted.

He spins his chair toward me. "What are you going to do now?"

It might piss him off again, but I need to be truthful. "I want her to give me a chance."

"Even though you're leaving?" His hard gaze bores into mine. "She has a job, Liam. One she loves. She won't give it up to follow you wherever you end up playing ball. That's not Gia. You go after her, you better be damn serious about a relationship."

"I wouldn't expect her to pick up and follow me."

He leans forward, pressing against his desk. "Then why bother pursuing something with her? You have to know it'll only end badly." His gaze narrows and the pissed off expression returns full force. "Are you just looking to screw around until you leave?"

The question is like a slap to my face. "Hell no! I like her, Coach. I've never felt this way about anyone before. But the age difference…" I shake my head before continuing. "It's been an issue from the beginning. Gia can't move past it. And she doesn't want to get in the way of our relationship. She knows how fucked-up everything is at home." Coach understands that my family issues aren't something I share lightly. I'm careful about who I confide in. "She doesn't want me to lose anyone else."

He nods as his expression turns pensive. "Yeah, that sounds like Gia. Always thinking about what's best for everyone."

"Look, Coach, I don't know where I'll end up playing football, but I want to make it work with Gia. Once she's mine, letting her go is the last thing I want."

With a shake of his head, he mutters, "I don't know what to tell you, Liam. I really don't."

This has to be the first time in seven years that I've heard him say that. The guy always knows what to do. I've come to depend on him for solid advice. To be a sounding board for all the issues I'm dealing with.

It seems like this time, I'm on my own.

CHAPTER 36

GIA

We sit in a diner across the street from the garage Liam's friend owns. As a personal favor to him, Tony is going to patch my tire today. It should be ready in about an hour.

Even though he doesn't necessarily need to stay and babysit me, Liam has made it clear he isn't leaving until the tire is taken care of. I should feel thankful, instead his presence makes me feel skittish and on edge.

Especially after yesterday. He hasn't touched me today, but still… my body is tense. It's driving me crazy. My nerves are stretched thin, and I feel like I'll shatter at any moment.

The waitress brings two mugs of steaming coffee before silently retreating. Neither of us bother to order anything to eat.

In a last-ditch effort at self-preservation, I say one more time, "You don't have to stay. It doesn't sound like it'll take all that long and then I'll be on my way."

He takes a sip of his coffee before flashing me a smile. One dark brow rises. "Are you trying to get rid of me?"

The edges of my lips curl up, because we both know that's *exactly* what I'm attempting to do. "Maybe."

He adds a packet of sugar to his mug, not looking offended by my honesty. "And why would you want to do that?"

I roll my eyes.

He watches me from across the table.

"You know the reason, Liam," I say quietly. "It's not a good idea for us to be alone together. There are too many feelings between us."

Emotion flashes in his eyes, as if my words have managed to hit their mark. Maybe he assumed I would continue to tap dance around the subject. The look he drills me with makes my breath catch at the back of my throat. It takes every ounce of strength I have to drop my gaze to the cup now warming my palms.

"It won't work."

My attention jerks back to him as my mouth turns cottony. "What's not going to work?" The words are nothing more than a croak as they leave my lips.

"You getting rid of me," he says easily.

That's all it takes for my heartbeat to pick up its pace beneath my breast. When I remain silent, he reaches across the table before snagging my fingers with his own. "I'm not walking away from this. Even though you keep doing your damnedest to push me away, I'm not going anywhere."

My gaze drops to our connected hands. The way his fingers swallow mine up has my belly hollowing out. What he does to me—the way he makes me feel—it's beyond comprehension.

In all honesty, it hurts to sit here. Maybe I'm the one who pushed him away, but that doesn't mean I don't want him. *Desperately.* I want Liam in my life. This might have started out as a no-strings-attached one-night stand, but it morphed into something infinitely deeper.

More than anything, I wish everything could be different. I wish he were a few years older. Or that I was younger. That he was sticking around and not leaving for the NFL. That he didn't have a personal relationship with my ex-boyfriend.

Liam doesn't need any more issues clouding his future. This is his chance to finally break free and spread his wings. I don't want to be the one weighing him down or holding him back. I don't ever want him to look at me and secretly wish he'd made different choices.

My heart couldn't survive that.

With a sigh, I shake my head. I can't do this with him again. It's too painful to keep dredging up our relationship. We both need to move on.

"What do you want me to say?" Because I'm at a loss. He wants me, and I want him, but sometimes that's not enough.

Sometimes *love* isn't enough.

"I want to know how you feel, Gia. I want you to be honest about your feelings."

"Why? What would be the point?" Baring my soul won't do either of us any good.

"I think we both need to be truthful about our feelings." As I open my mouth, he cuts me off. "Here, I'll make it easy and go first."

I don't know if I can bear to hear any of it. He hasn't spoken one word, and already my heart is shattering into a million jagged pieces.

"I know you have a problem with the difference in our ages, but it doesn't matter to me." He leans forward, gaze locked on mine. As much as I want to glance away, I can't. Was it ever a choice? "Not one damn bit. And I won't be in college after this semester."

"Where will you be living?" I force out the question in order to drive home the point that he could be anywhere in the country.

"I'll know next Saturday," he says calmly. "No matter where I end up, if you're willing to give us a chance, we'll find a way to make it work. I've never made any promises to a woman, but I'm making them to you. I want this. I want *you*. I want *us*. Whatever this is, it's rare. And I'm not willing to walk away from it. I'll keep on fighting."

His words, the raw honesty of them, steal the air from my lungs. And just like I knew it would, everything in me wavers. When we're together, I can block out all the white noise in my head. Liam has the strange ability to make me believe that what we feel for one another is all that will ever matter.

Even though I want to believe what he's telling me, I force myself to say, "But you could end up across the country. Do you realize how difficult that will be?"

"Yeah, I do. But I'm willing to take the chance. Living my life without you isn't an option I'm willing to consider. We'll do what we have to." He takes a deep breath before gradually releasing it back into the world. "Maybe after that first year, we can figure something different out. Maybe after that, we'll be able to make more of a commitment to each other. I'm in this for the long haul, Gia. If that means trying to get back to where you are or you considering a move to where I am, that's something we can deal with down the road. This isn't a casual relationship for me. I'm not burning time until I leave." His gray depths pierce mine. "If you're being completely honest, you'll admit that what we've found has turned out to be more meaningful than any other relationship that's come before it."

Almost desperately—because I can feel the walls crumbling—I say, "I don't understand this. We haven't been together that long. How—"

Liam presses forward, swallowing up the distance between us until the world fades and he's all I'm cognizant of. "Don't you feel it? Whatever you want to call it. Don't you feel it burning brightly between us? Didn't you feel it the first moment we saw each other? I know I did."

The last thing I want to do is encourage him, but I can't keep the truth buried in my heart any longer. Even though I know it would be so much easier for both of us if I did.

How can I not respond in kind when Liam is sitting here, baring his heart so completely?

"Yes," I whisper, "I feel it." I feel it throbbing in the air every moment we're together. Every time I look into his eyes or he grabs hold of my hand. Something magnetic passes between us. Something powerful. Elemental. Almost magical. It sounds ridiculous. Trust me, I know it does. But there's no other way to describe it. "I've always felt it."

"Then you have to realize this is special. And I'll be damned if I throw it away because it's not easy. Or there are obstacles standing in our way. I've always fought for what I wanted, Gia. And this here is *me* fighting for *you.*"

Tears prick my eyes. "I want to, Liam, I really do—"

"I told Coach about our relationship," he says.

My eyes widen as I stare in stunned silence before forcing myself to ask, "You did?" I almost cringe, imagining how blindsided Tyler must have felt.

His gaze never wavers from mine. Even when all I want to do is bury my face in my hands, his attention stays locked on mine. "I ran into him at the athletic center last night."

"Why would you do that?" My voice comes out sounding choked. "We're not together anymore. There was no point in telling him."

I don't want Liam to destroy such an important relationship.

Not for me.

"Don't you get it?" His brows draw together as he shakes his head. "You mean way too much for me to let you walk away without a fight. Whether you like it or not, I'm going to continue to bulldoze my way through all the roadblocks you're so intent on throwing up between us. You think there's so much standing in our way, but I'm going to do everything in my power to prove you wrong."

I nibble at my lower lip as confusion swirls through me. "I don't know what to say."

He squeezes my hand, drawing my attention back to him. "Say that you'll give us a chance, Gia. A real chance to make this work."

There is so much chaos warring inside my head. More than anything, I want to do what he's asking. I want to give this relationship a chance to flourish.

Even though he's eight and a half years younger than I am.

Even though he'll be leaving for God knows where in two months and poised for NFL greatness.

Even though my ex-boyfriend is his mentor. His coach. The one man in his life he can't afford to lose.

"I...I don't know," I whisper.

As he leans back in the booth, his hand falls away from mine. Almost immediately, I feel the loss of his warmth.

"I want you, Gia. I've always wanted you. More than anything, I want *us*. But you have to want it too." His gaze holds mine captive. "You have to want *me*."

CHAPTER 37

GIA

Three days have passed since the conversation with Liam in the coffee shop. Even though everything in me is screaming to reach out and say—*yes, yes, yes*! I haven't. I keep vacillating. If this were solely about me following my heart, it would be a no brainer.

But it's not that simple. Life is never that simple. I have to do what's best for both of us. The dark-haired football player is leading with his heart. I can't allow myself to do that. No one in Liam's life has cared enough to put him first. And he deserves that. More than anything, he deserves to have someone make decisions based solely on what's best for him and him alone. That's what I'm trying to do.

I care too much about him to do anything less.

Tango is curled up on my lap, purring away. I'm about to delve into a stack of papers to grade when the doorbell rings. With a glance at the door, I set down my blue marking pen and scoop up the cat before moving him to the other side of the couch. If the look on his furry face is any indication, he's not pleased by the abrupt relocation.

I can't say I blame him.

"Sorry, buddy." I give him a scratch between the ears because I know he likes it. Within moments, his chainsaw purr starts up again.

Since I'm not expecting anyone, I glance through the peephole in the door before jerking back with a frown.

Tyler.

I can only imagine what his unannounced appearance on my doorstep means. The last thing I want is to get an earful from my ex-boyfriend. Even though I feel like a chicken, I retreat from the door, hoping that if I remain silent, he'll give up and go home.

"Come on, Gia," he says, raising his voice to be heard from the other side of the thick wood, "I know you're in there. I can hear you moving around."

Crap.

When I fail to respond, he tries again. "Gia, please open the door so we can talk."

Other than shame me for sleeping with a guy in college, I'm not sure what we have to discuss.

My belly churns as I huff out a breath and crack open the door. I don't really want to invite him inside. Maybe he can spit out whatever he came here to say from the front porch.

His gaze locks on mine as he shoves his hands in the pockets of his jeans, as if he's as uncomfortable as I am. One of his brows rises when I don't budge from my position in front of the door. "Aren't you going to invite me in?"

I was hoping not to.

Unfortunately, the good manners that have been drilled into me since I was a kid dictate otherwise. I waver before taking a reluctant step backward and allowing him inside. I haven't seen or heard from Tyler since we grabbed dinner and I admitted to being involved with someone else.

Clearly, he now knows who that someone else is.

He looks around, as if to make sure I'm alone. I see the moment his gaze lands on Tango. A resigned look settles over his face. It's one that tells me he's not pleased to see my furry, four-legged friend again.

"Still have your cat, huh?"

I glance at Tango. I swear his bright, green eyes narrow as he studies Tyler in return.

Perturbed by the comment, I fold my arms across my chest. "Yup. He's not going anywhere."

Tyler releases a sigh as his shoulders slump. "Look, I just want to talk. That's it. Give me ten minutes and I'll be out of here."

Even though it's difficult, I force myself to push out the words. "I'm guessing this has to do with Liam?"

He jerks his head in response. "Yeah."

Resigned to this unwelcome interruption, I wave Tyler into the living room. He slides past me, making his way to an overstuffed chair while I settle on the couch by Tango. It's strange to see Tyler look so out of place in my house. He spent two years practically living here. More times than I can remember, he sat in that very chair with his feet kicked up on the ottoman, watching Monday night football with a beer in hand, yelling in frustration when a player did something he didn't like.

But that's no longer the case. The person I thought I might one day marry, now feels like a stranger.

He sits perched on the edge of the cushion. His fingers are threaded tightly together, and his elbows are propped on his knees. He looks uncomfortable. And just as unsettled to be here as I am to find myself parked across from him at seven o'clock on a Wednesday night.

"I don't know if Liam mentioned it, but he stopped by a few days ago to talk with me." His gaze bounces around the room, settling on mine before skittering away.

I give a stiff nod in acknowledgement.

"I can't say I wasn't shocked…"

Heat floods my cheeks. Instead of defending myself, I press my lips tightly together. Obviously, I didn't know Liam was a football player the night we met at O'Brien's. I wouldn't have gone home with him if I'd suspected he was in any way involved with Tyler or the Barnett football program.

That being said, I realized who he was when he showed up at my classroom. I'd put the pieces together before I agreed to have dinner with him, but by that time it was too late.

"I mean, the two of you." Tyler drags a hand through his sandy blond hair before his gaze returns to mine. *"Together—"*

"Yeah," I cut in, wishing he would get to the point, "I get it. You were shocked I was seeing one of your players. Trust me, I was just as surprised when I figured out who he was."

Tyler cocks his head. "But that didn't stop you from starting up a relationship with him. You knew who he was when you decided to get involved."

I nod. There's no denying it—I knew. And it still wasn't enough to stop me. Maybe it should have been. Maybe I wouldn't be stuck in this emotional quagmire if I'd held firm and sent him on his merry way.

But I couldn't do it. Not with the overwhelming attraction that pulsed between us like a living, breathing entity.

Or all the thoughtful gifts he'd sent to the school.

Or getting a firsthand glimpse at the dedication and love he feels for his family.

And certainly not after spending more time with him, getting to know who the man buried beneath the hype is.

I won't even mention the sex.

By that point, there was nothing I could do about my feelings or the deep attraction I felt for him.

"I didn't want to stop seeing him." Embarrassed, I glance at my hands. "I couldn't."

"Liam is a really good kid, Gia."

Him saying that only reinforces everything running rampant through my head. Tyler thinks I took advantage of the younger man.

"He's had a hard time," he continues. "His life hasn't been easy."

"I know. I've seen it firsthand."

Whatever he came here to say, I want him to spit it out and leave. Does he really think I don't know what he's about to unload on me? I've been struggling with it from the beginning. There hasn't been a single day that I didn't tell myself to let Liam go.

I squeeze my eyes tight before biting out, "Why are you telling me this?"

A puff of air leaves his lips. "To a certain extent, I feel responsible for him. I've known Liam since he was a freshman in high school. I've made it my job to watch out for him. I was there. I saw how it broke him when his mother walked away. I also saw how he stepped up to take care of things. How he's continued to do that the entire time he's been going to school. He's not your typical twenty-one-year-old college student."

"I know," I murmur thickly.

When you take the time to get to know Liam—to scratch beneath the surface—it becomes clear that he's had to deal with more hardship than most guys his age. Without those experiences, he wouldn't be the man he is today.

It's part of what attracts me to him. He's been taking care of his family for so long. There's been such a heavy burden on his young shoulders. It makes me want to wrap my arms around him and take care of him. I don't think anyone has done that in a long time, if ever, and he deserves it. He deserves to have someone love him. He deserves to have a soft place to land.

More than anything, I want to be that soft place.

"Why did you come here?" I ask.

For a fleeting moment, Tyler looks as lost and unsure as I feel. "Look, I know I'm not saying this the right way, or maybe it's just not coming out the way I want it to, but I'm okay with you and Liam being together."

What?

"I mean," he rushes to say, "when he first told me, I wasn't good with any of it. The whole thing pissed me off. I realized that I'd been trying to win you back and you were already with someone else. You were falling for *him*." He pauses. Almost as if he's waiting for me to confirm that's precisely how it played out.

"Yes," I admit, "I was seeing Liam at that point."

He sucks in a sharp breath. "Liam deserves to be with someone who loves him for the man he is. He needs someone who can be a true partner to him. In the seven years I've known him, I've seen him go out with numerous girls, but there's never been anyone serious. He's never bothered to show any of them who he really is. He keeps all of it buried beneath the charm and smiles. Those girls were dating Barnett's star quarterback. A future NFL prospect. But it's different with you, Gia. Even though we only spoke about you once, I could tell his feelings for you run deep." There's a pause. "You matter to him."

Now I'm the one left to suck in a sharp breath. "What do you mean?"

He stares down at his fingers. "This is really hard for me. We were together for three years, and part of me still loves you. I don't like to think about you with someone else. Falling in love with someone else."

"Tyler," I murmur, "it was never my intention to hurt you. I never wanted to come between you two."

He glances up, his gaze skewering mine. "I know, Gia. It took me a few days to calm down. Once I did, I realized that what happened between you two had nothing to do with me. You didn't set out to hurt me." He shrugs. "I guess what I'm trying to say is that if you feel there's a future for your relationship, you should take it."

I search my brain for a response, but there's nothing. I never imagined that Tyler would be okay with this situation.

It takes a moment for me to force out the question. "You don't have a problem with him being so much younger than I am?"

"Honestly?" He cocks his head.

I brace myself before nodding.

He releases a steady inhalation. "No, I don't. In fact, him wanting to be with someone older doesn't surprise me at all. I think Liam comes across as laid back—someone out for a good time—but that's not who he is. It's nothing more than a persona. I don't think anyone has ever taken the time to see beneath the surface to the man he truly is." He pauses. "If you two really like each other, then you shouldn't let the age difference get in the way of that."

Even though it's surreal to sit here with Tyler and have a discussion about my love life— hell, sit here and listen to him encourage me to get involved with another man—I can't help but admit, "There's more than just our ages standing in our way."

"Life is too damn short not to be with the person you really want.

If you care for Liam, then all the other bullshit keeping you apart is just that—*bullshit*. And it shouldn't matter. I think you need to ask yourself if you can really walk away and let him go."

Emotion squeezes my heart as I consider the possibility of doing exactly that. "I don't want to."

"Then you have your answer, Gia."

CHAPTER 38

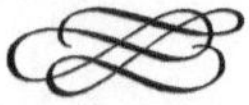

GIA

"Ms. Monroe?"

I glance at Isabella, who has snuck up on me when I wasn't paying attention. It's not something that happens often, but this situation with Liam has thrown me off my game. And I hate it. I hate that I'm so easily distracted and not giving one hundred percent to my kids.

"Yes, Bella?"

"Are we having a guest today?"

I frown, wondering why she would ask the question. One of the first things we do in the morning is go over our schedule for the day. If there's a change, that's the time it's mentioned. The class functions better when they know what to expect.

"Nope. Today is a normal day. No speakers or assemblies." I tilt my head. "Why do you ask?"

She points a finger toward the door.

Air rushes from my lungs as my gaze collides with a gunmetal-gray one.

Liam.

What's he doing here?

He holds up his hand in tentative greeting. "Hi."

As he stands at the threshold of the room—looking so damn sexy in a navy Henley and jeans with his leather jacket hanging open in the front—I realize how thrilled I am to see him.

The draw I feel is inescapable, and I take two steps in his direction before turning toward the kids. Most of them are sitting at their tables, waiting patiently for further instructions. "All right," I say, pausing until all eyes are on me. "Why don't you take out your independent chapter books, find your reading spots, and we'll flip reading with math today. Does that sound like a plan?"

The kids cheer, just as I suspected they would.

We're starting to work on triple digit subtraction and borrowing. For some of them, it's a difficult concept to wrap their little eight-year-old brains around. With enough practice, they'll all get there.

Once the children are settled around the room in their special spots, my gaze fastens on Liam as I close the distance between us. My legs turn rubbery, and I'm reminded of the first time he showed up in my classroom. I can't help but twist my fingers nervously in front of me. All I really want to do is reach out and grab hold of him.

When there's no more than a foot separating us, I force myself to stop. "What are you doing here?"

Even though it's only been a few days since I saw him, it feels like forever. I want to stand here and soak up every little detail. He's like bright sunlight filtering down on my face. I can't help but want to be near him.

"I didn't want to leave town without saying goodbye in person, especially since I don't know where we stand. I can't go into the draft with all these questions lingering in my mind. I need to lay them to rest, Gia." He shifts his weight. "One way or the other."

When I remain silent, he steps closer.

"The NFL draft is probably one of the greatest things that has ever happened to me. And yet..." His voice dips until it sounds as if it's been dredged from the bottom of the ocean. "You're all I can think about. The draft will change my world, but you've already done that. You're more important than anything else."

Liam walking into my room had my heart melting. His softly

spoken words, the power of them, makes it crumble. The walls I've tried to keep cemented in place tumble down like a cheap house of cards. Everything he does, everything he says, makes it impossible for me to keep my distance.

To hold myself back.

To make the right decision.

The one that sets him free to live his life.

I open my mouth to tell him what he means to me, but nothing comes out.

His face turns ashen as he jerks his head toward the roomful of kids. A few peek at us from behind the books they're pretending to read.

"It wasn't my intention to interrupt. I know you're in the middle of your day." The hope filling his eyes when he first walked into my room has been extinguished. "I should probably take off." He takes a step away from me. "Stopping here was a mistake."

As he swings away, my body kicks into high gear and I lunge for him. "No! Don't leave!" My heart thumps a painful staccato as I eat him up with my eyes.

Unsure what to say or where to start, I ramble. "I was going to call. I wanted to talk with you, but I wasn't sure..."

He nods, as if attempting to understand what I'm so desperate to tell him. The vulnerability that had been shining in his eyes is no longer present. He glances away before running his hand over his hair. It's styled in its trademark fauxhawk. My fingers itch to plow their way through it.

"I'm not trying to rush a decision from you. In fact, I didn't have any intention of stopping here, but then I found myself in the parking lot. And I knew I couldn't leave without seeing you. Without talking to you in person." There's a beat of silence. "At least one more time."

Those words are my breaking point. With it, every last doubt gets swept away on a rising tide of need. No longer am I able to deny or hold it in.

"If you still want me, then yes, I'm ready to do this. I want to make this work. You were right about everything you said. About me throwing up roadblocks because I was scared. That's exactly what I was doing. I was afraid to let go. Afraid there was too much stacked against us for this to work out in the end. And I was afraid to put my trust in your hands. But I'm not afraid anymore. You're the best thing that's ever happened to me, Liam Garrison. I don't want to lose you."

His gaze darts to the kids scattered around the room before cutting to mine. I get the feeling if he could drag me into his arms, that's exactly what he would do. When his voice rumbles up from deep in his chest, it's low and full of need. "You have no idea how badly I want to kiss you right now. It feels like I've been waiting forever to hear you say those words."

I can only shake my head at my own stupidity. Because that's exactly what I've been. Stupid. Misguided. Scared. I'm lucky he stuck around this long and isn't telling me to go to hell. How did I find such a wonderful man?

"I'm sorry I put you through this and made you wait. It was never you I was uncertain of." I gulp and force out the rest. "It was me."

I can only wonder why it took me so long to realize that.

Liam is perfect.

He's absolutely perfect for me.

Maybe that's the part that scared me the most.

"I'm sorry I gave you any reason to question my feelings. I care more than you'll ever know. I always have. Even when I was fighting against myself, trying to convince myself that I shouldn't be with you, that we weren't right for one another, I still had feelings for you."

Even though he tries to keep his distance—for propriety's sake—he steps closer. He leans toward me, staring into my eyes until he's all I'm aware of.

"What about the age difference? It'll always be there, Gia. Nothing will ever change it. You'll always be eight and a half years older than I am. I don't want to get in any deeper with you, open myself up even more, if you're only going to push me away in the end."

"I won't," I whisper. "I've already tried to let you go, and I couldn't do it."

"And Coach Bauer?"

I suck in a sharp breath at the mention of Tyler, and scan the quiet classroom, making sure everyone is still on task, doing what they're supposed to. For the most part, they are.

This isn't the time or place to discuss Tyler. "He won't be a factor."

For the first time since stepping foot inside my classroom, Liam's jaw unclenches as his expression relaxes. I didn't realize how tense he'd been until now.

"Good." His voice drops until I have to strain to hear his words. "You're mine, Gia. You always have been. Don't think for a moment that I'll ever allow anything to come between us. From the beginning, I knew you were special. And that will never change."

Unconsciously, my body strains toward him. All I want is to be wrapped up in his arms. But that's not possible. Not with twenty-six pairs of eyes watching us.

Liam clears his throat, and a smile curves his lips. It's as if he can read my mind.

"Are you going to kiss Ms. Monroe?" Isabella asks.

"Yeah, are you going to kiss her or what?" Aiden calls out.

Surprised by the comments, we turn toward the kids. All those little faces peering up at us with excitement.

"Do you think I should?" Liam asks, as if he's seriously debating the question. It's kind of hilarious. I love how at ease he is with them.

All twenty-six kids cheer so loudly that I can't help the gurgle of laughter that escapes.

"All right, then," he says, sliding an arm around my waist, "I should probably kiss her, right?"

They cheer even louder this time.

As Liam lowers his face to mine, I can almost hear their collective breaths catch in their throats before he abruptly pulls away. He glances at the children again as uncertainty flickers across his face. "You really think I should kiss Ms. Monroe?"

Another rousing cheer rings through the classroom. It's even louder than before. I'm half afraid Mrs. Davies, the principal, will poke her head inside the door, wondering what we're up to.

Liam laughs before holding up a hand. "All right, all right. I'll do it." He rolls his eyes. "Sheesh."

I wait with wide eyes, unable to believe he'll kiss me in front of my second-grade class. I can only imagine the calls and emails I'll be bombarded with after they go home and excitedly share what happened today.

As Liam leans in for a second time, his lips scant inches from my own, the door connecting my room with the other second grade classroom, flies open.

"What's going—"

Harper skids to a halt as her gaze lands on us. Her eyes widen as she stands there with her mouth hanging open. All the kids groan and complain about her untimely interruption.

She quickly pulls herself together again. "I was, ah, going to give my kids a fifteen-minute recess for doing so well on their math test yesterday. I thought maybe your class would like to join us out on the playground."

All interest in the kiss is now forgotten as they stare pleadingly at me.

"I don't know…" I begin before they all start begging. The classroom fills with beseeching voices.

"Please, Ms. Monroe?"

"Come on, Ms. Monroe!"

"Yeah, we need to get all our sillies out. Then we'll be ready for math."

Unable to hold it back any longer, I unleash a smile. "That's an excellent point, Aiden. I suppose you should go with Ms. Bennet so you can get out some of that energy."

They jump up and down excitedly, pumping their fists in the air. A second recess is a rare reward they get when they've been exceedingly good.

Once I hold up my hand, all of them freeze, waiting for further instructions. "Very quickly, grab your jackets and line up at the door."

No one utters a peep as they follow my directions. I nod and smile at them as Harper disappears to get her class ready. When all her kids have been outfitted with winter jackets, and mine are waiting eagerly, Harper meets them outside the classroom door. Quietly, they file into the hallway.

When the last child disappears around the corner, Liam walks to the exit before locking us inside. His gaze holds mine as he stalks toward me. My heart skitters with every step that's swallowed up between us. When he's close enough, he pulls me into his arms.

His warm breath feathers over my hair as he inhales deeply. "I thought I'd lost you, Gia. When I didn't hear anything, I figured you decided I wasn't worth taking a chance on."

I untangle myself from his embrace until I can meet his gaze. "I wanted you from the beginning, but I was scared of everything that stood in our way. My heart always belonged to you."

"You know I'll be careful with it, right?"

I think I've always known that. "I trust you, Liam. I trust you with every piece of me."

With that, he tugs me back into his arms. "I would never do anything to hurt you. You've owned my heart since you first walked into O'Brien's."

He tips my chin until my gaze can lock on his. "I don't know what the future holds or where I'll end up playing next year. The only thing I know for sure is that I want to face the future with you at my side."

"I want that too," I whisper. More than I ever allowed myself to believe.

As those words fall from my lips, his mouth crashes down on mine. Even though we're standing in the middle of my empty classroom, I open to him. His tongue slips inside my mouth as everything around us goes silent.

Until it's just the two of us.

The way it was always meant to be.

EPILOGUE

LIAM

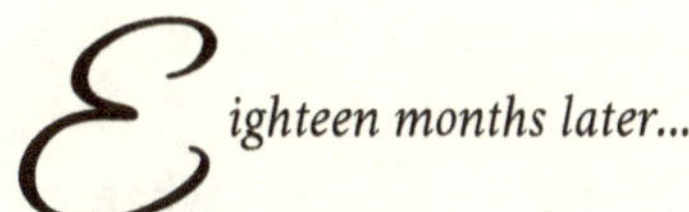

ighteen months later...

"Here you go, babe."

I open the sliding door that leads out to the brick paver patio, and hand Gia a glass of decaf unsweetened iced tea.

She flashes a grateful smile. I'm not sure if the expression is because she's happy to see me or for the tea. Although, I'm going with the latter. I'm beginning to suspect that Gia might be addicted to the stuff.

After swallowing down half the glass, she relaxes onto the plush lounger before a sigh of contentment escapes from her lips. "Thanks. That was *exactly* what I needed."

I chuckle and cock a brow in her direction. "Oh, really? I seem to recall those being your exact words last night. For the record, it wasn't tea I gave you."

Her smile broadens as a sexy glint ignites in her eyes as they stay focused on me. I'm not going to lie, that's exactly where I like them. "But this time I actually mean it. I had a serious craving for that tea."

I drop onto the seat next to her and bark out a laugh. "I'll remember that the next time you're coming on to me in the middle of the night, whining about how horny you are. Know what I'm going to tell you? Go find your damn tea."

"Awww," she says, giving me her best pouty face, "don't be like that."

I have a hard time resisting that look. And she knows it. The woman has me wrapped around her little finger.

And you know what?

I wouldn't have it any other way.

"You know I've developed a real craving for unsweetened tea over the last couple of months."

"Yeah." I snort before shaking my head. "Not to mention grilled bratwursts and smoked string cheese."

"Oh, that sounds good!" She pats her tummy. "I think the baby wants you to fire up the grill tonight."

Now that makes me laugh. "Well, the baby can have whatever he—"

"Or *she*," Gia cuts in like she always does. It's become a bit of a thing between us.

"Or *she* wants," I concede with a nod like I always do, because at this point, I don't give a damn what we have as long as he or she is healthy. I've been doing a lot of reading this offseason about all the things that can go wrong. It's pretty amazing there are any healthy babies born at all.

Gia beams from the lounger she's sprawled on. The patio is one of her favorite spots in the house. The yard backs up to a wooded nature preserve where there's an abundance of wildlife. I've never seen Gia look so relaxed or happy.

I have a sneaking suspicion I've got the same contented smile etched across my face because I've honestly never been happier in my life. And that has everything to do with the woman at my side. This pregnancy may have been unplanned and one hell of a surprise, but I wouldn't have it any other way. I love Gia with all my heart. And I couldn't be more ecstatic about this baby.

Once she told me, I hustled her adorable ass onto a plane bound for Vegas so we could make this official. Gia didn't fight me at all. Since I'd already proposed marriage, hastening things didn't really seem like a big deal.

After getting drafted to Green Bay as their backup quarterback, I finished out my junior year of college and then stayed with Gia until I left for training camp. Since I knew I was never going to let this woman go, I convinced her to road trip to Green Bay so she could help me pick out a house. She stayed in Wisconsin until the end of August when it was time for her to head back for the upcoming school year.

I'm not going to lie, the separation was hard as fuck.

The last thing I wanted to do was let her go.

I'll admit I did my best to convince her to put in her notice and find a teaching position in Green Bay. I even looked into what she would have to do to transfer her teaching license to the state of Wisconsin, which means I left paperwork all over the house.

But Gia was having none of it. She said she'd made a commitment to North Hill, to the district, not to mention her incoming students, and wasn't about to leave them scrambling for a new teacher at this point in the summer.

How could I argue with that?

My sweet girl is always thinking about what's best for her students. Gia Garrison is a woman who takes her commitments seriously. It's one of the things I love about her. And trust me, I love her something fierce. She's the best damn thing that's ever happened to me. The life we're building together is more than I could have dreamed possible.

Once she headed back, we spent the season FaceTiming, calling, and visiting when we could. She spent breaks with me at our house in Green Bay, and when I had a bye week, I flew to see her. Once my rookie season was over, I stayed with Gia at her house, and we discussed what our future looked like.

Proposing was a no brainer.

I knew Gia was special from the first moment I laid eyes on her, and nothing has convinced me otherwise. She's the perfect woman for me. All I'm trying to do is be the perfect man for her.

With August right around the corner, I can't help but ask, "Are you having second thoughts about moving here?"

She rubs her baby bump before shaking her head. Have I mentioned how much I enjoy kissing that adorable little belly of hers?

"Nope." Even she looks surprised by her answer. I know how much she loved teaching second grade at North Hill. "I'll miss being in the classroom this year, but there's no point when this little one is going to be born in five months. I'd have to take a maternity leave and miss the last part of the year."

It's hard to believe our entire world will be irreversibly rocked in five months.

"I can always look for a new position the following year." She shrugs, as if it's no big deal. "We'll play it by ear."

I like that she's keeping an open mind about going back to work. No matter what her decision is, I'll support her the same way she supports me. After the initial shock of the pregnancy test, Gia settled quickly into the idea of motherhood. She seems happy and content with the way our life is unfolding.

I love that she's here with me. It's amazing how everything has fallen into place. Sure, there've been a few bumps in the road. That's called being in a relationship. But we stuck it out and overcame all the obstacles in our way.

Sometimes you just gotta have faith that everything will work out the way it was meant to.

Gia and I are in this for the long haul, and with her by my side, there's nothing I can't accomplish. There's nothing we can't achieve together. We make a great team. And we make a great family.

If I've learned anything from this, it's that when you find that person—the one who changes everything—you don't let go.

Not ever.

***

Thank you so much for reading Gia and Liam's story! I hope you enjoyed One Night Stand as much as I loved writing it! The Barnett Bulldogs Series continues with Claire & JT's story.
One-click If You Were Mine now!

Know what's worse than being a twenty-one-year-old virgin?

Having the bad boy of the NFL, who also happens to be my brother's teammate, offer to take care of that pesky little problem.

Excuse me while I cue the laughter.

If there's one person I can barely tolerate —it's JT Higgins.

He might be talented on the field, but he's even more notorious for his bar brawls, drunken antics, and the women who flock to him in droves.

I've spent the last three years shutting down his every advance.

So, ignoring him should be a piece of cake, right?

Wrong.

JT was given an ultimatum at the end of last season—clean up his act or get traded. For some strange reason, my brother decided to take the younger man under his wing. Now the golden-haired, green-eyed mountain of muscle is around all the time. If he's not parked across from me during Thursday night family dinners, he's knocking on the door and maneuvering his way inside when I'm babysitting my niece and nephews. Or he's popping up at the shop where I grab coffee on my way to school.

What I'd like to know is when his gaze began to feel like a physical caress.

It's enough to make me scream.

It's also enough to send my pulse skyrocketing and my resolve to the brink of shattering.

Here's the problem...this new and improved JT—the one who doesn't whore around or drink—is more difficult to resist.

Especially when his attention is focused solely on me.

One-click If You Were Mine now!

Turn the page for an excerpt to If You Were mine...

IF YOU WERE MINE

CLAIRE

I watch him with narrowed eyes from my covert position inside the house. Even when we're nowhere near one another, the man is still able to burrow deep under my skin. Like an itch I just can't scratch. It's irritating as hell.

No, *he's* irritating as hell.

Someone needs to explain to me why he even bothered to show up today.

This is hardly his scene.

He's lounging on the patio in a pair of vibrantly colored board shorts. His thickly muscled legs are stretched out lazily in front of him. Even though there's a smile curving his lips, he can't possibly be enjoying himself. He's probably bored out of his ever-loving mind. This is a G-rated, Disney-esque family barbecue. Not a wild, drunken orgy where women will be abandoning their bikinis in an hour or two once they're liquored up.

In case you were wondering, JT Higgins is definitely more of a drunken orgy kind of guy. Trust me, my conclusions haven't been drawn from a few questionable lapses in judgment on his part.

It's taken *years* for him to cultivate this kind of reputation. He was already making a name for himself at whatever Big Ten university he attended before being drafted by Green Bay three years ago. He may play professional football, but he's even more notorious for his alcohol-induced antics, bar brawls, and, of course, the females who flock to him in droves.

For the life of me, I can't figure out why any self-respecting woman would actually want to be with him, let alone broadcast it to the world at large. It's a well-known fact that the guy dips his wick in anything that moves.

Gross.

It's not just groupies who lose their minds over him. He's been linked with his fair share of actresses and models as well. I think he was even seeing two chicks from the US Women's National Soccer Team last year.

At the same time.

From what I read online, it didn't end well.

The only possible upside I can see to all his *activity* is that he's probably keeping some clinic in business with penicillin and swab tests.

"Why is *who* here?"

Not realizing that I muttered the question out loud, my brother's wife, Gia, steps beside me and scans the backyard as if she can pick out who I'm talking about, all the while bouncing four-month-old baby Max in her arms.

Yanked from my thoughts, I attempt to cover my slip up. "Hmmm? What? Did I say something?"

Since her arms are full, she nods toward the patio where roughly seventy people are enjoying the early September sunshine. They're definitely a loud, boisterous group. It's football players and their wives or girlfriends along with offspring. People are lounging in the pool or playing bocce ball in the sand pit. A volleyball net has also been set up on the wide, expansive back lawn. Others are hanging out at the many tables that have been scattered around the brick paver patio.

My roommate, Holly, tagged along with me today. She's busy soaking up the sunshine on a lounger near the pool and enjoying all the man candy on display. This is our second year living together. We spent last year in the dorms and recently moved into an apartment off campus.

It's a tradition for Liam to host a Labor Day party at his place. Everyone from the team is invited. Since it's an open house, friends and teammates will drop by throughout the day. The party starts around two, lasting well into the night before ending with a professional firework display.

It's something I look forward to all summer long. Everyone always has a good time. Liam and Gia are gracious hosts and go out of their way to make everyone feel welcome and included. There's plenty of food and drinks being served. If you walk away hungry at the end of this party, it's your own fault.

Gia gives me a knowing look before asking again, "Who were you talking about?"

A slight blush creeps its way up my cheeks as the fib slides off my lips. "No one. Just mumbling to myself."

She narrows her blue eyes and gives me one of those deep, speculative stares that would normally leave me squirming. It's a relief when she doesn't push the issue.

As far as I'm concerned, JT is a complete ass and not worth wasting my breath on. Especially when there's a party in full swing. I'm just going to ignore him. Should be simple enough. It's not like I haven't had lots of practice.

Out of all the players on the team, why did my brother have to take an interest in JT Higgins?

It was bad enough when I occasionally ran into him at team events and functions, but now he's hanging around all the time. It probably wouldn't be so bad if he weren't always trying to strike up a conversation with me.

But that's exactly what he does.

Even though he knows perfectly well that I don't care for him.

I'm so lost in thought that I don't realize I'm still staring until clear green eyes collide with mine. A jolt of electricity spears through my body as my breath gets lodged at the back of my throat before I rip my gaze away.

Gia points toward a group of football players. "Looks like Ryan is here."

Careful to avoid JT's gaze, I cautiously glance back out the window, only to find my boyfriend standing in the midst of all that testosterone.

He looks completely awed by the company he's keeping.

I'm not sure if I should be miffed that he couldn't be bothered to find me first and say hello.

I met Ryan freshman year. His dorm was situated next to mine, so I'd see him frequently in the cafeteria or walking to and from class. He introduced himself after the first few weeks of school, and occasionally, we'd get together to study. Sometimes, he would invite me to a party, but I always declined.

Ever since I can remember, school has been a challenge. I'm not one of those people who can cram for a few hours and sail through a test with an A. In fact, that's a surefire way for me to flunk an exam. I've always had to work harder and longer than my friends to get the same grades. And I knew college was going to be more rigorous than high school. Instead of getting caught up in all the social stuff, I concentrated on my studies.

This semester, I'll start student teaching. I'm excited to finally step into a classroom. Now that I'm in the program and have the first three years of college under my belt, I feel like I can finally loosen the reins just a smidge. Maybe even have more of a social life than I've allowed myself in the past.

It's the reason I finally caved to Ryan after three years. We've been seeing each other for two months. We're definitely not the kind of couple who has to spend every waking moment together. Since we're both busy, we usually see each other a few times a week. We go out to dinner, grab coffee, see a movie, or hit a few parties.

I've yet to invite him to stay over at my place now that I finally have an apartment off campus, even though he keeps hinting at it.

I almost snort.

All right, he does way more than hint.

Up until this point, I haven't been ready to take our relationship further. I don't know what's holding me back, but something is. Maybe it's just first-time jitters.

I certainly didn't set out to save myself for someone special. I've been so focused on school and spending time with my brother and his family that sex was never a priority. But now, suddenly, I'm a senior in college. It's like I blinked and realized that I'll be graduating this spring.

Just as I'm about to respond to Gia, my gaze is ensnared by green ones for a second time. Another reluctant shiver shimmies down my spine as I yank my attention away yet again.

I really wish he would stop staring.

"I'm going to head out and say hello to Ryan." I force a bright smile before tickling the chubby baby in Gia's arms.

At this point, Max's eyes appear to be a gorgeous, deep gray. Even though they could still change, I don't think they will. Both Liam and I have the exact same shade.

"Want me to take Max?" There's nothing I love more than spending time with my niece and nephews. The two older kids are bundles of boundless energy. I don't know where they get it from. They're exhausting, but in the best way possible.

The question isn't even all the way out of my mouth when she drops the baby into my arms. "Sure, why don't you give him to Liam so I can get more food out onto the table? Looks like things are running low."

"No problem." I cuddle his wiggly four-month-old body close to mine before inhaling a great big breath of baby. As I do, everything inside me settles, just like it always does.

Max is like taking a handful of Xanax.

Totally addictive and completely necessary.

Especially when JT Higgins is in the vicinity.

One-click If You Were Mine now!

LOVE TO HATE YOU

DAISY

*L*ogan brushes a stray lock of hair away from my face.

"I had fun tonight," he says.

His husky voice sends a shiver of desire careening down my spine. I love that feeling. The one you get when you're out with someone new, and you're really clicking. And you think, *Yeah, this could actually go somewhere.*

That's exactly what I'm feeling right now. That little voice inside my head is screaming, *Ding, ding, ding, we have a winner.*

"Me, too," I murmur before shoving the key into the lock of the apartment door.

This is going to sound corny as hell, but time stands still as we gaze into each other's eyes. Have I mentioned that Logan has the dreamiest eyes? They're deep and soulful. I can practically feel myself getting lost in them.

His eyes were the first thing I noticed.

The second?

That he's cute.

Cute boys have always been a weakness of mine. He's handsome in a frat boy kind of way, with perfectly styled blond hair and an athletic build that's not overly muscular. I'm a sucker for that look. It should *not*, however, be confused with the douchey frat boy look.

There's a fine line between the two.

It takes a bit of effort for me to tamp down my rising excitement. The last thing I want to do is jump the gun. This is only the third time we've hung out together, but so far, it looks extremely promising. Even better than that, it feels like we're both on the same page.

I like him, and he seems to return the interest.

My fingers are crossed that my roommates have vacated the premises for the evening. If I were a betting woman, I'd say the odds were in my favor. After all, it's almost ten o'clock on a Friday night. Everyone with a social life at BU knows that's prime party time.

That's the only reason I chanced it and invited Logan up. I want to spend time alone with him, so we can get to know each other better. Since he lives at the Pi Kappa house, the idea of going over to his place was immediately nixed. I may be a lot of things, but stupid isn't one of them.

For the time being, it's my place or making out in his Ford Escape. And since I only live a few blocks from campus, police patrol the area on a regular basis. The last thing I need is a ticket for public indecency.

Ummm, no thank you.

I open the door and almost pump my fist at the silence that greets us. But I refrain, wanting to play it cool. Instead, I turn to Logan with an overly bright smile and he grins in response.

See? We *are* on the same page.

I flick on the hallway light and point toward the living area. "Make yourself comfortable. Do you want something to drink?" I head to the kitchen which is separated from the living area by a breakfast bar with three stools tucked under the faux granite counter.

"Sure, whatever you have is fine." Rather adorably, he shoves his hands into the pockets of his khakis and surveys the apartment.

I can't help but stop and take him in. He really is cute. I'm tempted to do a little happy dance in the kitchen but I'm afraid he'll catch me. I'll have to content myself to a mental jig until later.

"This is a really nice place," he says.

"Thanks. We just moved in a few weeks ago."

Our apartment has three bedrooms and two bathrooms. I was lucky enough to snag the master bedroom, so I have a private bathroom all to myself. The living room has a small dining room connected to it. While the kitchen isn't spacious, it's open to the main living area, which makes it feel bigger. It's perfect for the three of us.

I grab two bottles of water from the refrigerator and head back to where Logan has settled on the couch. He's tall. Probably around six feet. His legs are stretched out in front of him. I hand over a plastic bottle and sit next to him. Close, but not too close.

He twists off the cap and takes a long swallow before leaning forward and setting it on the coffee table. Then he relaxes on the couch and throws an arm across the top of the cushions. His fingers brush against my shoulder, and his mouth lifts into a sexy smile.

Mine does the same as my gaze drops to his lips. We've kissed a few times and Logan is a good kisser.

I'm pretty sure that I'm giving him the green light to lean in and plant one on me again.

At least I hope I am.

Logan raises his other hand to my cheek as the arm around my shoulder pulls me toward him.

"You're so pretty," he murmurs, gradually moving in for the kill.

Anticipation floods my system. Other than Logan, there hasn't been much making out going on. I spent most of the summer with my mother—

Best to stop that thought in its tracks. Thinking about Mom will kill the mood, so I'm not going to dwell on her. All my thoughts are on Logan and his very kissable lips that are oh-so-slowly descending toward mine.

My eyes are on the verge of drifting shut when an audible click shatters the silence, and the living room is flooded with bright light. Logan and I leap apart like guilty teenagers who've just been caught having sex in the basement by my parents. My hammering heart is lodged somewhere in my throat.

What the—

I blink, focusing my attention on the muscular form leaning against the wall with his arms crossed over his broad chest and hiss out an exacerbated breath.

Goddamn it.

I should have known better.

Carter fucking Prescott. Or better known as the biggest pain in my ass.

What the hell is he doing here?

He's supposed to be out getting his drunk on with Noah and holding court with his fan club. I overheard them discussing their plans earlier this afternoon.

Was I eavesdropping?

Please, as if…

What I was doing is a little something called recon. I humph out an irritated breath for all the good it did me. This is precisely the situation I was hoping to avoid.

I blink and realize with another wave of shock that Carter isn't wearing any clothes. How did I miss that? He casually rests against the wall in a pair of white, torso-hugging briefs stamped with red and black roosters.

What.

The.

Hell?

I could seriously die right now. Someone needs to shoot me and put me out of my misery before this gets any worse.

Too late.

Logan stiffens beside me. And not in the way I was hoping for, either.

Before I have a chance to blast Carter into next week, he saunters into the room and plops himself down on the ugly, oversized recliner situated across from us. I hate that eyesore and opposed it being moved into the apartment.

I was overruled.

Unaware, or—more accurately—uncaring that I'm about to blow a gasket, Carter lifts his chin in Logan's direction. "Hey, what's up?"

I sputter in anger. Carter's all nonchalant, as if he's not strutting around practically naked and interrupting my date.

Poor Logan doesn't know what to make of the situation.

"Ahhh…" he falters and stares wide-eyed as if Carter is a horrific traffic accident that he's unable to rip his eyes away from.

I feel much the same way.

We're talking bodies strewn across the pavement and several fatalities.

You can bet that once I get my hands on Carter, he's going to be one of them.

Carter sits with his legs spread wide. Unfortunately, both Logan and I are treated to an excellent view of his rather impressive package.

Crap. Did I seriously just think that?

Logan averts his gaze and mutters from the side of his mouth, "Who *is* this guy and what's he doing in your apartment?"

Wanting to downplay the situation, I wave a hand in Carter's direction as if what's happening is perfectly normal. "Oh…him?" I force out a chuckle. "He's just one of my roommates."

Logan's brows skyrocket across his forehead as his eyes pop wide. Under different circumstances, the expression would be comical. Sadly, this is not one of those occasions. My prospects for the evening have officially tanked. A smirk settles around the corners of Carter's lips as if he's reached the same conclusion.

Grrrr.

Logan shoots me a confused look. "You live with a dude?"

I bite my lower lip, racking my brain for a plausible explanation that will smooth over the situation and get us back on track. But my mind remains blank. There's nothing but crickets chirping up there.

"Actually, she lives with two dudes," Carter unhelpfully supplies.

Logan's face contorts with shock. "Is that true?"

Heat floods my cheeks, and I clear my now bone-dry throat. "Well, um, yes."

"Are you two like," Logan narrows his eyes and waggles a finger between us, "*a thing*? Because I'm not getting in the middle of some weird dating situation."

"What? No!" I let loose a high-pitched, nervous giggle that sounds ridiculously loud in the stillness of the apartment and babble, "We're not a thing! Not at all!"

I wait for Carter to jump in and open his big fat trap, but he remains quiet. I'm going to throttle him with my bare hands. It's the only thought getting me through the moment.

"I live with my cousin," I mutter. "And his friend."

Logan flicks a skeptical look in Carter's direction, but since he's still reclining with his legs spread and his manhood proudly on display, my date quickly averts his eyes. "Please tell me this is your cousin," Logan pleads.

"It's not." As soon as I mumble the words, I know that as promising as our evening started out, this is the end.

As if to confirm my silent musings, Logan shoots to his feet and whirls toward me. "Sorry, Daisy. Whatever you've got going on here is a little too complicated for me." He straightens his shoulders.

Did I mention that Logan has amazing shoulders?

Broad and sculpted?

Yeah...

"I'm out," Logan says.

The firm set of his jaw tells me that there's no point in arguing.

Not sparing Carter another glance, Logan beelines for the door as if he's just discovered that I'm a serial killer intent on making lampshades out of his hide. I don't bother getting up to escort him out. Instead, I glare at Carter, who sits nonchalantly across from me.

Maybe if I focus my attention hard enough he'll burst into flames.

No such luck.

The apartment door closes with a resounding thud.

Carter scratches his shadowed jaw. "Well, that was certainly odd. Why do you think he took off so quickly?" A smile hovers around the edges of his lips, and I grit my teeth. It takes everything I have inside not to grab the lamp on the end table and heave it in his direction.

"Yes," I bite out. "Him leaving was definitely the odd part of the evening." I tap my chin a few times. "Whereas you prancing around in your underwear with your cock on display was not."

His shoulders tremble with silent mirth. He clears his throat and admonishes, "I hope you're talking about the roosters and not—"

"What are you even doing here?" I snap. There's only so much I can take before I totally lose it. And I've just approached the limit. I'll never understand why Carter enjoys messing with me. It's maddening.

"Umm, I live here." He arches a brow as if I'm slow on the uptake. "Remember?"

"It would be impossible to forget." I fold my arms across my chest and scowl. "Why aren't you out with Noah?"

Noah is my cousin. He's also Carter's friend and teammate, which is how I got roped into this disastrous living situation in the first place.

Think about how awesome it'll be, Daze. Senior year will be a blast.

Yeah…not so much.

Carter shrugs, looking perfectly at ease lounging around in his super-tight, leaving-absolutely-nothing-to-the-imagination undies. "Guess I wasn't feeling it."

I snort. *Yeah, right.* "Since when?"

I've known Carter for three years. When *isn't* he up for a party or heading to the bars and dragging home a one-night stand?

All right, fine. There's usually no dragging involved. Women flock to him in droves. His short dark hair, piercing gray eyes, and athletic build honed from years of playing football and lacrosse is college girl catnip. And the fact that he's headed to the NFL only ups his hotness factor.

According to other girls.

Not me.

Carter takes a moment to study his blunt-tipped fingernails as if they're extremely interesting. "Maybe I wanted to spend the evening at home, relaxing in my Calvin Kleins." His gaze shifts toward mine.

A sizzle of unwanted energy zips through my body as they collide. I clench my teeth against the onslaught, desperate to ignore the sexual tug I feel for him. It's been there, simmering in the background, since freshman year and has yet to wane. I've told myself repeatedly that it's not a big deal to feel attracted to someone you're barely able to tolerate. But secretly, it bothers me on a deep level because I don't want to feel it. Carter annoys the hell out of me. My reaction to him is always instantaneous and visceral.

For the hundredth time, I curse my cousin, Noah. If it weren't for him, I wouldn't be stuck sharing space with Carter. But there's nothing that can be done about it now. I'm locked into the rental agreement and the academic school year has only begun. I've got eight long months ahead of me…

To not kill him.

With my bare hands.

We'll see if I'm able to get through it.

I tap my foot against the polished wood floor and scowl. Humor flashes in his eyes as he unfolds himself from the chair and stands, stretching his arms overhead. All of his muscles ripple and tighten. My mouth dries, and I force my eyes away. It's not quick enough, and I catch an eye-popping amount of chiseled strength.

Ugh. Why does he have to be so good-looking?

Carter isn't even my type—he's really not—and a throbbing ache has already taken up residence in my lower region. It's frustrating.

"I think I'll get dressed," he says.

My head snaps up. "What?"

He shrugs, a smirk hovering around the edges of his lips. "I've changed my mind. I'm going to head out after all." The smirk broadens into a grin. "Looks like your plans fell through for the evening. Any interest in tagging along?"

This time, I don't give it a second thought. I grab the television remote from the coffee table and hurtle it at his head.

Without breaking eye contact, he catches the sleek black controller in his hand. "I take it that's a no?"

I growl in frustration as he drops the remote onto the recliner and retreats to his bedroom.

Goddamn it!

I knew he stayed here on purpose. He wasn't tired or wanting to spend an evening at home chilling out. He was lying in wait, hanging around the apartment, ready to pounce. And I fell right into his trap.

I shake my head and bury my face in my hands.

Deep breaths, I tell myself. *I need to take deep breaths, or I'm going to commit a felony and go to prison for second-degree murder.*

I'm less than a month into this living arrangement, and already I know it's going to be a long year.

One-click Love to Hate You now!

MORE BOOKS BY JENNIFER SUCEVIC

<u>The Campus Series</u> (football)

Campus Player (Demi & Rowan)

Campus Heartthrob (Sydney & Brayden)

Campus Flirt (Sasha & Easton)

Campus Hottie (Elle & Carson)

Campus God (Brooke & Crosby)

Campus Legend (Lola & Asher)

<u>Western Wildcats Hockey</u>

Hate You Always (Juliette & Ryder)

Love You Never (Carina & Ford)

Always My Girl (Viola & Madden)

Dare You to Love Me (Stella & Riggs)

Never Mine to Hold (Fallyn & Wolf)

Never Say Never (Britt & Colby)

Mine to Take (Willow & Maverick)

Break my Heart (Ava & Hayes)

<u>The Barnett Bulldogs</u> (football)

King of Campus (Ivy & Roan)

Friend Zoned (Violet & Sam)

One Night Stand (Gia & Liam)

If You Were Mine (Claire & JT)

<u>The Claremont Cougars</u> (football)

Heartless Summer (Skye & Hunter)

Heartless (Skye & Hunter)

Shameless (Poppy & Mason)

<u>Hawthorne Prep Series</u> (bully/football)

King of Hawthorne Prep (Summer & Kingsley)

Queen of Hawthorne Prep (Summer & Kingsley)

Prince of Hawthorne Prep (Delilah & Austin)

Princess of Hawthorne Prep (Delilah & Austin)

<u>The Next Door Duet</u> (football)

The Girl Next Door (Mia & Beck)

The Boy Next Door (Alyssa & Colton)

<u>What's Mine Duet</u> (Suspense)

Protecting What's Mine (Grace & Matteo)

Claiming What's Mine (Sofia & Roman)

<u>Stay Duet</u> (hockey)

Stay (Cassidy & Cole)

Don't Leave (Cassidy & Cole)

<u>Stand-alone</u>

Hate to Love You (Hockey) (Natalie & Brody)

Just Friends (Hockey) (Emerson & Reed)

Love to Hate You (Football) (Daisy & Carter)

The Breakup Plan (Hockey) (Whitney & Gray)

<u>Collections</u>

ABOUT THE AUTHOR

Jennifer Sucevic is a USA Today bestselling author who has published twenty-five new adult novels. Her work has been translated into German, Dutch, Italian, French, Portuguese, and Hebrew.
She has a bachelor's degree in History and a master's in Educational Psychology from the University of Wisconsin-Milwaukee. Jen started out her career as a high school counselor before relocating with her family and focusing on her passion for writing. When she's not tapping away on the keyboard and dreaming up swoonworthy heroes to fall in love with, you can find her bike riding or at the beach. She lives in Michigan with her family.

If you would like to receive regular updates regarding new releases, please subscribe to her newsletter here-
Jennifer Sucevic's newsletter

Or contact Jen through email, at her website, or on Facebook.
sucevicjennifer@gmail.com

Want to join her reader group? Do it here -)
J Sucevic's Book Boyfriends | Facebook

Social media links-
https://www.tiktok.com/@jennifersucevicauthor
www.jennifersucevic.com
https://www.instagram.com/jennifersucevicauthor

https://www.facebook.com/jennifer.sucevic
Amazon.com: Jennifer Sucevic: Books, Biography, Blog, Audiobooks, Kindle
Jennifer Sucevic Books - BookBub